John Henry Overton

John Wesley

John Henry Overton

John Wesley

ISBN/EAN: 9783337399078

Printed in Europe, USA, Canada, Australia, Japan

Cover: Foto ©Raphael Reischuk / pixelio.de

More available books at **www.hansebooks.com**

JOHN WESLEY

BY

J. H. OVERTON, M.A.

Methuen & Co.

18, BURY STREET, LONDON, W.C.

1891

PREFACE.

IT is obviously impossible, within the compass of two hundred short pages, to give anything like a full account of a life which was all but commensurate with the eighteenth century, and which was certainly the busiest, and in some respects the most important life in that century—a life about which the most divers views have been taken, and in which the interest, so far from having slackened through lapse of time, is as keen if not keener than ever it was. All that can be attempted is to select the salient points of John Wesley's life and character, and to draw as vivid a picture of the man and his work as space will permit. As a native of the same county, a member of the same University, on the foundation of the same college in that University, a Priest of the same Church, a dweller in the same house, a worker in the same parish, a student for nearly twenty years of the Church life of the century in which John Wesley was so prominent a figure, the present writer has naturally for a long time taken the deepest interest in his subject, but whether he has succeeded in communicating that interest to his readers is quite another question. It only remains for him to return his hearty thanks to the Rev. L. H. Wellesley Wesley and Edward Riggall, Esq., for placing at his disposal a vast number of portraits, out of which one has been selected belonging to the former gentleman.

CONTENTS.

JOHN WESLEY.

CHAPTER I.

EARLY YEARS.

JOHN WESLEY[1] was born on June 17th (O. S.), 1703, at Epworth Rectory, his father, Samuel Wesley, being rector of the parish from 1696 to 1735. He was of gentle birth on both sides. The Wesleys were an ancient family settled in the west of England from the time of the Conquest. The Annesleys, his mother's family, were an equally ancient and aristocratic stock. The fact that Wesley was a gentleman born and bred was no slight help to the influence he afterwards acquired. The native delicacy of such a man gives him a certain tact in dealing with the poor, which is rarely acquired by those who are not to the manner born. He had no temptation to flatter the great, and was not intoxicated by being brought into contact with them. But John Wesley owed much more to his parents than the good blood in his veins. Both Samuel and Susanna

---

[1] He was christened John Benjamin, but the second name was always dropped both by himself and all the family.

B

Wesley were people of real piety and considerable
abilities, which had been improved by culture ; both felt
keenly their responsibility in bringing up their numerous offspring in the fear and love of God ; both had
thought out the great problem of religion for themselves, for both had been reared in the ranks of Noncon-
formity, and both had come over at an early age to the
Church of England, from a deliberate conviction that it
was the more excellent way. To the mother chiefly was
consigned the task of the early training both of sons and
daughters ; and that regard for discipline, those method-
ical and orderly habits, that sense of the value of time
and of the duty of cultivating his talents to the utmost,
above all, that intense realization of an overruling
Providence and of the supreme importance of religion,
which marked the whole career of John Wesley, may be
clearly traced back to his mother's training at Epworth
Rectory. Of all her children, she felt it her duty to
bestow the greatest pains upon John, who had been
providentially preserved to her when he was all but
burnt to death in the fire which consumed the Rectory
in 1709. "I do intend," she writes in her private
meditations under the heading of "Son John," "to be
more particularly careful of the soul of this child, that
Thou hast so mercifully provided for, than ever I have
been, that I may do my endeavour to instil into his
mind the principles of Thy true religion and virtue.
Lord, give me grace to do it sincerely and prudently,
and bless my attempts with good success!" Upon John
himself his deliverance from the fire made a deep impression ; though he was only six years old at the time,
he remembered all the circumstances perfectly well,
and many years afterwards (1750), when he happened to

be holding a watch-night service on the anniversary of his rescue, "it came into my mind," he says, "that this was the very day and hour (11 p.m., Feb. 9) in which, forty years ago, I was taken out of the flames. I stopped, and gave a short account of that wonderful providence." Three years later (1753), when he thought he was dying, "to prevent vile panegyric" he wrote his own epitaph, in which he described himself as "a Brand plucked out of the burning."

As he was thoughtful beyond his years, it is quite possible that other events which occurred at Epworth during his childhood may really have helped to shape his future career. It has been suggested, for instance, that the serious weekly conversations which Mrs. Wesley used to hold with each of her children individually may have been present to his mind when he established the class-meeting. That he remembered and valued them is certain, for when he was a Fellow of Lincoln, he wrote to his mother begging her to give him that time which she had formerly given him on a Thursday. Again, it has been conjectured that the gatherings at the rectory on Sunday afternoons, at which Mrs. Wesley, in the absence of her husband on Convocation business in London, attracted and affected the rude people of Epworth in a way that the rector had never been able to do from the pulpit, impressed upon John the desirableness of supplementing the regular work of the Church by the formation of Societies. He certainly did intimate very often in after-life that the disheartening results of his good father's efforts in his parish led him to think lightly of the parochial system. But these were probably the inferences of later years; at any rate they cannot be directly

traced back to his childhood. What we *can* say for
a certainty is, that he most thoroughly appreciated the
excellent training, moral, spiritual, and intellectual,
which he received at Epworth Rectory, all his life long.
When he was quite an old man (1771), he wrote with
rapture about an admirable household he had become
acquainted with in Ireland, and added, "Their ten
children are in such order as I have not seen for many
years; indeed, never since I left my father's house." It
is also clear that he attributed the benefits of his early
training chiefly to his mother. For though he never
spoke but with the greatest reverence and love of his
father, it is to Mrs. Wesley that he most frequently and
most warmly alludes. One of the reasons why he
resolved that he would never marry (it is a pity that
he did not keep his resolution), was because he despaired
of finding any woman equal to his own mother; and he
more than once expressed a wish that he might not
survive her. So highly did he value her method of
bringing up her family, that he persuaded her with
some difficulty to write a full account of it to him in
1732. From this account we learn how "the children
were put into a regular method of living, in such things
as they were capable of, from their birth;" how "when
turned a year old (and some before), they were taught
to fear the rod and cry softly," how she insisted "upon
conquering their will betimes, because this is the only
strong and rational foundation of a religious education,
without which both precept and example will be in-
effectual," and many other details which are too long to
quote.

Mrs. Wesley's reluctance to write this account
arose from a reason which seven years' residence at

Epworth Rectory enables the present writer heartily to endorse. "It cannot," she says, "be of any service to any one to know how I, that have lived such a retired life for so many years, used to employ my time and care in bringing up my children. No one can, without renouncing the world in the most literal sense, observe my method; and there are few, if any, that would entirely devote twenty years of the prime of life in hopes to save the souls of their children, which they think may be saved without so much ado; for that was my principal intention, however unskilfully managed." Now the geographical position of Epworth shows to some extent its isolation; but its ecclesiastical position is still more isolated. It is cut off from its own proper diocese by the rapid river Trent, which it is sometimes difficult and even dangerous to cross. The rector of Epworth would be naturally drawn to the Lincoln side (on one side his parish touched Yorkshire), being a prominent man in the diocese, and the representative of its clergy in Convocation; but his family would be quite cut off from Lincolnshire—(though we are Lincolnshire people, we talk about "going into Lincolnshire," as though we were no part of it, to the present day). There would be few neighbours with whom the Wesleys could associate on terms of equality; they would therefore be left very much to their own resources. But, as all the family—father, mother, and all the brothers and sisters—were above the average in point of abilities and attainments, this would be no detriment to John Wesley's intellectual culture, while at the same time it would lay the foundation of that simplicity, guilelessness, and unworldliness which were his strongly-marked

characteristics all through life. His early home training
also combined the double advantage of giving him the
culture and refinement of a thorough gentleman, and
also a hardiness and power to endure poverty. For
from circumstances into which it is not necessary to
enter, the Wesleys were always poor, sometimes even
to the verge of destitution.

John Wesley had not been reared in the lap of luxury,
and his habit of roughing it in his childhood stood him
in good stead in his hard after-life. All the little traits
of him at Epworth indicate that the boy was father of
the man. He was so far beyond his years that his
father, who would be a strict censor in such a matter,
admitted him to the Holy Communion when he was
only eight years of age. He had the small-pox shortly
after (April 1712). "Jack," writes his mother, "has
borne his disease bravely, like a man, and indeed like
a Christian, without any complaint, though he seemed
angry at the small-pox when they were sore, as we
guessed by his looking sourly at them, for he never
said anything." "I believe," he writes himself, "till I
was about ten years old I had not sinned away that
washing of the Holy Ghost which was given me in
baptism." One pictures John Wesley at Epworth as
a grave, sedate child, always wanting to know the
reason of everything, one of a group of remarkable
children, of whom his sister Martha was most like him
both in appearance and character, each of them with a
strong individuality and a very high spirit, but all well
kept in hand by their admirable mother, all precise and
rather formal, after the fashion of the day, in their
language and habits. Mrs. Wesley complains, that
after the fire of 1709, when the children had to be

billeted out among the neighbours, the arrangements became disorganized; but she soon put them into order again when they settled down in their new house, which is now standing.

Before leaving John Wesley's first home, mention must be made of the famous Epworth ghost, although he did not commence his antics until John had left Epworth for Charterhouse. "Old Jeffery" is to some extent answerable for a marked feature of Wesley's character—his love of the marvellous, and his intense belief in the reality of apparitions and of witchcraft. The noises which disturbed the Wesley household in the winter of 1715-16 have never been satisfactorily explained; the Wesleys themselves undoubtedly attributed them to supernatural causes, and both Mr. and Mrs. Wesley's comments upon what happened show how thoroughly both believed in the active interference of spiritual agents in the affairs of this life. What some have thought a weakness in John Wesley he clearly inherited from his parents, who fostered it both by precept and example.

CHAPTER II.

On January 28, 1713-14, John Wesley was admitted on the foundation of Charterhouse, on the nomination of the Duke of Buckingham, who had already shown himself a kind friend to the Wesleys. At this famous school he remained for more than six years, during the whole of which time Dr. Thomas Walker was the head-master, and Mr. Andrew Tooke "usher," or second master.[1] His quietness, regularity, and industry made him a favourite with his teachers, and the scholarship which he showed in after-life indicates plainly that his school-days were not wasted. He kept up his health by following his father's sensible advice, to run round the Charterhouse garden three times every morning; and the tyranny of the elder boys, who used to appropriate the meat apportioned to the younger, and thus forced him in the earlier part of his school-life to live chiefly on dry bread, unwittingly contributed to prepare him for the hard, ascetic life which he afterwards led. "From ten to fourteen," he says, "I had little but bread to eat, and not great

---

[1] Mr. Tooke was the author of a once well-known book, *The Pantheon.*

plenty of that. I believe this was so far from hurting me, that it laid the foundation of lasting health." The story of his propensity to associate with, and domineer over, boys younger than himself, and of his answer to Mr. Tooke, who remonstrated with him for so doing, "Better rule in hell than serve in heaven," rests upon slender foundations, and may well have arisen from a prevalent but in my opinion a mistaken view of his character. Nor is it quite clear how far he lost the religious impressions which he carried with him from Epworth. The removal from home, and such a home as Epworth Rectory, to a public school, as public schools then were, could hardly fail to be perilous; and from John Wesley's own vehement condemnation of the public school system in his sermon on the education of children, written many years later, we may fairly presume that his own experience of Charterhouse did not commend that system to him. He describes his own state both as a school-boy and an undergraduate as that of one who was living without any real sense of religion, and who habitually indulged in outward though not flagrant sin; but he never ceased to read his Bible daily, and to say his prayers morning and evening. And surely it was greatly to Wesley's ultimate advantage that he had been a public-school boy. For, after all, it is not a healthy training to bring up a boy, as it were, under a glass case; and in spite of their many evils,—and in the eighteenth century these evils were *very* many,—public schools afford a mental and moral discipline which cannot be found elsewhere; in a rough way they brace the tone of the character, impart a sort of undefinable readiness to give and take, and encourage a larger way of looking at things than any other system

does. Moreover, the knowledge which they convey, if
narrow in its range, is thoroughly sound of its kind;
for, after all, public-school masters are, and always have
been, the picked men of England. *Exceptis excipiendis*,
you can tell at a glance one who has had a public-
school and university education from one who has not.
We have only to compare the two Wesleys in these
respects with some other leaders of the Evangelical revival to find a striking illustration of what is meant.

During the last four years of John's stay at Charterhouse both his brothers were at Westminster—Samuel
as usher, Charles as a young scholar. Their father had
good reason to boast that he had given his three sons
the best education that England could afford. Charterhouse had not quite the splendid reputation of
Westminster, which school, under the régime of Dr.
Busby, continued by his successor, Dr. Freind, had
attained to an eminence which no school ever had
reached in England. But Charterhouse too had grand
traditions of its own; when John Wesley was there,
only a few years had passed away since Joseph Addison
and Richard Steele were being nurtured in its
cloisters; a little later two other eminent men, whose
names were afterwards to be strangely linked with
Wesley's own, Archbishop Potter and Bishop Benson,
were educated there; and many other great names
might be found on the roll of its worthies. John Wesley
himself conceived such a love for the place, that when
he was in London he always made a point of walking
round it every year. His elder brother Samuel, who
really seems to have been a kind of second father to the
whole family, kept a watch over his progress from Westminster, invited him to his house, and sent reports of

him home. "My brother Jack," he writes to his father in 1719, "I can faithfully assure you, gives you no manner of discouragement from breeding your third son [Charles] a scholar;" and in the same year, "Jack is with me, and a brave boy, learning Hebrew as fast as he can." How many boys of sixteen in these examination-ridden days arc learning Hebrew as fast as they can ?

On July 13, 1720, John Wesley entered as a commoner at Christ Church, Oxford, bringing with him from Charterhouse a school exhibition of £40 a year. We must multiply by four to find the true value of this aid. £160 a year should have been nearly enough to maintain an economical undergraduate; but at this period John Wesley seems to have been rather too like his father, who never was a good manager of money. There is really no reason for supposing that he was at all extravagant at Christ Church ; but his correspondence shows that he was constantly in monetary difficulties. It is hardly necessary to dwell upon the reputation of "The House," which in the days before Wesley had completed the education of the majority of the foremost men in England. It had the pick of Westminster, and Dr. Fell crowned the edifice which Dr. Busby had begun to raise. Its repute was not, perhaps, quite so high when Wesley was an undergraduate, but still it was a grand society to belong to. We have an interesting description of John Wesley at this period by a contemporary, Mr. Badcock, according to whom he was "the very sensible and acute collegian, baffling every man by the subtleties of logic, and laughing at them for being so easily routed; a young fellow of the finest classical taste, of the most liberal and manly sentiments;" "gay

and sprightly, with a turn for wit and humour." This
is very different from the grave child at Epworth of
fifteen years before, and it quite bears out what Wesley
says about his own state at school and college. Only
we must beware of laying too much stress upon what
he regards as a deterioration; the reaction from the
severe restraint at Epworth was inevitable; he was
passing through a crisis which all except a very few
have to encounter. There is absolutely no proof of any
grave moral delinquency; he was simply the lively,
careless young man, but certainly not the mere idler,
for his well-stored mind forbids any such notion, and
still less, the profligate. He dabbled in poetry; he was
troubled, for almost the only time in his life, about his
health, and adopted the severe regimen recommended
by the famous Dr. Cheyne. His tutors were, first a
Mr. Wigan, and then a Mr. Sherman, but they do not
seem to have made much impression upon him. There
is little more to be said about his life at Christ Church,
except that it is surely not fair to blame the authorities
because they failed to touch, as those at Charterhouse
had failed to touch, Wesley's higher nature, and because
neither enabled him to keep up, under new and far
more trying circumstances, the high standard which had
been set before him at Epworth. If the tree is to be
judged by its fruits, his days at Charterhouse and
Christ Church could not have been idly spent, for he
carried away with him an amount of mental culture
which would compare favourably with that of some of
the best specimens of these days of incessant examination.

Mental culture, however, is one thing, spiritual growth
another. There are abundant traces of the former,
none of the latter, between his leaving Epworth and

his last year at Christ Church. Then, when he was
twenty-two years of age, a great change came over him.
The question now arose as to whether he was to enter
the sacred ministry or not. No thoughtful man, who
had been trained as John Wesley had been trained at
Epworth, could possibly contemplate so momentous a
step without serious consideration.

It was early in 1725 that the thought of taking
Holy Orders occurred to him. He wrote home on
the subject; his father counselled delay, fearing lest
his motive might be, " as Eli's sons, to eat a piece of
bread;" but his mother judged his character better,
and saw that the change was real. "I was much pleased,"
she says, " with your letter to your father about taking
orders, and liked the proposal well; but it is an un-
happiness almost peculiar to our family, that your father
and I seldom think alike. I approve the disposition
of your mind, and think the sooner you are a deacon
the better. . . . God Almighty direct and bless you!"
Mr. Wesley, however, soon yielded to the stronger
mind of his wife, and wrote, advising his son to seek
Holy Orders without delay. John Wesley's own conduct cannot be so well described as in his own
words :—

" When I was about twenty-two my father pressed
me to enter into Holy Orders. At the same time, the
providence of God directing me to Kempis' *Christian
Pattern*, I began to see that true religion was seated
in the heart, and that God's law extended to all our
thoughts as well as words and actions. I was, however,
angry at Kempis for being too strict, though I read
him only in Dean Stanhope's translation. Meeting
likewise with a religious friend, which I never had till

now, I began to alter the whole form of my conversation, and to set in earnest upon a new life. I set apart an hour or two a day for religious retirement; I communicated every week; I watched against all sin, whether in word or deed. I began to aim at, and to pray for, inward holiness; so that now, doing so much and living so good a life, I doubted not that I was a good Christian."

The last sentence is of course ironical; but is it not right in this case to defend John Wesley against John Wesley? While thoroughly believing in the reality and importance of a later change, can any one deny that from this time forward to the very close of his long life, John Wesley led a most holy, devoted life, aiming only at the glory of God, the welfare of his own soul, and the benefit of his fellow-creatures? and if that is not to be a good Christian, what is? His mother gave him, as usual, excellent advice about the *De Imitatione*, and also advised him to read another devotional work, now little known, but well worth reading, *The Life of God in the Soul of Man*, by Scougal, a clergyman of the Scotch Episcopal Church, which John Wesley loved. Most interesting letters also passed between mother and son, and father and son, about such subjects as the minatory clauses of the Athanasian Creed, the thorny question of Predestination, and other difficult points. The upshot was, that John Wesley was ordained deacon by Dr. Potter, Bishop of Oxford, in the September Ember week, 1725.

CHAPTER III.

On March 17, 1726, John Wesley was elected Fellow of Lincoln College, on the Lincolnshire foundation. He owed his success chiefly to the interest made by his father and others with Dr. Morley, rector of the college, to whom he always acknowledged a deep debt of gratitude; but he certainly might have been elected on his merits, if such had been the custom of those days. There was, however, an examination of some kind; for his father writes to him in the preceding summer—"Study hard, lest your opponents beat you." These opponents or their friends tried to make capital out of his serious behaviour, but in vain. His election threw a gleam of light upon the somewhat gloomy life of his worthy father, who addressed him exultingly on March 21st, as "Dear Mr. Fellow-elect of Lincoln" (the expression "Fellow-elect" refers to the fact that at first a man is only elected probationary Fellow); and on April 1st wrote—"What will be my own fate before the summer be over, God only knows—*sed passi graciora.* Wherever I am, my Jack is Fellow of Lincoln."

John Wesley's connection with Lincoln College lasted for more than a quarter of a century. "Sometime Fellow of Lincoln College" is the designation by which he describes himself in the title-page of all his works. He frequently refers to the college with pleasure and gratitude, and he was deeply and permanently influenced in more respects than one by his connection with it.

"Lincoln" is only the popular name, its proper designation being "Collegium Beatæ Virginis Mariæ et Omnium Sanctorum Lincolniense." The last epithet was added because it was founded by a Bishop of Lincoln, Richard Fleming, in 1427, and its resources greatly augmented by another Bishop of Lincoln, Thomas Rotheram, who was afterwards Archbishop of York and Lord High Chancellor of England.[1] It differed from other colleges, inasmuch as it was to be exclusively a college of theologians, "a college of divines," says John Wesley himself, "(so our statutes express it,) founded to overturn all heresies, and defend the Catholic Faith," which, being interpreted, means that it was founded for the express purpose of putting down the Lollards, whose increasing influence alarmed Bishop Fleming. It was the duty of the individual members of the college to preach against Lollardism throughout the huge diocese of Lincoln.

Lincoln, though a small and comparatively poor college, has always held its own among its statelier and richer sisters in the University. In the seventeenth century it had numbered among its Fellows men who had been distinguished both by learning and by piety of a pronounced Anglican type. One of the very best of the Bishops of Lincoln, Robert Sanderson, had been Fellow of Lincoln for thirteen years (1606—1619), and his college lectures as "Reader of Logic in

[1] The Bishop of Lincoln for the time being was always to be *ex officio* visitor.

the House," had been the standard work on Logic at Oxford until they were superseded by the far inferior manual of Dean Aldrich. Though more than a hundred years had elapsed between the resignation of Robert Sanderson and the election of John Wesley, the fragrance of so great a name may still have lingered about the college.

Passing from the earlier to the later part of the seventeenth century, we find the Rector of Lincoln College, Dr. Marshall, among the foremost of the Church-men who helped to revive Church principles after the Restoration. Then, a little later, that staunch Church-man and most able and learned man, George Hickes, was among the Fellows of Lincoln College; and his friend, John Kettlewell, saintliest as well as soundest of English Churchmen. The good Bishop also who ordained John Wesley, Dr. Potter, had been a Fellow of Lincoln College ; and the Lincolnshire Fellowship to which John Wesley was elected had been vacated by John (afterwards Sir John) Thorold, scion of a very ancient and aristocratic family, and known in the family as "the good Sir John,"[1] a very pious man.   And

[1] The following information has been kindly supplied to the present writer by Dr. Trollope, Bishop of Nottingham, who is great-grandson to this Sir John Thorold, on his grandmother's side, as Dr. Thorold, Bishop of Rochester, is on his father's side.

"Sir John Thorold of Marston and Syston, eighth baronet, entered Lincoln at the age of eighteen, and resigned his Fellowship there, May 3rd, 1725. He was afterwards a friend of Wesley, and is thus described in a letter to the Honourable Grace Granville, daughter of Lord Lansdown, dated November 1st, 1738, and sent from Windsor to Miss Ann Granville, Mrs. Delany's sister.

"According to your desire, I have inquired after our new 'Star of Righteousness.' He does deserve in every particular the charac-ter you give him. His name is Thorold ; he has at present a very plentiful fortune, £3000 (that is, per annum), will have £10,000 after his father's death. He has a wife and five children, preaches

among those who were actual Fellows with John Wesley,
but very much his senior, was Richard Hutchins, who
became an Oxford Methodist, and was afterwards known
as "the Methodist Rector." Hence there would be, to
say the least, a tradition of learning and piety about the
college when Wesley was elected. Wesley's own inci-
dental remarks fully bear out this theory. Speaking
in 1756 of the chapel service at Trinity College,
Dublin, he says—"I never saw so much decency
at any chapel in Oxford; no, not even at Lincoln
College;" and writing to his brother Samuel soon
after his election, he says—"As far as I have ever observed, I never knew a college besides ours whereof the
members were so perfectly satisfied with one another;
and so inoffensive to the other part of the University.
All I have yet seen of the Fellows are both well-natured
and well-bred; men admirably disposed as well to
preserve peace and good neighbourhood among themselves, as to promote it wherever else they have any
acquaintance."

Wesley seems to have made an equally good impression upon his brother Fellows, as appears from the
following letter from one of them :—

"Lincoln College, Dec. 28th, 1727.
   "SIR,

         "Yesterday I had the satisfaction of receiving
your kind and obliging letter, whereby you have given

---

twice a week (Monday and Friday), reads a chapter, explains
every verse. He has got a young gentleman from Oxford to live
with him, who follows his example."
   To this it may be added, that on Mr. Thorold's resigning his
Fellowship, he restored all the money that he had received from
it to the college. He preached in connection with the Moravian .
brotherhood. Several letters from him to John Wesley are extant.

me a singular instance of that goodness and civility
which is essential to your character, and strongly con-
firmed to me the many encomiums which are given of you
in this respect by all who have the happiness to know
you. This makes me infinitely desirous of your acquaintance. And when I consider those shining qualities
which I hear daily mentioned in your praise, I cannot
but lament the great misfortune we all suffer in the
absence of so agreeable a person from the college. But
I please myself with the thoughts of seeing you here on
Chapter-day, and of the happiness we shall have in your
company in the summer.

" Your most obliged and most humble servant,
                         " LEW. FENTON."

This is anticipating; but the letter is inserted here
to show that we must not take quite literally some of
the observations which Wesley makes about himself.

With his newly-awakened earnestness, he found no
sympathizers among his acquaintance at Oxford. "Even
their harmless conversation so-called," he says, " damped
all my good resolutions. I saw no possible way of
getting rid of them unless it should please God to
remove me to another college. He did so, in a manner
contrary to all human expectation. I was elected
Fellow of a college where I knew not one person; " and
he determined to know none except those who were
walking on the same road as himself. But the letter
of Mr. Fenton, written after Wesley had been Fellow
for a year and a half, shows that we are not to gather
from this that he became an ascetic and a recluse. Nor,
though he henceforth considered everything in subordination to the one thing needful, did he fall into the

foolish error of despising human learning. On the
contrary, he mapped out his time so methodically that
he was able to embrace a most wide and varied range
of studies. Monday and Tuesday were to be devoted
to Greek and Latin; Wednesday to logic and ethics;
Thursday to Hebrew and Arabic; Friday to meta-
physics and natural philosophy; Saturday to oratory
and poetry; Sunday to divinity.

In the October term of 1726 he was in harness at
Lincoln College, being appointed Greek lecturer and
moderator of the classes. These appointments have
been strangely misunderstood; perhaps a Lincoln man
may be allowed to explain them. Greek lecturer does
not mean teacher of Greek generally; it is a technical
term, the explanation of which illustrates what has been
written above respecting the tradition of piety as well
as learning which belonged to Lincoln College. The
object was to secure some sort of religious instruction to
all the undergraduates; and for this purpose a special
officer was appointed, with the modest stipend of £20 a
year, who was to hold a lecture every week in the College Hall, which all the undergraduates were to attend,
on the Greek Testament. As became a learned society,
the lecture was to be on the original language, but the
real object was to teach divinity, not Greek.

The duty of " Moderator of the Classes " was to sit in
the college hall, and preside over the "Disputations "
which were held at Lincoln College every day in the
week except Sunday. Bishop Rotheram lays great
stress upon these disputations in his Statutes for the
College, and gives minute directions as to how they
are to be conducted ; it will be remembered that John
Locke found " Disputations " prevalent at Christ Church

seventy years before, and lamented the "unprofitable-
ness of these verbal niceties." John Wesley seems to
have thought otherwise, at any rate so far as the
moderator himself was concerned. The plan was this:
a thesis was proposed; the disputants argued on one
side or the other; the moderator had to listen to the
arguments, and then to decide with whom the victory
lay. "I could not avoid," says Wesley, "acquiring
thereby some degree of expertness in arguing, and
especially in discovering and pointing out well-covered
and plausible fallacies. I have since found abundant
reason to praise God for giving me this honest
art."

Wesley had only been three terms at Lincoln, when
he was called away to another duty which would
assuredly be sacred in his eyes. His father was growing
old, and the duties of his two parishes, Epworth and
Wroote, were so heavy that he felt he must have a
curate upon whom he could thoroughly depend; and
who was so fitting as his son John? Mrs. Wesley was
equally anxious that John should return home; and the
wishes of the two were—as they ought to have been—
law to John Wesley. So from the summer of 1727 to
the autumn of 1729 we find him again in the Isle of
Axholme, at Epworth or Wroote, living for the most
part at the latter place, but officiating sometimes at
one and sometimes at the other. That Wesley was an
earnest and active parish clergyman goes without saying; he tells us himself that "he took some pains with
this people," and his father speaks of "the dear love they
bore him." But it is also clear that this, the sole experience he ever had in England of work as a parish priest,
did not at all commend to him the parochial system.

He made visits now and then to his beloved Oxford
during these two years—once to vote at an election,
another time to be ordained priest in 1728.   There is
little to be said about this period; no doubt he felt it a
comfort to be able to help his father, but that was all.
He was not in his element; and, what is rather curious,
there is not the slightest trace of his attempting to carry
out the Church system in all its fulness as he afterwards
did in Georgia.   The church arrangements at Epworth
and Wroote seem to have all been after the old-fashioned
style of the eighteenth century.   Doubtless respect for
his father would have deterred him from making any
radical change, even if he had desired to do so; but I
am inclined to think that he himself had not as yet
realized what he afterwards considered of so great
importance ; he was simply a high and dry Churchman
of the old school; and influences were brought to bear
upon him on his return to Oxford which he had never
yet felt.

    That return was in consequence of a summons from
Dr. Morley, the rector of his college.   It came, as
Wesley intimates, unexpectedly.   " I was," he writes in
1745, " safe, as I supposed, in a little country town, when
I was required to return to Oxford without delay, to take
the charge of some young gentlemen, by Dr. Morley,
the only man then in England to whom I could deny
nothing." ˙Dr. Morley's letter was kind, but firm.   " We
hope," he says, " it may be as much to your advantage
to reside at college as where you are, if you take pupils,
or can get a curacy in the neighbourhood of Oxon.
Your father may certainly have another curate, though
not so much to his satisfaction ; yet we are persuaded
that this will not move him to hinder your return to

college, since the interest of college and obligation to statute requires it."

Accordingly, in the autumn of 1729, Wesley returned to Lincoln College, resuming his old office of Greek Lecturer, and taking other college work. It should be noted that the office of college tutor, as now understood, did not then exist; and that the private tutor then differed widely from what irreverent undergraduates now term "a coach." If he were a conscientious man, he considered himself responsible for the moral as well as the intellectual training of his pupils; Dr. Morley, with his wonted kindness, placed eleven pupils under Wesley's charge, and it is almost needless to say that Wesley took the highest standard of duty in his relations to them. From several who were his private pupils in this sense from 1729 to 1735, we have strong and even enthusiastic testimony to the effect that he was not only an able and conscientious, but also a most kind and considerate tutor. Many years later, he tells us that in those days the undergraduates used to stay at college all the year round, and that he should as soon have thought of committing a highway robbery, as of failing to give them instruction six days in every week. The testimony of James Hervey, John Whitelamb, and others fully bears out this account of his diligence.

But it is not as lecturer or tutor or moderator that John Wesley's career at Oxford from 1729 to 1735 is most interesting. When he returned to the University he found established one of those little societies or clubs for mutual edification which at all times have been very common.

Little, no doubt, did the club which John Wesley

now joined, dream that their small meetings would become world-renowned. They were "The Oxford Methodists," and the formation of this society is the first instance of what hereafter we shall frequently have to notice, viz. that John Wesley was the originator of scarcely anything that is specially connected with his name, but that all arose either from apparently accidental circumstances, or from the suggestions of others. Strictly speaking, Charles Wesley, not John, was the Founder of Methodism; if we date the commencement, as John Wesley almost invariably does, from 1729, not from 1739. Nothing could be more simple and natural than its origin. Charles Wesley had now been a Westminster student at Christ Church for some three years. During his brother's absence in Lincolnshire he had become deeply impressed with the vital importance of religion, and, like John, had devoted himself to a strictly religious life. What was more natural than that he should gather round him a small band of like-minded young men, who should meet together for mutual improvement, both spiritual and intellectual? On week-days they read the classics, on Sundays divinity; they attended most punctually all the means of grace, especially the Holy Communion,—and that was all. It was also quite natural that when John Wesley joined them he should take the lead; his age, his experience, his University position, his superior learning, and, above all, the ascendancy which he had always exercised over his younger brother, made this a matter of course.

Accordingly, in John Wesley's rooms at Lincoln College, which tradition points out as the first-floor rooms on the south or right-hand side of the first quadrangle, shaded by the famous Lincoln vine,[1] and opposite the clock-tower, "in November 1729, four young gentlemen of Oxford—Mr. John Wesley, Fellow of Lincoln College; Mr. Charles Wesley, student of Christ Church; Mr. Morgan, commoner of Christ Church; and Mr. Kirkham, of Merton College—began to spend some evenings together in reading chiefly the Greek Testament." Mr. Morgan was the first who combined with this practical work. "In the summer of 1730," writes Wesley, " Mr. Morgan told me he had called at the gaol, to see a man who was condemned for killing his wife; and that, from the talk he had with one of the debtors, he verily believed it would do much good if any one would be at the pains of now and then speaking with them. This he so frequently repeated, that on the 24th of August, 1730, my brother and I walked with him to the Castle. We were so well satisfied with our conversation there, that we agreed to go thither once or twice a week; which we had not done long, before he desired me to go with him to see a poor woman in the town who was sick. In this employment too, when we came to reflect upon it, we believed it

---

[1] An anecdote is preserved in the old MS. Statutes of Bishop Rotheram, which is worth quoting in connection with the Lincoln vine :—" They say that when, according to custom, in the visitation of his diocese, Bishop Rotheram had come to Oxford, a certain one of the Fellows of Lincoln College, or perhaps the Rector, Fristhorpe, exhorted him in a sermon preached before him, to finish the College, taking his text, Psalm lxxx. 14, 15—'Behold and visit this vine, and perfect it which Thy right hand hath planted,'—with which words he so moved the Bishop, that straightway he answered the preacher that he would do that which he sought."—I am a little doubtful, however, as to whether Wesley's vine is *the* Lincoln vine ; but the subject, though interesting to a Lincoln man, is not of sufficient general interest to be discussed here.

would be worth while to spend an hour or two in a
week, provided the minister of the parish, in which any
such person was, was not against it. But that we
might not depend wholly upon our own judgments, I
wrote an account to my father of our whole design;
withal begging that he, who had lived seventy years in
the world, and seen as much of it as most private men
have ever done, would advise us whether we had yet
gone too far, and whether we should now stand still or
go forward."

The father replied (Sept. 21, 1730), "As to your
designs and employments, what can I say less of them
than *Valde probo*, and that I have the highest reason to
bless God that He has given me two sons together in
Oxford, to whom He has given grace and courage to
turn the war against the world and the devil? . . . You
have reason to bless God, as I do, that you have so fast a
friend as Mr. Morgan, who I see in the foremost difficult
service is ready to break the ice for you. I think I
must adopt him as my son, together with you and your
brother Charles; and when I have such a Ternion to
prosecute that war, wherein I am now *miles emeritus*,
I shall not be ashamed when they speak with their
enemies in the gate!" After some other excellent
advice, he says, "Go on, then, in God's name, in the
path to which your Saviour has directed you, and that
track wherein your father has gone before you. For
when I was an undergraduate at Oxford, I visited those
in the Castle there, and reflect on it with great satisfaction to this day." He then counsels him to "walk as
prudently as he can, though not fearfully," to gain the
approbation of the proper authorities, and signs himself
"your most affectionate and joyful father."

Other letters followed, and John Wesley felt and expressed the greatest satisfaction in having his father's approval. The four (for Mr. Kirkham was also with them) went steadily on "in spite of the ridicule which increased fast upon them during the winter." They were also joined the same year by John Gambold of Christ Church, and in 1732 by John Clayton of Brasenose, Benjamin Ingham of Queen's, Thomas Broughton of Exeter, and Westley Hall of Lincoln. James Hervey of Lincoln, an attached pupil of John Wesley, joined them in 1733. John Kinchin, Fellow of Corpus, John Whitelamb of Lincoln, and Richard Hutchins, Fellow, afterwards Rector, of Lincoln, also joined; and then a poor servitor of Pembroke, who had never been in such grand company before, but who in later years became *the* one whose name was even more prominently connected by his contemporaries with Methodism than that of John Wesley himself—George Whitefield. All the members of the little society were the staunchest of staunch Churchmen; they kept scrupulously all the Fasts of the Church, including every Wednesday and every Friday; they made a point of communicating every Sunday and every Festival; they spent upon themselves only sufficient money for bare subsistence, exercising the severest self-denial, and giving away all they could in charity; they visited the poor and sick in their homes, the prisoners in the Castle, and the poor debtors in Bocardo; they paid for the education of poor children, and educated some themselves.

But John Wesley shall describe the movement in his own words. On laying the foundation of "the new Chapel, near the City Road, London," April 21, 1777, he thus refers to "the rise of the extraordinary

work God had wrought in England":—"In the year
1725 a young student at Oxford was much affected
by reading Kempis' *Christian Pattern*, and Bishop
Taylor's *Rules of Holy Living and Dying*. He found
an earnest desire to live according to those rules, and
to flee from the wrath to come. He sought for some
that would be his companions in the way, but could
find none; so that for several years he was con-
strained to travel alone, having no man either to guide or
to help him. But in the year 1729 he found one who
had the same desire. They then endeavoured to help
each other, and, in the close of the year, were joined by
two more. They soon agreed to spend two or three
hours together every Sunday evening. Afterwards they
sat two evenings together, and in a while, six evenings in
the week, spending that time in reading the Scriptures,
and provoking one another to love and to good works.
The regularity of their behaviour gave occasion to a
young gentleman of the college to say, 'I think we have
got a new set of *Methodists*,'—alluding to a set of physicians who began to flourish at Rome about the time of
Nero, and continued for several ages.[1] The name was new
and quaint; it clave to them immediately; and from that
time both those four young gentlemen, and all that had
any religious connection with them, were distinguished
by the name of *Methodists*. In the four or five years
following, another and another were added to the

---

[1] But Charles Wesley says that the name of Methodist "was
bestowed upon himself and his friends because of their strict
conformity to the method of study prescribed by the statutes of
the University," and this seems to me a much more likely explanation; for what would a giddy undergraduate know about a sect
of physicians in the reign of Nero? In another passage John
Wesley also gives this as an alternative explanation.

number, till in the year 1735 there were fourteen of them who constantly met together. Three of these were tutors in their several colleges; the rest Bachelors of Arts or undergraduates. They were all precisely of one judgment, as well as of one soul; all tenacious of order to the last degree, and observant, for conscience' sake, of every rule of the Church, and every statute both of the University and of their respective colleges. They were all orthodox in every point, firmly believing, not only the Three Creeds, but whatsoever they judged to be the doctrine of the Church of England, as contained in her Articles and Homilies. As to that practice of the Apostolic Church (which continued till the time of Tertullian, at least in many Churches), the having all things in common, they had no rule, nor any formed design concerning it; but it was so in effect, and it could not be otherwise, for none could want anything that another could spare. This was the infancy of the work. They had no conception of anything that would follow. Indeed, they took 'no thought for the morrow,' desiring only to live to-day."

When John Wesley says, "A young gentleman of the college" nicknamed the Methodists, he does not mean his own college. A Lincoln man may be pardoned for remarking with satisfaction, that Lincoln had nothing to do with the feeble jokes which were made upon these good, earnest youths. Christ Church and Merton must divide the honour between them. The Holy Club, Bible Bigots, Bible Moths, Sacramentarians, Supererogation men, Methodists,—all these titles were invented by the fertile brains of "the wits" to cast opprobrium, as they thought, but really to confer honour, upon a perfectly inoffensive little band of young men who

only desired to *be* what they and their opponents were
alike *called*—Christians. An Oxford man may indeed
blush for his University when he reflects that these
young men could not even attend the highest service
of the Church without running the gauntlet of a jeering
rabble principally composed of men who were actually
being prepared for the sacred ministry of that Church.

In the last part of his account John Wesley touches
upon a point which is really the most important and
interesting feature of this period of his career. He
refers to the Primitive Church; and it seems to me that
it was during these years at Oxford that the idea first
gained a hold upon his mind which it never lost, of
modelling all his doctrines and practice after that
pattern. It is a far cry from Ritualism (so-called) to
Methodism (so-called); but it is not fancy, but plain
historical fact, that Wesley derived his ideas about the
Mixed Chalice, Prayers for the Faithful Departed, and
the observance of the Stations, from precisely the same
source from whence he derived his ideas about the Class-
meeting, the Love-feast, the Watch-night, and the tickets
of membership; and they date from this period. He
had hitherto been content to take the Church of England
just as it was in the eighteenth century. He now went
back hundreds of years, to the times when Christianity
was in its infancy; and henceforward through all his
long life he never ceased to refer everything to those
early days. Let us see how this came about. Among
the Oxford Methodists one of the least known, but one
who exercised by far the deepest and most permanent
influence over John Wesley, was John Clayton. He
was a Hulmeian Exhibitioner, and afterwards tutor, of
Brasenose, and he was also a nonjuror and a Jacobite.

He encouraged him to study more thoroughly than he had ever done before the lives and writings of the early Fathers, and he probably introduced him to a still more able and distinguished man than himself, who took precisely the same line, Thomas Deacon, " the most unworthy of Primitive Bishops," as he is termed in his epitaph. The subject is so important in connection with John Wesley's mental history, that some extracts from Clayton's letters may be fitly inserted. In July 1733 he writes—" As to your question about Saturday, I can only answer it by giving an account of how I spend it. I do not look upon it as a preparation for Sunday, but as a festival itself; and therefore I have continued festival prayer for the three primitive hours, and for morning and evening, from the Apostolical Constitutions, which, I think, I communicated to you whilst at Oxford. I look upon Friday as my preparation for the celebration of both the Sabbath [that is, of course, Saturday] and the Lord's Day; the first of which I observe much like a common saint's day, or as one of the inferior holidays of the Church. I bless God I have generally contrived to have the Eucharist celebrated on Saturdays as well as other holidays, for the use of myself and the sick people whom I visit. Dr. Deacon gives his humble service to you, and lets you know that the worship and discipline of the primitive Christians have taken up so much of his time, that he has never read the Fathers with a particular view to their moral doctrines, and therefore cannot furnish you with the testimonies you want out of his collection. However, if you will give me a month's time, I will try what I can do for you. I have made some progress in the earliest authors, and should have made more had I

not been interrupted; first with the public ceremony of
the bishop's triennial visitation; and secondly, with the
blessing of a visit which the truly primitive Bishop
of Man [that is, Bishop Wilson] made to our town
[Manchester], with both which affairs the clergy have
been wholly taken up for a week. I was at Dr. Deacon's
when your letter came to hand, and we had a deal
of talk about your scheme of avowing yourselves a
society, and fixing upon a set of rules. The Doctor
seemed to think you had better let it alone, for to what
end would it serve? It would be an additional tie upon
yourselves, and perhaps a snare for the consciences of
those weak brethren that might chance to come among
you. Observing the Stations and weekly communion
are duties which stand upon a much higher footing
than a rule of a society; and they who can set aside
the command of God and the authority of His Church,
will hardly, I doubt, be tied by the rules of a private
society. As to the mixture, Mr. Colly told me he
would assure me it was constantly used at Christ
Church. However, if you have reason to doubt it,
I would have you to inquire; but I cannot think
the want of it a reason for not communicating. If
I could receive when the mixture was used I would;
and therefore I used to prefer the Castle to Christ
Church; but if not, I should not think myself
any further concerned in the matter than as it
might be some way or other in my power to get it
restored."

This letter shows how anxiously Wesley was now
studying the history of the Early Church. His questions
about the proper way of spending the Sabbath as well
as the Lord's Day (the early Christians often observed

both), about the moral doctrines of the Fathers, about the mixed chalice, which John Wesley seems to have thought not only lawful but necessary,—an idea which quite accords with the undoubted practice of the Early Church,—show plainly enough what was the bent of his mind.

Six weeks later followed another letter from Mr. Clayton, in which he dwells upon the Epistles of St. Clement, St. Ignatius and St. Barnabas, Hermas' Pastor, and the Apostolical Constitutions. And then, referring evidently to some anxious inquiries of Wesley, "How," he writes, "shall I direct my instructor in the school of Christ? or teach you, who am but a babe in religion? However, I must be free to tell you my sentiments of what you inquire about. On Wednesday and Friday, I have for some time used the Office for Passion week out of *Spinckes' Devotions*, and bless God for it. . . . Refer your last question to Mr. Law. I dare not give directions for spending that time which I consume in bed; nor teach you, who rise at four, while I indulge myself in sleep till five."

Nathaniel Spinckes was a pious nonjuror, and his *Devotions* are a collection in the very spirit of the early Church. The last sentence introduces us to another name which will always be associated with that of John Wesley. William Law was, of course, a nonjuror and staunch Churchman. Both the Wesleys had been deeply impressed with his *Christian Perfection* and *Serious Call*, and had made his personal acquaintance. They paid several visits to him at Putney, where he was in the house of Mr. Gibbon as tutor to his son. All these visits were for the sake of religious guidance, and Mr. Law was "a sort of oracle" to Mr.

D

Wesley; he was highly valued also by other Oxford Methodists, one of whom, Mr. Ingham, terms him "a divine man."

The two others of the little band who were certainly the highest in University standing were Mr. Kinchin, Fellow of Corpus, and Mr. Hutchins, Fellow of Lincoln. Mr. Kinchin took a country living, Dummer in Hampshire, and there strove to present the Church's system in all its fullness to the people; Mr. Hutchins has left behind him one sermon (*Concio ad clerum*), in which he advocates the most strictly sacramental interpretation of the sixth chapter of St. John's Gospel. These would be the Methodists who would influence John Wesley most. But for a picture of him as he was in his capacity of "Curator of the Holy Club" we must turn to another of the band, Mr. Gambold, from whose long and extremely interesting description, written when Wesley was in Georgia, the following extracts are taken:—

"Mr. Wesley, late of Lincoln College, has been the instrument of so much good to me, that I shall never forget him. Could I remember him as I ought, it would have very near the same effect as if he was still present; for a conversation so unreserved as was his, so zealous in engaging his friends to every instance of Christian piety, has left now nothing new to be said." Then he describes how, "about the middle of March 1730," he became acquainted with "Mr. Charles Wesley of Christ Church;" and after dwelling upon his own spiritual difficulties, proceeds:—"After some time he introduced me to his brother John, of Lincoln College. 'For,' said he, 'he is somewhat older than I, and can resolve your doubts better.' This, as I found afterwards,

was a thing which he was deeply sensible of; for I
never observed any person have a more real deference
for another than he constantly had for his brother.
Indeed, he followed his brother entirely. Could I
describe one of them, I should describe both." After
explaining the nature of the little society he says—
"Mr. John Wesley was always the chief manager, for
which he was very fit, for he not only had more learning and experience than the rest, but he was blest with
such activity as to be always gaining ground, and such
steadiness that he lost none. What proposals he made
to any were sure to charm them, because he was so
much in earnest; nor could they afterwards slight
them, because they saw him always the same. What
supported this uniform vigour was, the care he took to
consider well of every affair before he engaged in it,
making all his decisions in the fear of God, without
passion, humour, or self-confidence; for though he had
naturally a very clear apprehension, yet his exact
prudence depended more on humanity and singleness
of heart. To this I may add, that he had, I think,
something of authority in his countenance; though, as
he did not want address, he could soften his manner,
and point it as occasion required. Yet he never
assumed anything to himself above his companions.
Any of them might speak their mind, and their words
were as strictly regarded by him as his were by them."
The meetings "at his chamber or one of the others,"
the visits to the poor, the prisons, the schools, and the
workhouse, the endeavours to influence for good "the
younger members of the University," are then described,
and the writer adds: "Though some practices of Mr.
Wesley and his friends were much blamed,—as their

fasting on Wednesday and Friday, after the custom of the Primitive Church,—their coming on those Sundays when there was no sacrament in their own colleges, to receive it at Christchurch—yet nothing was so disliked as these charitable employments. They seldom took any notice of the accusations brought against them; but if they made any reply, it was commonly such a plain and simple one, as if there was nothing more in the case, but that they had heard such doctrines of their Saviour, and believed and done accordingly." [1]

Then follows a defence of Wesley's conduct as " Curator." " What I would chiefly remark upon is, the manner in which Mr. Wesley directed his friends. Because he required such a regulation of our studies as might devote them all to God, he has been cried out upon as one that discouraged learning. Far from that; the first thing he struck at in young men was that indolence which would not submit to close thinking." It is unnecessary to repeat in Mr. Gambold's words what has already been said respecting the doings of the Society; but there is a personal matter on which he represents Wesley in so very different a light from that in which he is sometimes regarded that it should be noticed. " If any one," he writes, " could have provoked him, I should; for I was slow in coming into his measures, and very remiss in doing my part. I frequently contradicted his assertions; or, which is much the same, distinguished upon them. I hardly ever

[1] The unpopularity of the Oxford Methodists was increased by the premature death of Mr. Morgan, who was falsely represented as having destroyed his health by his ascetic practices. His father thought so at first, and was very angry; but John Wesley convinced him that this was not the case.

submitted to his advice at the time he gave it, though I relented afterwards. One time he was in fear that I had taken up notions that were not safe, and pursued my spiritual improvement in an erroneous, because inactive, way. So he came over and stayed with me near a week. He accosted me with the utmost softness, condoled with me the incumbrances of my constitution, heard all that I had to say, endeavoured to pick out my meaning, and yielded to me as far as he could. I never saw more humility in him than at this time. It was enough to cool the warmest imaginations that swell an overweening heart. It was, indeed, his custom to humble himself most before the proud, not to reproach them; but, in a way of secret intercession, to procure their pardon.

"He had not only friends in Oxford to assist, but a good many correspondents. He set apart one day in the week, at the least—and he was no slow composer—for writing letters; in which, without levity or affectation, but with plainness and fervour, he gave his advice in particular cases, and vindicated the strict original sense of the Gospel precepts."[1]

And this is the man who a few years later affirmed that in his Oxford days he was not a Christian! But in his old age he thought differently. "I often cry out," he writes in 1772, "*Vitæ me redde priori!* Let me be again an Oxford Methodist. I am often in doubt whether it would not be best for me to resume all my Oxford rules, great and small. I did then walk closely

---

[1] See *The Oxford Methodists*, by the Rev. L. Tyerman. This is the fullest and best account we possess of this interesting little body of men; but the writer is of course quite out of sympathy with their principles. Could not some Oxford resident, in sympathy with the movement, write something about it?

with God, and redeem the time. But what have I been
doing these thirty years?"

Wesley's six, or rather, off and on, ten years' residence
at Oxford, left a marked influence upon his character.
In a way that is exceedingly difficult to define, one can
trace the University man in him all through his life.
The *genius loci* affected him, and one can quite understand what he means when he says nearly fifty years
later (1781), "I love the very sight of Oxford; but," he
adds, "my prejudice in its favour is considerably abated;
I do not admire it as I once did." He owed, however,
very much to his training there. What was said above
of the public school is still more true of a great University like Oxford. It gives a man a larger way of
looking at men, books, and things in general, which is
clearly distinguishable in John Wesley. The College
Don frequently appears in his dealings with his followers; and, if one may read between the lines, traces
of the influence of the college may frequently be found
in his writings. Is it fanciful, for instance, to suppose
that his love of the Festival of All Saints had something
to do with its being the great day at Lincoln College—
or rather, "The College of the Blessed Virgin Mary and
All Saints," "quod vulgo vocatur Lincoln College"?
On All Saints' Day all the Fellows were present at
morning chapel, and the Senior Fellow read the First
Lesson and the Junior the second (it was the wrong
order, but we did not understand much about ritual
in those days), and all the benefactors of the college
from Richard Fleming and Thomas Rotheram down-
wards were duly commemorated. And then at 11 a.m we
all walked in solemn procession to All Saints' Church,
which was originally the College Chapel, the Rector and

Fellows leading the way, all surpliced, and then the scholars, also surpliced, and then the exhibitioners, and then the commoners—the wrong order again. And a special sermon was preached by the Rector or one of the Fellows, and then the procession returned in the same order. All this went on, according to statute, in Wesley's time. Can one help thinking that it was impressed, though perhaps unconsciously, upon his mind when he wrote—

"1756, November 1, was a day of triumphant joy, as All Saints' Day generally is. How superstitious are they who scruple giving God solemn thanks for the lives and deaths of His Saints!

"1767, November 1. Being All Saints' Day (a Festival I dearly love), I could not but observe the admirable propriety with which the Collect, Epistle and Gospel are suited to each other"?

He always made a point of preaching on "The Communion of Saints" on All Saints' Day. He thoroughly realized the doctrine of the Intermediate State, and to his dying day used to speak of his departed Christian friends, not as "having gone to heaven," in the popular phraseology, but as being in Paradise, or in Abraham's bosom.

His attachment to Oxford was strongly brought out by a dilemma in which he found himself in the year 1734. The health of the Rector of Epworth was obviously failing, and he was naturally anxious that one of his sons should succeed him, so that the old home might not be broken up. Samuel was, of course, the one first thought of. As early as Feb. 28, 173$\frac{3}{4}$, his father wrote to him, expressing his wish to resign Epworth, "provided you could make an interest to

have it in my room." " My first and best reason for
it," he adds, "is, because I am persuaded you would
serve God and His people here better than I have done ;
though, thanks be to God, after near forty years' labour
among them, they grow better, I having had above one
hundred at my last Sacrament, whereas I have had less
than twenty formerly. My second reason relates to
yourself, taken from gratitude, or rather from plain
honesty. You have been a father to your brothers and
sisters, especially to the former, who have cost you great
sums in their education, both before and since they
went to the University. Neither have you stopped
here ; but have showed your pity to your mother and
me in a very liberal manner, wherein your wife joined
with you when you did not over-much abound yourselves, and have ever done noble charities to my children's children." The Wesleys generally, and John
Wesley in particular, had reason to be grateful to
Samuel ; and though the two brothers differed widely
as to the later proceedings of the younger, no diminution
of their mutual affection resulted.

Samuel had but lately settled at Tiverton, and was
naturally unwilling to leave it. Then the two Samuels,
father and son, did their utmost to persuade John Wesley
to seek the post which in all probability would be too
soon vacant. A long and interesting correspondence
ensued, in which John gave his father no less than
twenty-six reasons why he should not leave Oxford.
The elder brother's comment was that he could see in
his brother's arguments his love to himself, but could
not see his love to his neighbour ; and his father wrote
in the same tone—" It is not dear self, but the glory of
God, and the different degrees of promoting it, which

should be our main consideration and direction in the
choice of any course of life." His brother then urged
that his ordination vow obliged him to undertake parish
work, and that he had positively perjured himself if he
refused to do so. This was touching John Wesley on a
tender point; for, however some may disagree with his
sentiments at this period, none can deny that his conscience was most sensitive. His reply was very characteristic—" I own," he writes, " that I am not a proper
judge of the oath I took at ordination ; so I referred it
to ' the high-priest of God,' before whom I contracted
that engagement, proposing this single question to him :
whether I had, at my ordination, engaged myself to take
care of a parish or no ? His answer runs in these words—
' It doth not seem to me that at your ordination you
engaged yourself to undertake the care of any parish, if
you can better serve God and His Church elsewhere !'
Now that I can as a clergyman better serve God and
His Church in my present station, I have all reasonable
evidence." John Wesley took a high, but surely not
an unreasonably high, estimate of the good he could do
at Oxford, in influencing young men at the most pliable
and critical epoch of their lives, and especially young
men, many of whom were in preparation for the sacred
ministry. "Here," he says, "are the schools of the
prophets ; he who gains one does as much service to
the world as he could do in a parish in his whole life ;
in him are contained all who shall be converted by
him ; he is not a single drop of the dew of heaven, but
a river to make glad the city of God." Moreover, if he
desired parish work, he might have it without leaving
Oxford. "I do not," he says, "nor ever did, resolve
against undertaking a cure of souls. There are four

cures belonging to our college, and consistent with a
fellowship. I do not know but I may take one of them
at Michaelmas." This was not a mere flourish of
words. It is literally true that there are no less than
four parochial charges, viz. All Saints' and St. Michael's
in Oxford, and Combe Longa and Forest Hill, villages
in the neighbourhood, which may be, and often are,
held by resident Fellows without resigning their Fellow-
ships. Nor can I see that Wesley laid himself open to
the charge of selfishness, when he pleaded that it would
be better for his own soul for him to remain at Oxford.
Surely to " work out one's own salvation " is a scriptural
precept ; and his bitterest enemies could not accuse
John Wesley of leading a selfish life at Oxford.

However, the earnest pleadings of his father and
brother, and no doubt also the mute appeals of his
mother and sisters, who must otherwise lose their home,
ultimately prevailed. John Wesley consented to accept
Epworth, and one of his own pupils and disciples, Mr.
Broughton, made interest with those in whose gift Crown
livings like Epworth practically lay. The application
was unsuccessful ; the good old rector died in April 1735,
having received the last offices of the Church from his
son John, and the living was given to a gentleman who
appears never to have resided on his cure. John Wesley's
only parish work was done far away from Epworth.

CHAPTER IV.

GEORGIA.

In the year 1732 a Royal charter was granted, for the establishment of a colony "in that part of Carolina which lies from the most northern part of the Savannah river, all along the sea-coast to the southward." A corporation was formed, called *The Trustees for Establishing the Colony of Georgia in America*—the name being of course given in honour of the reigning monarch. The idea originated with James Edward Oglethorpe, a Member of Parliament, and "a gentleman of unblemished character, brave, generous and humane," who had been educated at Corpus Christi College, Oxford, and had then entered the army. He took a great interest in the relief of unfortunate debtors, and the correction of abuses in the conduct of prisons. He was made chairman of a committee of the House of Commons to visit prisons and to suggest a reform. One great difficulty arose as to what was to become of the released debtors, who through no fault of their own had suffered from the cruel laws then in force. The new colony was to be made a refuge for them ; it was thought that it might be beneficial to the mother country as well as to the colonists, since the latter would

protect the southern frontier of Carolina against the
inroads of the Indians. Each male inhabitant was to
be regarded both as a planter and a soldier; each lot
was to be held as a military fief. The colony received
an accession from a party of Salzburghers who were
driven from their homes on account of their religion by
the Roman Catholics. Oglethorpe "gratefully acknowledged the sympathy and valuable co-operation of the
Society for the Propagation of the Gospel in the
accession of colonists from this source," and saw in it
"the rapid conversion of nations, relief from religious
persecution, and the increase of the wealth and trade
of Great Britain." The religious element was very
important in the foundation of the colony. Liberty of
conscience was to be allowed universally to all, except
Papists, in the worship of God. To the west of the
province lay the French, to the south the Spaniards,
who were "all Papists." Hence there was great "fear
of introducing into the colony persons opposed to the
Protestant religion, the maintenance of which was
regarded as all important." The native Indians not
only gave up all opposition to the scheme, but showed a
desire to be instructed in the religion of the white man.
Writing of one of their tribes in 1733, General Oglethorpe says—"Their king comes constantly to church,
is desirous to be instructed in the Christian religion, and
has given me his nephew, a boy who is his next-of-kin,
to educate." This king was named Tomo-chi-chi; he
was of great assistance to the infant colony, and was
evidently quite open to instruction. "We do not," he
said, "know good from evil, but desire to be instructed
and guided by you that we may do well with, and be regarded amongst, the children of the Trustees." Nor did

he stand alone. Another chief declared that "though they were poor and ignorant, He who had given the English breath, had given them breath also; that He who had made them both, had given more wisdom to the white man; that they were firmly persuaded that the Great Power which dwelt in Heaven and all around" —and then he spread out his hands and lengthened the sound of his words—"and which had given breath to all men, had sent the English thither for the instruction of them, their wives and children." Tomo-chi-chi visited England, and made a great impression here. In fact the whole of the Georgian scheme appealed to the best feelings of the nation, and found many sympathizers. Among these were the two Samuel Wesleys, father and son, the former of whom had a correspondence with Oglethorpe on the subject, in which he declared that had he been ten years younger, he would have joined the colonists himself; while the latter presented a set of communion plate for the church at Savannah.[1]

These details have been dwelt upon at some length, because upon them hinges the whole of John Wesley's future history in Georgia, which really influenced his whole after-life. His ardent imagination was evidently fired by the prospect of a glorious work for God to be wrought among the Indians. And what has been said above shows that this was no unreasonable expectation. " I hope," he said, "to learn the true Gospel of Christ by preaching it to the heathen. They have no comments to construe away the text; no vain philosophy to corrupt it; no luxurious, sensual, covetous, ambitious expounders

---

[1] A full and interesting account of the establishment of the Georgian Colony will be found in *The History of Georgia*, by Charles C. Jones, LL.D., 2 vols., Boston, U.S., 1883.

to soften its unpleasing truths. They are as little
children, humble, willing to learn, and eager to do the
will of God, and consequently they shall know of every
doctrine I preach, whether it be of God. By these,
therefore, I hope to learn the purity of that faith which
was once delivered to the saints, the genuine sense and
full extent of those laws which none can understand
who mind earthly things." "Why, Mr. Wesley, if they
are all this already, what more can Christianity do for
them?" replied the lady to whom Wesley expressed his
glowing anticipations, with something of a lady's logic,
for John Wesley based all his hopes upon their *reception*
of Christianity. In short, John Wesley's great object in
going to Georgia was to be a *missioner* (it is his own
word) among the Indians.

The circumstances which led to his appointment were
these:—On his father's death he went to London to present the Rector's volume on the Book of Job to Queen
Caroline. There he fell in with some of the Georgian
Trustees, who were in search of persons who would
preach the gospel to the settlers and the Indians. Dr.
Burton, an Oxford friend of Wesley's, introduced him
to General Oglethorpe as a man eminently qualified for
the work. Wesley hesitated, principally on his mother's
account. "I am the staff," he said, "of her age, her
support and comfort." But he consulted his brother
Samuel, and William Law; and made a special journey
to Manchester to ask the advice of Mr. Clayton and Dr.
Byrom, and then went to Epworth -to lay the case before
his mother. "Had I twenty sons," was her noble reply,
"I should rejoice that they were all so employed, though
I should never see them more." This settled the matter;
but it is a remarkable illustration of the bent of Wesley's

mind, that the only persons he consulted outside his own family in this momentous crisis of his life were Nonjurors and Churchmen of the most advanced type.

John Wesley was sent out as a missionary by the Society for the Propagation of the Gospel, with a stipend of £50 a year. With his characteristic disregard for money, he purposed to refuse the stipend, and live wholly on his Fellowship. But the prudent Samuel prevented him from doing this, very properly arguing that it would be unfair to his successor, and that if he did not require the stipend for his own use he might spend it in doing good. His brother Charles determined to go out with him in the capacity of secretary to the Governor. Two other young men joined them—Benjamin Ingham, the Oxford Methodist, to whom Wesley wrote in his own curt way, " Fast and pray; and then send me word whether you dare go with me to the Indians"; and Charles Delamotte, the son of a London merchant, " who had a mind to leave the world, and give himself up entirely to God." The spirit in which they went forth is thus described by Wesley himself— " Our end in leaving our native country was not to avoid want (God having given us plenty of temporal blessings), nor to gain the dung and dross of riches and honour; but singly this, to save our souls; to live wholly to the glory of God."

Their manner of life on board ship shows how steadily from the very first they kept this end in view. " We resolved," writes one of them, " to rise early, and to spend our time regularly and carefully. The first hour we allotted to ourselves, was to pray for ourselves and absent friends. The next, we read the Scriptures; and from six to breakfast we generally read something

relating to the Primitive Church. At eight we had
public prayers. The forenoon *I* [Ingham] spent either
in teaching and instructing the children, or reading
antiquity; *Mr. John Wesley,* in learning German; *Mr.
Charles Wesley,* mostly in writing; *Mr. Delamotte,* in
learning Greek or Navigation. At twelve we all met
together to join in prayer, and to exhort one another,
consulting both how to profit our neighbours and ourselves. After dinner I taught the children or conversed
religiously with some of the passengers, as also Mr.
Wesley constantly did. At four we had public prayer.
From five to six we spent in private; then we supped."
They afterwards abandoned this luxury. "At seven I
read to as many of the passengers as were willing to
hear, and instructed them in Christianity. Mr. John
Wesley joined with the Moravians in their public
devotions. At eight we all met together again, to give
an account of what we had done, whom we had conversed
with, deliberating on the best method of proceeding
with such and such persons; what advice, direction,
exhortation, or reproof was necessary for them; and
sometimes we read a little, concluding with prayer;
and so we went to bed about nine, sleeping soundly
upon mats and blankets, regarding neither the noise of
the sea or sailors. 'The angels of the Lord are round
about them that fear Him.' "

The Moravians mentioned in the above passage were
an important factor in John Wesley's mental history.
They were twenty-six in number, and were going to
join the Georgian colony, having been driven out of
their own country on account of their religion. Their
simple piety, their humble readiness to do servile work
which the English passengers refused to do, and, above

all, their undaunted courage in facing death when a storm arose (their very women and children showing that they were not afraid to die), impressed John Wesley deeply; and all the more so because they seemed to him to be an exact reproduction in the eighteenth century of the early Christians of the first three centuries. "They are," again to quote Mr. Ingham, "more like the Primitive Christians than any other Church now in the world; for they retain both the faith, practice, and discipline delivered by the Apostles. They have regularly ordained bishops, priests, and deacons. Baptism, Confirmation, and the Eucharist are duly administered. Discipline is strictly exercised without respect of persons. They all submit themselves to their pastors, being guided by them in everything. They live together in perfect love and peace, having, for the present, all things in common. They are more ready to serve their neighbours than themselves. In their business they are diligent and industrious; in all their dealings strictly just and conscientious. In everything, they behave themselves with great meekness, sweetness, and humility." One can readily understand how fascinating such a spectacle would be to John Wesley; it appealed to the two dominant feelings of his mind—his love of practical piety, and his love of Church doctrine and discipline. It was to converse with these Moravians that John Wesley set himself, and accomplished, on shipboard the difficult task of learning German. He had, in an eminent degree, that most useful gift of learning new languages with little trouble.

On February 5th, 1736, the vessel after a stormy voyage reached its destination, and John Wesley at once began, we cannot say to put on his harness, for

E

he had never taken it off, but to work as vigorously for
his Divine Master on land as he had never ceased to
do on board ship.   The newly-raised town of Savannah
was his special sphere; but he was more or less responsible for the spiritual guidance of the whole colony of
Georgia.   His brother Charles had, as we have seen,
come merely as the Governor's secretary, much to John
Wesley's annoyance.   But Charles was now in Holy
Orders, and he worked as a clergyman at Frederika, as
John did at Savannah.   With characteristic promptitude and vigour, John Wesley commenced at Savannah
to carry out the Church system in its most pronounced
form.   He at once established the double daily service
and the weekly Communion.   On Sundays, he "divided
the public prayers according to the original appointment of the Church;" he refused to baptize the child
of an influential parishioner except by immersion; he
formed a society which met on the evenings of Sunday,
Wednesday, and Friday for devotional purposes; he
commenced a system of house-to-house visitation, setting
apart three hours every day for this work; he preached
down the love of fine dress, so that, he says, "I saw
neither gold in the church, nor costly apparel, but the
congregation in general was almost constantly clothed
in plain, clean linen or woollen;" he learnt the Spanish
language that he might converse with his Jewish parish-
ioners, his knowledge of languages also enabling him to
hold a service in French for those who spoke that
tongue, and in Italian for some Vaudois who formed
part of the colony; he put a stop to the better class
of children jeering at their poorer school-fellows who
came to school without shoes and stockings by himself
attending the school bare-foot.   Ever ready to rush into

the breach, when he found that his brother Charles was
in difficulties at Frederika, he changed places with him
for a time. Here he was not so successful. At the end
of about a month one of the congregation said to him,
" I like nothing you do ; all your sermons are satires
upon particular persons. Besides, we are Protestants ;
but as for you, we cannot tell what religion you are of.
We never heard of such a religion before ; we know not
what to make of it. And then your private behaviour.
All the quarrels that have been since your arrival have
been because of you ; and there is neither man nor
woman in the town minds a word you say." As to
knowing what religion he was of, they had only to look
into their Prayer-books, and they would have found it
described plainly enough. But here the larger question
arises, Was the mission in Georgia a failure ? Surely
not ; and in his calmer moods John Wesley himself did
not think it was. His own language in Georgia as to
the hopefulness of his work is most sanguine.

About a fortnight after his arrival, he wrote to Charles
—" I have hitherto no opposition at all ; all is smooth,
and fair, and promising. Many seem to be awakened ;.
all are full of respect and commendation." About two
months later (April 20th, 1736), he wrote to Oglethorpe
—" Savannah never was so dear to me as now. I found
so little either of the force or power of godliness at
Frederika, that I am sincerely glad I am removed from
it." On February 16th, 1737, he wrote to a friend at
Lincoln College, Oxford—" There is great need that
God should put it into the hearts of some to come over
to us, and labour with us in this harvest ; " and then he
owns that the " difficulties we have hitherto met with
have been small." On June 15th, 1737, the Trustees

write, expressing their satisfaction with "your endeavours to suppress vice and immorality, and that a
reformation gains ground, as you observe it does." On
March 28th and 29th, 1737, he wrote two most hopeful
letters which are worth quoting, because they show that
the popular opinion that John Wesley was an unhappy,
disappointed man when he was in Georgia is an utter
fallacy. "I entirely agree with you," he writes to Mr.
Wogan, "that religion is love and peace, and joy in the
Holy Ghost; that, as it is the happiest, so it is the
cheerfullest thing in the world; that it is utterly inconsistent with moroseness, sourness, and indeed with
whatever is not according to the softness, sweetness,
and gentleness of Christ Jesus. I believe it equally
contrary to all preciseness, stiffness, affectation, and
unnecessary singularity." And to Mrs. Chapman—
"You seem to apprehend that I believe religion to be
inconsistent with cheerfulness, and with a social friendly
temper. So far from it, that I am convinced that
religion has nothing sour, austere, unsociable, unfriendly
in it; but, on the contrary, implies the most winning
sweetness, the most amiable softness and gentleness.
Are you for having as much cheerfulness as you can?
So am I. Do you endeavour to keep alive your taste
for all the truly innocent pleasures of life? So do I.
Do you refuse no pleasure but what is a hindrance to
some greater good, or has a tendency to some evil? It
is my very rule"—with much more to the same effect.
And finally, in summing up what had been done in
Georgia during his ministry, he writes—"All in Georgia
have heard the word of God, and some have believed
and begun to run well. A few steps have been taken
towards publishing the glad tidings both to the African

and American heathens. Many children have learned how they ought to be useful to their neighbour. And those whom it most concerns have an opportunity of knowing the state of their infant colony, and laying a firmer foundation of peace and happiness for many generations." His friend and successor, Mr. Whitefield, declared—" The good Mr. John Wesley has done in America is inexpressible. His name is very precious among the people, and he has laid a foundation that I hope neither men nor devils will ever be able to shake. Oh that I may follow him as he has followed Christ!"

Does all this look like a failure? But, it may be asked, how is it that the idea that John Wesley's Georgian mission was a failure has become so prevalent? The answer is, that among those best acquainted with John Wesley's history it is *not* prevalent. But among those who are not so well acquainted, it is quite easy to see how the mistake arose; and John Wesley's own words are to a great extent responsible for it.

In the first place he was, through no fault of his own, disappointed in the object which he had chiefly in view when he left his native land. He went forth to evangelize the Indians, and the project then appeared by no means Quixotic. Their chiefs seemed quite open to instruction, and his first interview with Tomo-chi-chi a few days after his landing was not discouraging. " Ye are welcome," said the chief; "I am glad to see you here. I have a desire to hear the Great Word, for I am ignorant. When I was in England, I desired that some might speak the Great Word to me. Our nation was then willing to hear. Since that time we have been in trouble. The French on one hand, the Spaniards on the other, and the traders that are amongst us, have

caused great confusion, and have set our people against
hearing the Great Word. Their tongues are useless;
some say one thing, and some another. But I am glad
that ye are come. I will assemble the great men of our
nation, and I hope, by degrees, to compose our differences; for without their consent I cannot hear the Great
Word. However, in the meantime, I shall be glad to
see you at my town; and I would have you teach our
children. But we would not have them made Christians as the Spaniards make Christians, for they
baptize without instruction; but we would hear and be
well instructed, and then be baptized when we understood." To which John Wesley replied with characteristic brevity—"God only can teach you wisdom, and if
you be sincere, perhaps He will do it by us." One
hindrance to the work of evangelizing the Indians is
hinted at by the chief; they had of late received so
unfavourable an impression of Christianity as presented
by the French and Spaniards that they were prejudiced
against any further teaching; they had also become em-
broiled in wars among themselves, and hence were not
in a position to hear "the Great Word." And moreover,
John Wesley quite unexpectedly found his time pre-
occupied with work for which he had never bargained.
Instead of being a missionary to the heathen, he was
forced, by the withdrawal of another clergyman, Mr.
Quincy, to become simply the parish priest to the
settlers; that is, to do the very work from which he had
shrunk at Epworth when he was impelled to it by the
strongest and purest of earthly motives, the unanimous
wishes of the Wesley family. No wonder that he was
disheartened; and, instead of being surprised that he did
not accomplish more, one is astonished that he was able

to do so much, considering that the work was uncongenial to him, and that the people among whom he did it were, one would have thought, the very last to sympathize with what would now be called his extremely high Church principles.

Again, his new friends the Moravians unsettled him as to his own spiritual state. Almost immediately after his arrival, one of them subjected him to a cross-examination, which, considering the position and attainments of the respective parties, seems to an outsider, in plain words, rather impertinent. John Wesley however thought far otherwise. He submitted to it humbly and thankfully, and while he taught others in a very authoritative way he was content to attend the Moravian services as a simple learner. The more he saw of them, the more closely they seemed to him to resemble the Primitive Christians. He was present when they elected a Bishop for Georgia, and the proceedings made him "almost forget the seventeen hundred years between, and imagine himself in one of those assemblies, where Paul the tent-maker or Peter the fisherman presided." Their Christian conduct thoroughly won his heart; but withal, they made him dissatisfied with himself, and they must certainly be regarded as one of the causes why he afterwards wrote so despondingly of his work in Georgia. They were also in some degree responsible for the final fracas which brought his residence in Georgia to an abrupt termination; for he consulted them on a most delicate question connected with his private life, and submissively yielded to their decision. The story is a painful one, but it is illustrative alike of John Wesley's strength and his weakness, and must be briefly told.

Miss Sophia Christina Hopkey, the niece of Mr. Causton, the chief magistrate of the place, was intro-duced to John Wesley, soon after his arrival, as an anxious inquirer. She frequently consulted him about her spiritual state; she received lessons in French from him; she dressed in simple white, because he abhorred finery; she was a regular member of his congregation at Savannah both on week-day and Sundays; she nursed him through an illness; in fact the intimacy between the two was very close. It was a strictly religious intimacy—of course; but when a handsome young clergyman and an attractive young lady are thus engaged, an engagement of another kind is apt to be the result. Wesley, with a guileless simplicity which one hardly knows whether to be provoked at or to admire, consulted the Moravians as to whether he should marry her or not; and when the answer was unfavour-able, meekly replied, "The will of the Lord be done." The lady soon consoled herself by marrying a Mr. Williamson, and here the matter ought to have ended. But unfortunately it did not. Wesley still continued his parochial ministrations to Mrs. Williamson, and the husband, not unnaturally perhaps, objected. Wesley had not a high opinion of Mr. Williamson's piety, and probably thought that he influenced his wife against religion. To cut a long story short, he at last felt it his duty to repel Mrs. Williamson from the Holy Communion, and was prosecuted by her husband for so doing in a Civil Court, whose authority in spiritual matters Wesley, as a staunch Churchman, could not recognize. Then the storm burst. A list of grievances, which reminds one of those of the "aggrieved par-ishioner" in the present day, was drawn up. They may

No.

be almost all explained by the fact that Wesley strove
to model his conduct, both in and out of church, on
what he deemed the lines of the Primitive Church.
The great majority of the indictments he declared
"he could take no cognizance of, they being matters of
an ecclesiastical nature;" but he was ready to be tried
upon the only one that was of a secular nature. Mr.
and Mrs. Williamson now purposed going to England,
and Wesley was urged by his friends to go too, lest
they should misrepresent him at home. His brother
Charles and Mr. Ingham had already left Georgia; and
the matter was summarily settled for John by the
magistrates of Savannah appointing another clergyman
to take his place. So with a heavy heart John Wesley
left Georgia for ever; and, being joined by Delamotte,
made his way with great difficulty to Charlestown,
where he took ship on Dec. 22nd, 1737, and after a
stormy voyage reached England once again on Feb. 1st
1738.

On the voyage home, and after his return, he poured
forth the bitterness of his soul in language which in
after years he felt it necessary to modify, if not retract.
"I went to America," he writes, "to convert the Indians;
but oh! who shall convert me? I have a fair summer
religion. I can talk well, but let death look me in the
face, and my spirit is troubled. Alienated as I am from
the life of God, I am a child of wrath, an heir of hell."
Are we to take such expressions literally? If we are,
then we must in common fairness also take literally
quite as strong if not stronger language, which he used
eight months after he had had "the assurance given
him that Christ had taken away his sins." But Wesley
himself has left us in no doubt about the matter. To

the assertion that when he went to convert the Indians
he was not himself converted, he appended many years
later a note, "I am not sure of this"; and to the
words, "I am a child of wrath," another note, "I believe not." He explained himself further—"I had even
then the faith of a servant, though not that of a son"
—a distinction on which he enlarged in one of his
sermons, and in other passages of his works. He gives
us the clue to explain his use of such strong and, we
must add, unguarded expressions, when he calls, in the
very paper in which they occur, "inward feeling the
most infallible of proofs." This was the weak side of
the Moravian teaching, the exaggerated importance
they attached to inward feeling, as Wesley himself
afterwards found to his sorrow. In a most touching
passage in his second letter to Bishop Lavington (1752),
who had twitted him with this strange account of his
spiritual state in America, he himself deprecates the
too literal interpretation of what "was wrote," he says,
"in the anguish of my heart, to which I gave vent
between God and my own soul." If John Wesley was
not a true Christian in Georgia, God help millions of
those who profess and call themselves Christians!

CHAPTER V.

JOHN WESLEY'S mind was now clearly ripe for the powerful influence which was brought to bear upon it. He had failed in his cherished project of converting the Indians, and he seems most unjustly to lay the blame upon himself; he had failed also in that calm trust in God which would stand him in stead in the hour of need. The simple Moravians had not been afraid of facing death, but he had been. "I want," he says, "that faith which none can have without knowing it." In this unsettled frame of mind he met with another member of that Moravian brotherhood which had so fascinated him in Georgia. Within a week of his landing at Deal, he was introduced to Peter Böhler, who had just come to England from Germany. Böhler was ten years younger than Wesley, being only twenty-five, but Wesley was, in his hands, like a little child.

He was led on by him step by step, until he reached the consummation for which he had been yearning. But the remarkable history cannot be so well told as in his own words.

"Feb. 7th, 1738 (a day much to be remembered), at the house of Mr. Weinantz, a Dutch merchant, I met

Peter Böhler, Schulius Richter, and Wensel Naiser, just then landed from Germany."

This was in London, and Wesley found the strangers lodgings in Westminster, near Mr. Hutton's. The next meeting was at Oxford, when Böhler said to him, " My brother, my brother, that philosophy of yours must be purged away;" and forthwith commenced the process of purging.

"March 4th. I found my brother [Charles] at Oxford, and with him Peter Böhler; by whom (in the hand of the great God) I was on Sunday the 5th clearly convinced of unbelief; of the want of that faith whereby alone we are saved. Immediately it struck into my mind, 'Leave off preaching. How can you preach to others, who have not faith yourself?' I asked Böhler whether he thought I should leave it off or not. He answered, 'By no means.' I asked, 'But what can I preach?' He said, 'Preach faith *till* you have it; and then *because* you have it, you *will* preach faith.' Accordingly, Monday the 6th, I began preaching the new doctrine, though my soul started back from the work." On March 23rd, "I met Peter Böhler again, who now amazed me more and more by the account he gave of the fruits of living faith—the holiness and happiness which he affirmed to attend it." On April 22nd he met Peter Böhler again, who spoke to him about the witness of the Spirit, and about saving faith being given in a moment. Wesley rebelled against this, but consulted his New Testament, and found to his astonishment that "scarce any was so slow as St. Paul, who was three days in the pangs of the new birth;" he then objected that the times were changed, but Böhler was prepared to meet this objection by producing actual instances. "I

was beat out of this retreat too," writes Wesley, "by
the concurring evidence of several living witnesses.
Here ended my disputing. I could now only cry out,
'Lord, help Thou my unbelief.'" Peter Böhler left
England in May, but not till he had sown the seed in
Wesley's mind, which was destined to grow up and bear
much fruit. The last stage was reached on May 24th,
1738, in a meeting of a Society in Aldersgate Street,
"when a person read Luther's Preface to the Epistle to
the Romans, which teaches what justifying faith is."
"I felt my heart strangely warmed. I felt I did trust
in Christ, Christ alone, for salvation; and an assurance
was given me that He had taken away my sins, even
mine, and saved me from the law of sin and death; and
then I testified openly to all there what I now first felt
in my heart." The sum of what Wesley had learnt
from Peter Böhler was, that true faith in Christ was
inseparably attended by dominion over sin, and constant
peace arising from a sense of forgiveness; that that
saving faith is given in a moment; and that instantane-
ously a man is turned from sin and misery to righteousness and joy in the Holy Ghost. In later days Wesley
certainly did not insist upon the instantaneousness of
the change, and indeed his own experience did not
altogether bear out the theory.

It was not till several months had elapsed that he
was finally settled. He tells us of being "troubled,
and in heaviness"; of "grieving the spirit of God";
of "a want of joy"; of his not being able to "find in
himself the love of God or of Christ"; of his deadness
and wanderings in public prayer, and "even in the
Holy Communion having frequently no more than a
cold attention"; of "not having that joy in the Holy

Ghost, no settled, lasting joy "; nor "such a peace as
excludes the possibility either of fear or doubt." On
October 23rd, 1738, he writes to his brother Samuel,
" This witness of the Spirit I have not, but I patiently
wait for it." And on Jan. 4th, 1739, he uses these remarkable words—" My friends affirm that I am mad,
because I said I was not a Christian a year ago. I
affirm, I am not a Christian now. Indeed, what I might
have been I know not, had I been faithful to the grace
then given, when, expecting nothing less, I received
such a sense of the forgiveness of my sins as till then I
never knew. But that I am not a Christian at this
day, I as assuredly know as that Jesus is the Christ."
He then declares that he has neither the love of God,
nor the joy of the Holy Ghost, nor the peace of God,
and repeats over and over again that he is not a Christian. This, however, was the last outbreak; henceforth,
during the whole of his long life, hardly the shadow of
a doubt about his spiritual state crossed his path; clouds
and darkness constantly swept over his outer life, but
there was perpetual and unclouded sunshine within.

It has been thought well to anticipate in order to
trace out Wesley's spiritual history without a break.
But it is necessary to go back a little before proceeding
to describe that wonderfully active career which he
commenced soon after the memorable evening in
Aldersgate Street. On May 1st, 1738, when he was
yielding inch by inch to the arguments of his new
mentor, Peter Böhler, he turned upon his old mentor,
William Law, and upbraided him with not having taught
him the same lesson. Law was not the man to leave
such a charge unanswered. *He* too had had an interview with this wonderful German, and was evidently

not at all impressed by him; but he felt it necessary to vindicate himself to his old disciple. The correspondence between the two is most interesting, but too long to quote; and indeed there is little temptation to quote it, for it led to an estrangement, which cannot be too deeply deplored, between two of the holiest and ablest men of the day, who were both intensely in earnest about promoting one great object. It is more pleasant to dwell on the fact that in spite of this difference, John Wesley always spoke of William Law personally with the deepest respect, frequently recommended his practical works, and made them class-books for the two highest classes at Kingswood school; while Law, on his side, though he differed widely from Wesley's later views and practices, and though he certainly as a rule did not spare those from whom he differed, never once drew that terribly powerful weapon, his pen, to deal a blow at his old friend.

John Wesley was the most outspoken of men; whatever was in his mind was at once disclosed without the slightest circumlocution or disguise to all who cared to know it. As he disburdened himself to his old guide, William Law, so he made no secret whatever of his change to other old friends. Among these were the family of the Huttons, whose house in Westminster had been almost John and Charles Wesley's home in London, after Samuel Wesley, through whom they had made acquaintance with the family, had removed to Tiverton. On the Sunday evening after the Aldersgate meeting, John was present at a meeting of one of those religious societies of which more will be said presently, at Mr. Hutton's house, and during the reading of a sermon of Bishop Blackall's, he stood up and declared,

to the amazement of the company, that he had never
been a Christian till within the last five days; that he
was perfectly certain of this; and that the only way for
them to become Christians was to believe and confess
they were not so now. "Have a care, Mr. Wesley," said
Mr. Hutton, "how you despise the benefits received by
the two Sacraments." Hutton was, like William Law, a
nonjuring clergyman of the second generation, and, like
all the Nonjurors, an advanced Churchman. Mrs. Hutton
was still more vehement—"If," she said, "you have
not been a Christian ever since I knew you, you have
been a great hypocrite, for you made us all believe that
you were one." John's reply shows how strong the
Moravian influence was upon him—"When we renounce
everything but faith and get into Christ, then, and not
till then, have we any reason to believe that we are
Christians." John Wesley rarely offended against good
taste, and in later days he would have been the first to
revolt against such an expression as "get into Christ";
but this by the way. Mrs. Hutton wrote an account of
the startling incident to Samuel Wesley, who was her
first friend among the brothers. Samuel's reply was
very characteristic—"What Jack means by his not
being a Christian till last month, I understand not.
Had he never been in covenant with God? Then, as
Mr. Hutton observed, baptism was nothing. Had he
totally apostatized from it? I dare say not; and yet he
must either be unbaptized or an apostate to make his
words true"—and so forth. There was the true Wesley
ring of clearness and directness about the reply, which
also appears in the sharp and abrupt, but always truly
amicable, correspondence on the subject between the
two brothers themselves. Samuel Wesley's was a fine

character, and John Wesley always respected it, though
the divergences between the brothers widened with time.

There was yet one step which Wesley could not be
satisfied without having taken. He must see for himself in their own home these people who modelled their
lives after the Primitive Church. Accordingly, in the
middle of June 1738, he set forth, accompanied by his
old friend Ingham and another, on his pilgrimage. At
Frankfort he had the pleasure of conversing with the
natural father of him whom he now considered as his
own *spiritual* father, Peter Böhler. At Marienborn he
met a brotherhood of ninety persons presided over by
Count Zinzendorf, who was the leader of the whole
community of the United Brethren. Here he spent a
fortnight, and wrote a rapturous account of what he saw
to his brother Samuel, of all men in the world. "God
has given me at length the desire of my heart. I am
with a Church whose conversation is in heaven; in
whom is the mind that was in Christ, and who so walks
as He walked. As they have all one Lord and one
faith, so are they all partakers of one Spirit—the Spirit
of meekness and love, which uniformly and continually
animates all their conversation. I believe, in a week,
Mr. Ingham and I shall set out for Herrnhuth, about
three hundred and fifty miles hence. Oh, pray for
us, that God would sanctify to us all these precious
opportunities."

One of the most striking features in the character of
this remarkable man, is the blending of an almost
unique capacity for ruling with a readiness to submit
to indignities with the utmost meekness. One cannot
describe his treatment at Marienborn better than by
saying in homely phrase that he was made to eat

F

humble pie. He was not admitted to the Holy Communion because "the congregation saw him to be *homo perturbatus*, and that his head had gained an ascendancy over his heart," and also because they were desirous not to interfere with his plan of effecting good as a clergyman of the English Church; and the exclusion was the more marked because his friend Ingham *was* admitted. Count Zinzendorf, who combined the pride of a spiritual autocrat with that of a feudal baron, treated Wesley in the most lordly fashion. He ordered him to dig in his garden, and Wesley humbly obeyed him; he then told him to come with him just as he was to visit a neighbouring noble; and when Wesley asked to be allowed to make himself neat, forbade him, saying, "You must be simple, my brother."

On July 19th, the pilgrims set forth again; at Weimar Wesley was brought before the Duke, who desired to know why he was going to Herrnhuth. "To see the place where the Christians live," was the reply. Having arrived at Herrnhuth, Wesley sat at the feet of a pious carpenter, Christian David, who instructed him in what were thought the most elementary truths, as also did other members of the brotherhood. Wesley received it all with the intensest humility and thankfulness, and wrote, "I would gladly have spent my life here. Oh, when shall this Christianity cover the earth, as the waters cover the sea?" He was absent from England altogether about three months, and he carefully described all the minutest details of the Christian life and teaching which had so delighted him.

But now comes the strangest part of the story. On his return he began a letter to the Moravians at Marienborn and Herrnhuth, in which, after specifying

the many points of which he approved, he proceeded—
" But of some other things I stand in doubt, which I
will mention in love and meekness. Is not the Count
all in all among you ? Do you not magnify your own
Church too much ? Do you not use guile and dissimu-
lation in many cases ? Are you not of a close, dark,
reserved temper and behaviour ? " It is true the letter
was never sent, but it shows what Wesley thought all
the same, and it throws light on another letter which
he actually *did* send to Count Zinzendorf, in which,
having spoken of "the love and zeal of the brethren in
Holland and Germany, particularly at Herrnhuth," he
adds—" I hope to see them at least once more, were
it only to speak freely on a few things which I did
not approve, perhaps because I did not understand
them."

We find the same curiously mixed feelings in John
Wesley with regard to the Moravians in England.
There was, as we shall see, a complete breach between
them and the Wesleys; but another meeting with Peter
Böhler seems to have revived all John Wesley's admir-
ation for that body to which Böhler belonged. " I had,"
he writes (April 6th, 1741), "a long conversation with
Peter Böhler. I marvel how I refrain from joining these
men. I scarce ever see any of them but my heart burns
within me. I long to be with them, and yet I am kept
from them." Such discrepancies, instances of which
may be found in other matters, may be explained, I
think, by the fact that Wesley said or wrote just what
was uppermost in his mind at the moment; he was
frankness itself; and, as his brother Charles said many
years later, could never keep a secret in his life. But
the direct influence of the Moravians upon Wesley only

lasted for a few years at the most, though the indirect
effect of their teaching pervaded all his after life.

Before passing on from the important question of the
Moravian influence, it should be added that what
Wesley learnt from Peter Böhler did not in the least
shake his attachment to the Church of his baptism.
Shortly after the memorable Aldersgate meeting, he
published a pamphlet entitled, *The Doctrines of Salvation, Faith, and Good Works : Extracted from the Homilies of the Church of England*, to show that what he
taught was in accordance with the teaching of his
spiritual mother; and on June 11th, he preached a
sermon at St. Mary's, Oxford, on the text: " By grace
are ye saved, through faith," in which he clearly set
forth his views.   St. Mary's, it should be remembered,
is the University pulpit; his audience would of course
be a critical one; and this sermon must be regarded as
a manifesto, put forth in a place where, of all others, he
would, as a Fellow of a College, be most responsible for
every word he uttered, and where his language would
therefore be carefully chosen.   We find in this sermon
the germs of all his future teaching; but that teaching
is too important a matter to be discussed at the close of
a chapter; it requires and deserves a chapter to itself.

CHAPTER VI.

HAD John Wesley been asked what new doctrine he taught, he would assuredly have answered, "None whatever." Indeed he *did* say so in effect over and over again. He takes up quite eagerly a supposed objection. "'Why, these are only the common fundamental principles of Christianity!' Thou hast said; so I mean; this is the very truth, I know they are no other; and I would to God both thou and all men knew, that I, and all who follow my judgment, do vehemently refuse to be distinguished from other men by any but the common principles of Christianity."[1] And if any one had pressed him further, and desired to know how he would have those common principles interpreted, he would as assuredly have answered, "According to the Church of England." Two or three instances will suffice to show this. "I simply," he writes in 1739, "described the plain, old religion of the Church of England, which is now almost everywhere spoken against under the new name of Methodism." In 1744, "You are a member of the Church of England? Are you? Then the controversy is at an end." "'If this were done in

---

[1] "Character of a Methodist," *Works*, viii. 348.

defence of the Church.' That is the very proposition I undertake to prove." "'But why then do you leave the Church?' '*Leave the Church!* What can you mean?'"[1] In 1745, "But I have greater authority, and such as I reverence only less than the oracles of God; I mean that of our own Church." There was no discrepancy to his mind between these two authorities, the Bible and the Church; the one was but the exponent of the other. In a noble passage he tells us plainly what was the mainspring of all his teaching— "To candid, reasonable men, I am not afraid to lay open what have been the inmost thoughts of my heart. I have thought, I am a creature of a day, passing through life as an arrow through the air. I am a spirit come from God, and returning to God; just hovering over the great gulf; till, a few moments hence, I am no more seen; I drop into an unchangeable eternity! I want to know one thing—the way to land safe on that happy shore. God Himself has condescended to teach the way; for that very end He came from heaven. He hath written it down in a book. Oh give me that book! At any price, give me the book of God! I have it; here is knowledge enough for me. Let me be *homo unius libri*. Here then I am, far from the busy ways of men. I sit down alone; only God is here. In His presence I open, I read, His book; for this end, to find the way to heaven. Is there a doubt concerning the meaning of what I read? Does anything appear dark or intricate? I lift up my heart to the Father of Lights, 'Lord, is it not Thy Word? "If any man lack wisdom, let him ask of God." Thou "givest liberally, and upbraideth not."

[1] *Earnest Appeal to Men of Reason and Religion.*
[2] *Farther Appeal.*

Thou hast said, "If any man be willing to do Thy will, he shall know!" I am willing to do, let me know, Thy will.' I then search after and consider parallel passages of Scripture, ' comparing spiritual things with spiritual.' I meditate thereon with all the attention and earnestness of which my mind is capable. If any doubt still remains, I consult those who are experienced in the things of God ; and then the writings whereby, being dead, they yet speak; and what I thus learn, that I teach."[1]

And by this standard of Holy Scripture as interpreted by his own branch of the Church, he was not only prepared to abide in general terms, but was quite ready to submit every one of his tenets in detail to be tried by this touch-stone. Let us notice briefly what those tenets were.

Justification by faith was the hinge on which all his teaching turned; but it must not for a moment be confounded with what is termed in theological language, Solifidianism. If he was at all inclined to this, when the Moravian influence was yet fresh, he very soon corrected himself. "I fell," he says, "among some Lutheran and Calvinist authors, whose confused and undigested accounts magnified faith to such an amazing size, that it quite hid all the rest of the commandments." This would never suit the practical mind of John Wesley. Nor did this doctrine of justification by faith at all lead him to make light of the necessity of repentance. "Repentance absolutely must go before faith ; fruits meet for it, if there be opportunity." Justifying faith cannot exist without previous repentance. "Whoever

---

[1] Preface to *Sermons*.

desires to find favour with God should cease to do evil,
and learn to do well." [1]   In fact no one who reads
John Wesley's works candidly and intelligently can
for a moment charge him with exalting faith to the
disparagement of those good works which are its inseparable results.   John Wesley was a true preacher of
righteousness; and the most violent opposition he ever
aroused was on the score of his laying too much stress
upon good works.   Faith and holiness, justification and
sanctification, were separable in thought, but quite
inseparable in fact.   "The moment we are justified by
the grace of God through the Redemption that is in
Jesus, we are also born of the Spirit; but in order of
thinking justification precedes sanctification.   We first
conceive His wrath to be turned away, and then His
Spirit to work in our hearts.   Justification implies only
a relative, the new birth a real change.   God in justifying us does something *for* us; in begetting us again He
does the work *in* us.   By justification, instead of enemies
we become children; by sanctification, instead of sinners
we become saints.   The first restores us to the favour,
the other to the image, of God.   Justification, in short,
is equivalent to pardon, and the very moment we are
justified, sanctification begins.   In that instant we are
born again." [2]

This seems to me to be a fair summary of Wesley's
views, but the subject requires further amplification and
explanation.   It must, for instance, be clearly explained
that by faith Wesley meant far more than belief.   It

---

[1] For fuller evidence on this point see Canon Hockin's *John
Wesley and Modern Methodism*, pp. 107—112 (4th ed.).
[2] See *inter alia* Wesley's sermon on "Justification by Faith,"
Vol. I. Sermon V.

was at least as much a moral and spiritual as an intellectual act. "What," he asks, "is faith? Not an
opinion nor any number of opinions, be they ever so true.
A string of opinions is no more Christian faith than a
string of beads is Christian holiness." Opinions are
"feathers light as air, trifles not worth naming." This
taken by itself is rather startling language, and so also
is another passage which contains a strange gloss upon
the Athanasian Creed. "The fundamental doctrine of
the people called 'Methodists' is, Whosoever will be
saved, before all things it is necessary that he hold the
true faith; the faith which works by love; which, by
means of the love of God and our neighbour, produces
both inward and outward holiness. This faith is an
evidence of things not seen; and he that thus believes is
regenerate, or born of God; and he has the witness in
himself (call it assurance, or what you please); the
Spirit Itself beareth witness with his spirit that he
is a child of God. This is 'The true portraiture of
Methodism,' so-called. 'A religion superior to this'
(the love of God and man), none can 'enjoy,' either in
time or eternity." [1] If Wesley was led, as he was accused
of being led, into incautious language and into a mani-
pulation of a creed of the Church, it was not because
he really disparaged orthodoxy, but because he felt so
acutely the necessity of enforcing practical holiness, and
that the mere holding of right opinions in the head
would not suffice to affect the heart and the life. "'We
are saved by faith,' that is, the moment a man receives
faith, he is saved from doubt and fear; and from his
sins, of whatsoever kind they were, from his vicious

[1] Letter to the Editor of *Lloyd's Evening Post*, Nov. 17, 1760.

desires, as well as words and actions, by the love of God and of all mankind, then shed abroad in his heart. But nothing is more unreasonable than to imagine that such mighty effects can be wrought by that poor, empty, insignificant thing which the world calls faith." [1]

With the same view to practical results, he is very careful to explain that by being saved he understood far more than being rescued from future punishment. " By salvation, I mean not merely deliverance from hell, or going to heaven ; but a present deliverance from sin ; a restoration of the soul to its primitive health, its original purity ; a recovery of the divine nature ; the renewal of our souls after the image of God in righteousness and true holiness, in justice, mercy, and truth. Therefore holiness is not a *condition* of a present salvation from sin ; it is the thing itself. Faith is the sole condition." [2]

It was in the same practical spirit—one might almost say with the same intolerance of everything that had not a practical bearing—that he insisted so frequently upon the necessity of a *New Birth* as the beginning of holiness, using language about it which, taken by itself, certainly laid him open to the charge of holding views inconsistent with the Baptismal Service of that Church of which he was an ordained priest. But when we balance one passage with another in his works, we find that the inconsistency does not really exist.

The New Birth, however, is so prominent a feature in Wesley's teaching, that a little more must be said on the subject. He places it in importance on a level with that of justification. " If any doctrines within the

---

[1] *Earnest Appeal*, p. 10.   [2] *Farther Appeal*, p. 47.

whole compass of Christianity may be properly termed fundamental, they are doubtless these two—the doctrine of justification, and that of the new birth; the former relating to that great work which God does *for us*, in forgiving our sins; the latter to the great work which God does *in us*, in renewing our fallen nature." What he means by the New Birth is this—"It is that great change which God works in the soul when He brings it into life; when He raises it from the death of sin to the life of righteousness. It is the change wrought in the whole soul by the Almighty Spirit of God when it is 'created anew in Christ Jesus'; when it is 'renewed after the image of God, in righteousness and true holiness'; when the love of the world is changed into the love of God; pride into humility; passion into meekness; hatred, envy, malice, into a sincere, tender, disinterested love for all mankind. In a word, it is that change whereby the earthly, sensual, devilish mind is turned into the 'mind which was in Christ Jesus.'"[1] It would have saved some confusion if he had called this "conversion," but he was sparing in his use of the word conversion, because he says it does not often occur in the New Testament;[2] and he also seems to have preferred the term New Birth to conversion, because the former implies more necessarily the idea of pain, travail, effort; in a word, repentance, on which, again, as a practical man, he lays great stress. Thus in his first letter to Bishop Lavington, he speaks of "the sorrow and fear which usually attend the first repentance—called by St. Chrysostom, as well as a

[1] "The New Birth." Sermon XLV., Vol. ii. of *Sermons*, pp. 73 and 75.
[2] See second letter to Bishop Lavington.

thousand other writers, 'the pangs or throes of the New
Birth.'"

Here one might stop, for John Wesley expressly
declares—"Our main doctrines, which include all the
rest, are three: that of repentance, of faith, and of
holiness. The first of these we account, as it were, the
porch of religion; the next, the door; the third, religion
itself." The division, it will be seen, precisely corresponds with that of the Church Catechism; in the two
first parts verbatim; in the last, though not verbatim,
yet quite as really, for "love is the fulfilling of the law,"
and holiness and love to God and man were with John
Wesley one and the same thing.

This suggests an answer to another question which
thoughtful people will naturally ask—How is it that
John Wesley does not include among his fundamentals
those Sacraments which his own Church declares to be
"generally necessary to salvation"? The simple answer
is, He *does* include them, precisely in the same way as
the Church Catechism includes them in that threefold
division to which John Wesley's threefold division
exactly corresponds. They belong to God's law of love,
obedience, holiness. Those who desire to see this
idea exhaustively and beautifully worked out, may be
referred to Bishop Ken's *Exposition of the Church
Catechism, or Practice of Divine Love*, the alternative title
of which tells its own tale. All through his life John
Wesley attached the utmost importance to the Sacraments, and the way in which he dealt with them shows
how unaltered his views were from youth to old age
concerning them. For both with regard to Holy Baptism and the Holy Eucharist, he reprinted, for the edification of his followers in later days, works which belonged

to an earlier period. The *Treatise on Baptism*, which he published in 1756, was nothing else than his father's *Short Discourse on Baptism*, published in 1700, with a few verbal alterations. A single extract will suffice to show its tendency—"By Baptism we, who were 'by nature children of wrath,' are made children of God. And this regeneration, which our Church in so many places ascribes to Baptism, is more than barely being admitted into the Church, though commonly connected therewith; being 'grafted into the body of Christ's Church, we are made the children of God by adoption and grace.' This is grounded on the plain words of our Lord, 'Except a man be born again of water and of the Spirit, he cannot enter into the kingdom of God.' By water, then, as a means, the water of baptism, we are regenerated or born again. Herein a principle of grace is infused, which will not be wholly taken away, unless we quench the Holy Spirit of God by long-continued wickedness." [1]

But had not John Wesley forgotten all this when he preached to those who had been already baptized the necessity of a New Birth? Certainly not; for in his famous sermon on the New Birth, he distinctly repeats the same views—"It is certain our Church supposes, that all who are baptized in their infancy are, at the same time, born again; and it is allowed, that the whole Office for the Baptism of Infants proceeds upon this supposition. Nor is it an objection of any weight against this, that we cannot comprehend how this work can be wrought in infants. For neither can we comprehend how it is wrought in a person of riper years."

[1] On this point see further evidence in Canon Hockin's *John Wesley and Modern Methodism*, pp. 81—88.

What then does he mean by saying in the same sermon that "baptism and the new birth are not one and the same thing," and that "it is sure all of riper years who are baptized are not at the same time born again"? Clearly that, to those who are capable of it, faith must precede baptism to make it effectual. Let us remember that John Wesley's mind was permeated with the study of the Primitive Church, in which of course adult baptism was necessarily very common, but never administered without a distinct profession of faith. Let us remember also that the term regeneration (παλιγγενεσία), though applied to the New Birth in baptism, is not confined to that use, but is applied by our Lord (S. Matt. xix. 28) to another Birth. Finally, let us remember that John Wesley's mind was eminently practical, and that when he had found a term which exactly expressed what he meant to convey, he would not shrink from using it simply because another meaning was generally attached to it. He does not ignore or evade the difficulty, but boldly faces it, and then brushes it aside as of no practical import:—"The beginning of that vast, inward change is usually termed the New Birth. Baptism is the outward sign of this inward grace, which is supposed by our Church to be given with and through that sign to all infants, and to those of riper years, if they repent and believe the Gospel. But how entirely idle are the common disputes on this head! I tell a sinner, 'You must be born again!' 'No,' say you, 'he was born again in baptism; therefore he cannot be born again.' Alas, what trifling is this! What, if he was *then* a child of God? He is *now* manifestly a child of the devil; for the works of his father he doeth. Therefore do not play upon words.

He must go through an entire change of heart. In one not yet baptized, you yourself would call that change the New Birth. In him, call it what you will; but remember meantime that if either he or you die without it, your baptism will be so far from profiting you that it will greatly increase your damnation."[1] It should be added that Wesley attached the utmost importance to adult baptism. Such entries as the following are very frequent in his Journal—"I baptized a gentlewoman at the Foundery; and the peace she immediately found was a fresh proof that the outward sign, duly received, is always accompanied by the inward grace." "I baptized Hannah C——, late a Quaker. God, as usual, bore witness to His ordinance!" It is also a significant fact that John Wesley knows no such people as Baptists; he persistently calls them Anabaptists.

In 1788, John Wesley published a sermon on *The Duty of Constant Communion*—he strongly objects to the expression "frequent communion"—with this preface: "The following discourse was written above five-and-fifty years ago, for the use of my pupils at Oxford. I have added very little, but retrenched much; as I then used more words than I do now. But, I thank God, I have not yet seen cause to alter my sentiments in any point which is therein delivered." So the old man of 1788, the founder of the United Societies, was on this most important point entirely at one with the young man of 1733, the Oxford Methodist, Sacramentarian, Curator of the Holy Club! A few sentences from this sermon will suffice to illustrate Wesley's teaching on this point.

[1] *Farther Appeal*, &c., pp. 48, 49. Precisely the same line is taken in the sermon on *The New Birth.*

Having spoken of it as "the food of our souls," which "gives strength to perform our duty, and leads us on to perfection," "let every one, therefore," he goes on, "who has either any desire to please God, or any love of his own soul, obey God, and consult the good of his own soul, by communicating every time he can; like the first Christians, with whom the Christian sacrifice was a constant part of the Lord's service. And for several centuries they received it every day; four times a week always, and every Saint's day beside. Accordingly, those that joined in the prayers of the faithful never failed to partake of the blessed Sacrament. What opinion they had of any who turned his back upon it, we may learn from that ancient canon, 'If any believer join in the prayers of the faithful, and go away without receiving the Lord's Supper, let him be excommunicated, as bringing confusion into the Church of God.'"

In 1745, John and Charles Wesley published a volume entitled *Hymns on the Lord's Supper*, with a Preface concerning the *Christian Sacrament and Sacrifice*, extracted from Dr. Brevint. "Few of the books," writes Dr. Jackson in his *Life of Charles Wesley*, "which they (the brothers Wesley) published, passed through so many editions; for the authors had succeeded in impressing upon the minds of their Societies the great importance of frequent communion. They administered the Lord's Supper in London every Sabbath day." For the present purpose it is sufficient to observe that no one can read either the prose or the verse of this volume without perceiving that it would be difficult to find language strong enough to express the importance which John Wesley attached to the Holy Eucharist in the Christian scheme. Consistently with these high views of the Sacraments of the Gospel, he steadily refused, in spite of strong and persistent pressure, to suffer his preachers to administer either of them. In his famous sermon " On the Ministerial Office," written quite at the close of his life (May 1789), his trumpet gives no uncertain sound on this point. " I wish all of you," says he, "who are vulgarly termed Methodists, would seriously consider what has been said. And particularly you whom God hath commissioned to call sinners to repentance. It does by no means follow from hence that you are commissioned to baptize, or to administer the Lord's Supper. Ye never dreamed of this, for ten or twenty years after ye began to preach— ye did not then, like Korah, Dathan, and Abiram, ' seek the priesthood also.' Ye knew 'no man taketh this honour unto himself, but he that is called of God, as was Aaron.' O contain yourselves within your own bounds; be content with preaching the Gospel"—and so forth. In the same sermon he declares boldly—" The Methodists are not a sect or party ; they do not separate from the religious community to which they at first belonged ; they are still members of the Church ; such they desire to live and to die. And I believe, one reason why God is pleased to continue my life so long is, to confirm them in their present purpose, not to separate from the Church."

There are other specialities in John Wesley's teaching which must be noticed, although they do not stand at all on the same level with those already mentioned.

The doctrine of *Christian Perfection*—not *sinless* perfection as Whitefield and others would persist in calling it—brought upon John Wesley more odium than any

G

other. It was opposed by the old-fashioned orthodox, and still more by the new Evangelical School, as savouring of Pharisaism and spiritual pride. But John Wesley himself intended nothing less. He did *not* mean that any Christian could reach perfection in the sense of being free from ignorance, or from error, or from infirmities, or from temptation; but he *did* mean that they might be made free from outward sin, from evil thoughts, from evil tempers; he *did* mean that " Christians are called to love God with all their hearts and to serve Him with all their strength, which," he says, " is precisely what I apprehend to be meant by the scriptural term, *perfection*." In this sense he declares that he had held the doctrine of Christian perfection long before what is called his conversion. "After weighing this for some years, I openly declared my sentiments before the University in the sermon on the Circumcision of the Heart. About six years after, in consequence of an advice I received from Bishop Gibson, I published my coolest and latest thoughts, in the sermon on that subject." That is, he held the doctrine as early as 1729, preached on it before the University, on Jan. 1st (the Festival of the Circumcision), 1733, and about five years later published his latest thoughts on it. Twenty years afterwards the subject came prominently to the front; and Wesley, with his keen eye for practical results, saw that it was very necessary to guard against the obvious abuses to which the name, if not the thing, is liable. In 1759, he tells his followers that they all ought to wait for entire sanctification (the same as perfection), "not in careless indifference, or indolent inactivity, but in vigorous universal obedience, in a zealous keeping of all the commandments, in watchfulness and painfulness, in denying ourselves and taking up our cross daily; as well as in earnest prayer and fasting, and a close attendance on all the ordinances of God. If any man dreameth of attaining it in any other way, yea, or of keeping it when it is attained, he deceiveth his own soul." And in 1768 he administered what I have no doubt was a well-deserved rebuke to one who had misrepresented his views. "You never heard either from my conversation or preaching or writings that 'holiness consisted in a flow of joy.' I constantly told you quite the contrary; I told you it was love; the love of God and our neighbour; the image of God stamped in the heart; the life of God in the soul of man; the mind that was in Christ, enabling us to walk as Christ also walked. . . . This perfection cannot be a delusion unless the Bible be a delusion too; I mean 'loving God with all our heart, and our neighbour as ourselves.' I pin down all its opposers to this definition of it. No evasion! no shifting the question! where is the delusion of it?"

It was very cháracteristic of the man that while he never professed to have reached this stage of perfection himself, he gave an implicit and often too ready credence to those who maintained that they had reached it. He attached a growing importance to it as years went on, characterizing it as "the peculiar doctrine committed to our trust," though, at the same time, he certainly modified his views as to its nature.

Another doctrine which exposed Wesley to the charge of Pharisaism was the doctrine of *assurance*. By assurance Wesley meant something very different from the final perseverance of the Calvinists. It was simply the assurance of a present pardon, and might be, and very often was, lost. The Christian "has the witness in himself (call it assurance, or what you please); the Spirit itself beareth witness with his spirit that he is the child of God." This seemed to Wesley a necessary result of his view of faith. "Faith implies assurance; an assurance of the love of God to our souls, of His being now reconciled to us, and having forgiven all our sins."[1] But in his old age he vehemently retracted his earlier opinion that such assurance was absolutely necessary as a proof of salvation. "When," he writes, "fifty years ago, my brother Charles and I, in the simplicity of our hearts, taught the people that unless they *knew* their sins were forgiven they were under the wrath and curse of God, I marvel they did not stone us. The Methodists, I hope, know better now. We preach assurance, as we always did, as a common privilege of the children of God, but we do not enforce it under pain of damnation denounced on all who enjoy it not." One of the sources of the strength, and perhaps also sometimes of the weakness, of this remarkable man, was his perfect readiness to abandon, without the slightest hesitation or evasion, any doctrine or practice in which he found himself to have been mistaken.

The last tenet of John Wesley which must be noticed, is one that he derived directly from Peter Böhler, who convinced him with much difficulty, but at last quite completely, that the change of heart is an *instantaneous* process. Here, however, again Wesley by no means contended for the necessity of every one sharing his opinion—he never did that of any opinion except those which were of the very essence of Christianity. " ' So

----

[1] *Earnest Appeal.*

is the kingdom of God as if a man should cast seed into the ground,' &c. The first sowing of this seed I cannot conceive to be other than instantaneous, whether I consider experience, or the Word of God, or the very nature of the thing; however, I contend not for a circumstance, but for the substance. If you can attain it another way, do; only see that you do attain it; for if you fall short you perish everlastingly." [1] "The forgiveness of sins is one of the first unseen things whereof faith is an evidence. And if you are sensible of this will you quarrel with us concerning an indifferent circumstance of it? Will you think it an important objection that we assert that this faith is usually given in a moment?" [2]

Such is a brief, but it is hoped, a correct, and as far as it goes, complete, account of the teaching which from the year 1738 to 1791 John Wesley delivered throughout the length and breadth of the British Isles. The account of his wanderings, as he went about with indefatigable energy, charged with this message, will be the subject of the next chapter.

---

[1] *Farther Appeal*, p. 48.   [2] *Earnest Appeal*, p. 24.

CHAPTER VII.

As it was Charles Wesley, not John, who was the originator of Methodism, so it was George Whitefield, not John Wesley, who commenced the Evangelical Revival. During Wesley's absence in Georgia, Gloucester, Bristol, and London had been stirred by a course of preaching from Whitefield such as they had never heard before. Then, on Wesley's urgent appeal, Whitefield set forth for Georgia, leaving England just at the time when his friend was returning to it. Wesley took up Whitefield's work in England, as Whitefield took up Wesley's in Georgia; and Whitefield, on his return to London within a year, found that those who had been aroused by his preaching had "grown strong men in Christ by the ministrations of his dear friends and fellow-labourers, John and Charles Wesley."

And now (1738) commenced that incessant round of itinerant labours in every part of the British Isles, which makes the last fifty years and more of John Wesley's life a subject calculated to drive a biographer to despair. It is simply impossible to follow him step by step, although there are ample materials to enable one to do so. He seems to fly about like a meteor.

Town after town and village after village are visited by him with bewildering rapidity. A cursory glance at his Journals might lead the reader to think that there was no system in his wanderings; he seems to be here, there, and everywhere. But a closer inspection shows that the "mighty maze" was "not without a plan." The course of his journeys was guided by the direction of the places in which Societies were established, and as these increased in number, so his halting-places seem to have increased. Let any reader try the experiment in the locality with which he is best acquainted. He will soon find that when he knows where John Wesley is, he also knows approximately whence he has come and whither he is going.

The mere figures which represent John Wesley's itinerant labours are enough to take one's breath away. For a man to have commenced at the mature age of thirty-six, and to have travelled during the remainder of his life 225,000 miles, and preached more than 40,000 sermons, some of them to congregations of above 20,000 people, and most of them in the open air, is a *tour de force* to which it would be hard to find a parallel. And yet these figures represent but feebly John Wesley's toils. In order to estimate the mere physical exertion we must carry our thoughts back from the days of railways and good roads to times when there were no railways, and in some places no roads worthy of the name. Then again John Wesley was not the mere preacher. He could echo, indeed, the wish of his friend, Whitefield, "Oh, that I could fly from pole to pole, preaching the everlasting Gospel!" But that was not all; he had to organize and visit his numerous Societies; he kept himself well abreast of the literature of the day by a wide and varied course of reading; he was a most indefatigable writer and compiler; a frequent though most unwilling controversialist; a reformer of practical abuses, and an ardent philanthropist.

Surely such an active life, physical and mental, was never led before; and if we ask for the motive power of all this activity, there is but one satisfactory answer to be given. Facts will not bear out the theory that he was merely an ambitious man who undertook all this Herculean labour to make himself a name and become a great party leader. If this had been his motive, why did he persistently dwell on the fact that he was teaching "the people called Methodists" (he would never call them by any other distinctive name) nothing new? Why did he to the very last cling to the idea that his Societies should simply be an Order in the Church of England? Why did he do absolutely nothing to perpetuate his name, for such a title as Wesleyans was never thought of by him? "So far as I know myself," he said, "I care no more about Methodism than about Prester John." Why, again, if he had been merely an ambitious man, did he shrink to an almost ludicrous extent from intercourse with those who from their position would have been best able to promote his ambitious views, and devote himself to the poor, the uninfluential, the outcast? [1]

---

[1] Mr. Alexander Knox, who had a wonderful knack of hitting the right nail upon the head, asks also very pertinently, "Could John Wesley have been absorbed in a passion, at once as selfish and as fascinating as any which actuates corrupt statesmen, or more corrupt demagogues, and yet enjoy a 'cheerfulness' like 'perpetual sunshine,' from 'the approbation of his own mind, the certainty that he was employed in doing good to his fellow-creatures, and the full persuasion that the Spirit of God was with him in his work'?" The words in inverted commas are a

Nor again was it the mere love of excitement and novelty which led him to be always on the move. Such restlessness of mind and body is generally found in people who have no resources in themselves; but John Wesley, as a highly-educated scholar, had resources in abundance; and there are some touching passages in his Journals which show that if he had consulted his natural inclinations he would often have been thankful to be at rest. Witness the following—

" March 17, 1752. Mr. ——'s aunt could not long forbear telling me how sorry she was that I should leave all my friends to lead this vagabond life. Why, indeed, it is not pleasing to flesh and blood; and I would not do it if I did not believe there was another world."

" March 9, 1759. At the Foundery. How pleasing would it be to flesh and blood to remain at this little, quiet place, where we have at length weathered the storm! Nay, I am not to consult my own ease, but the advancing the kingdom of God."

" August 27, 1775. I went to Miss Bosanquet's [near Wigan], and prepared for the Conference. How willingly could I spend the residue of a busy life in this delightful retirement! But

'Man was not born in shades to lie!'

" Up and be doing. Labour on, till

'Death sings a requiem to the parting soul.'"

---

quotation from Southey's *Life of Wesley*. The whole of Knox's *Letter to Mrs. Hannah More*, on Mr. Southey's *Life of John Wesley* (*Remains*, iii. 457-470, from which the above is taken), and also his *Letter on the Life of John Wesley* (*Ib.* 471-480), are well worth reading. Mr. Knox seems to me to have understood Mr. Wesley better than any man, living or dead.

"September 11, 1788. I went over to Kingswood; sweet recess! Where everything is now just as I wish. But

> 'Man was not born in shades to lie !
> Let us work now : we shall rest by and by.' "

When he wrote this he was in his 86th year! *Solve senescentem*, &c., was not his maxim.

In fact, the more closely John Wesley's history is studied, the more clearly does it appear that his one object was to do good ; that his sole quarrel was with sin and Satan, and his sole ambition to promote the love of God and man, to restore the Divine Image in the souls of as many as he could influence. Those who knew him best testify to this the most warmly. There is a genuine ring about their language on this point which shows how thoroughly they were convinced of it. Let us take two instances out of many. Alexander Knox was the friend of later years, who combined, perhaps, above all others wide culture with ardent piety, and his testimony is all the more valuable because he was very far from being a blind admirer of Wesley. He had once belonged to one of his Societies, but had afterwards changed his sentiments and withdrawn. But difference of views made no difference in his conviction of the singleness and purity of Wesley's aim. It has always seemed to me most unfortunate that Knox's *Remarks* should have appeared merely as an appendix to Southey's *Life*. Readers, as a rule, rebel against appendices. It is exasperating to find, when you have reached the end of a book, that you have *not* reached the end, that there are " more last words," and you decline to read them. Now those last few pages tacked on to the second volume of Southey are, to a student of John Wesley, worth far more than all the rest of the two volumes (including Coleridge's Notes) put together. Knox knew Wesley intimately, Southey did not. Knox took the deepest interest in just those subjects which one most connects with the name of Wesley. Southey can scarcely be said to have done so; he simply took up the life, as he might have taken up any other life, in the way of business.[1] These are the terms in which Knox speaks of Wesley's motives—"The slightest suspicion of pride, ambition, selfishness, or personal gratification of whatever kind, stimulating Mr. Wesley in any instance, or mixing in any measure with the movements of his life, never once entered into my mind. That such charges were made by his opponents I could not be ignorant. But my deep impression was, and it certainly remains unimpaired, that since the days of the Apostles there has not been a human being more thoroughly exempt from all *those* frailties of human nature than John Wesley."[2] To the same effect Dr. Whitehead, Wesley's literary executor and biographer—"Having known him for twenty-five years, and having examined his private papers, I have no hesitation in declaring that I am fully convinced he used all his influence and power, to the best of his judgment, on every occasion to promote the interests of Christianity, the prosperity of the people he

---

[1] This is not intended as any reflection on Southey, whose *Life of Wesley* is, after all, by far the best, from a literary point of view, which we possess. But this very fact makes one regret all the more that a man of equal calibre with Southey (such as I venture to think Knox was), and of a more kindred tone of mind, did not give us the life *par excellence* of the great reformer.

[2] He repeated this still more emphatically in letters to Mrs. Hannah More published in his *Remains*.

governed, and the peace and welfare of his country,
disregarding any private concern or attachment whatever, when it stood in the way of his general purpose of
doing good." This is the unvarying strain of those who
knew Wesley best; they were outsiders who imputed
to him other motives.

Numberless instances might be given, but it is high
time that we began to grapple with the almost in-
superable difficulty of dealing with the details of
Wesley's itinerant work. Where are we to begin, and
where are we to end? One feels painfully the truth of
a remark made by one of Wesley's most acute critics—
"John Wesley's life was no life at all in the ordinary
sense of the word, but only a mere string of preachings,
&c. His Journals are like the note-books of a physician
—a curious, monotonous, wonderful narrative."[1] In
fact, it would simplify matters if, instead of inquiring,
"What places did John Wesley visit?" we inquired,
"What places of any importance in the British Isles
did he *not* visit?" Let us take the account of one single
week, extracted almost at hap-hazard from his Journal.

. "May 1747, *Sun.* 10.—I preached at Astbury at five;
and at seven proclaimed at Congleton-cross, Jesus Christ
our 'wisdom, and righteousness, and sanctification, and
redemption.' It rained most of the time that I was
speaking; but that did not hinder abundance of people
from quietly attending. Between twelve and one I
preached near Macclesfield, and in the evening at
Woodly-green.

"*Mon.* 11.—I preached at noon about a mile from
Ashton, and in the evening at Stayley-hall. *Tuesday*

---

[1] *Historical Sketches of the Reign of George II.*, by Mrs. Oliphant.
Vol. ii., *The Reformer*, p. 68.

12.—I rode to Bongs, and explained to a serious people the parable of the Prodigal Son. In the evening I exhorted them at Chinley, 'earnestly to contend for the faith once delivered to the Saints.' *Wed.* 13.—I preached at noon in the High-peak, and in the evening at Sheffield. *Thursday* 14.—I rode to Barley Hall. As soon as I had done preaching, William Shent told me he was just come from Leeds, where he had left Mr. Perronet in a high fever. I had no time to spare ; however, at three in the morning on *Friday* 15, I set out, and between seven and eight came to Leeds. By the blessing of God he recovered from that hour."

" Being willing to redeem the time, I preached at noon, and then hastened back to Barley Hall, where I preached at seven, on 'Glorify God in your body, and in your spirit, which are God's.' *Sat.* 16.—I spent an hour or two at Nottingham, and then rode on to Markfield. At eight I preached. The church was pretty well filled, and God gave a blessing with His Word."

And this is a sample of what went on for fifty-two years ! Cold or hot, wet or dry, good roads, bad roads, or no roads at all, it was all one to John Wesley ; there he was at his post, morning, noon, and night, to deliver, as best he might, the message of his Divine Master.

It is a somewhat invidious task to select out of so many a few particular places, which were connected with John Wesley's itinerant work. But the attempt must be made ; and there will, at any rate, be no difficulty in knowing where to begin. For during the first three or four years of his itinerant life, he had only two chief centres, London and Bristol.

Within five weeks of his return from Germany in 1738, he and his brother Charles had created such a

sensation by their preaching in the metropolis, that they
had to wait on the Bishop of London (Dr. Gibson), to
answer complaints which had reached him about their
doctrines.   There is a painful interest about this and
other interviews, which followed in rapid succession
between John Wesley and the Bishops, because one
feels that the future of Methodism in its relation to the
Church depended very much upon them.   It certainly
cannot be said that he was in any instance treated un-
kindly; what rather seems to have been wanting was
definite guidance, the natural result of that lack of a
firm grasp of Church principles, which is so terribly
conspicuous in the whole history of the Church in the
eighteenth century.   The points on which the discussion
between John Wesley and Bishop Gibson turned, were
the doctrines of "an absolute assurance of salvation"; of
justification by faith only, which might be so stated as
to lead to Antinomianism; the propriety of re-baptizing
those who had only received lay-baptism, on which
Wesley, quite characteristically, held stiffer views than
the Bishop; the nature of the "Religious Societies," and
whether the attending their meetings came within the
range of the Conventicle Act or not.   Now on the first
two points we have only to turn from John Wesley to
John Wesley, to see how useful definite guidance would
have been to him.   The first doctrine was the very one
for the unguarded preaching of which, just at this time,
he "marvelled" many years later that the people did
not stone him.   As to the second, we have only to turn
to the famous Conference Minutes of 1770 to see that
Wesley himself thought afterwards that there really
was a danger of its being so stated as to lead to Antinomianism; on the third point, the Wesleys would, in

plain words, have been all the better for a gentle snub, which the Bishop might with great advantage and propriety have administered to them; and on the fourth, when Wesley asked "if his reading in a Religious Society made it a conventicle," and "if Religious Societies are conventicles," the reply was miserably inadequate: "I think not, but I determine nothing; read the acts and laws on the subject for yourselves." But surely the Bishop might have "determined" something. The Religious Societies were excellent institutions, and valuable feeders of the Church. One of their earliest and chief promoters had been one of the best men and soundest Churchmen of his day, Bishop Beveridge. If John Wesley had been assured on high authority that these Religious Societies were things not merely to be winked at, but warmly encouraged, who can tell what might have been the effect upon him as one who sincerely desired to be loyal to the Church of his baptism? The close of the interview is more satisfactory. The brothers requested that the Bishop would not in future receive an accusation against them but at the mouth of two or three witnesses, and he replied, "No, by no means; and you may have free access to me at all times." They then thanked his lordship, and departed.

By the close of 1738 John Wesley was "almost uniformly excluded from the pulpits of the Established Church," that is, we may presume, in London, for that was the chief scene of his labours. "Be pleased to observe," he says, "I was forbidden, as by a general consent, to preach in any church (though not by any judicial sentence)."[1]

[1] *Farther Appeal*, p. 113.

Now let us clearly understand what this means. He
was excluded from churches in which, under any circumstances, he would have had no right to officiate
without the Bishop's and the incumbent's leave. And,
in common fairness to the clergy, it must be remembered that they did not know him as we know him. If
they had heard of him at all, it would only be as of
one who had set the ordinary routine of the Church at
defiance. This fact, which is far too frequently ignored,
is strikingly illustrated by another remarkable interview with a Bishop which will be noticed presently.
Indeed, this period might be described as the period of
"interviewing" Bishops. In February 1738-9, John
Wesley went with Whitefield to the Bishop of Gloucester
(Dr. Benson) to solicit a subscription for Georgia; then
the two brothers Wesley waited on the Archbishop of
Canterbury (Dr. Potter), who, as he had always done,
"showed them great affection." He "cautioned them
to give no more umbrage than necessary, to forbear exceptional phrases, and to keep to the doctrines of the
Church"—very sensible advice, but rather vague. They
said they expected persecution, but would abide by the
Church till her articles and homilies were repealed;
not a very likely contingency to arise. Then they went
again to Bishop Gibson, who "denied that he had condemned them, or even heard much about them, warned
them against Antinomianism, and dismissed them
kindly." And then, after a short interval, occurred
the most important episcopal interview of all.

But before touching upon this, we must retrace our
steps. On Feb. 17, 1738-9, Whitefield began to preach
in the open air to the colliers at Kingswood; day after
day, all through the cold months of February and

March, he repeated the experiment, now on Hannam Mount, now at Rose Green, now on a bowling-green in the heart of Bristol itself, and on various other spots. The effects were marvellous; the congregations increased from 200 to 20,000; and as he now wished to try what he could do elsewhere, he sent for his old friend John Wesley to take his place at Bristol and Kingswood. John writes in his Journal—"March 31, 1739. Reached Bristol, and met Mr. Whitefield there. I could scarce reconcile myself at first to this strange way of preaching in fields, of which he set me an example on Sunday, having been all my life (till very lately) so tenacious of every point relating to decency and order, that I should have thought the saving of souls almost a sin, if it had not been done in a church."

However, though to the last it was a cross to him, he *did* reconcile himself to it as " a thing submitted to rather than chosen, and submitted to because preaching even thus was better than not preaching at all." And so Hannam Mount, Rose Green, and the other parts about Bristol and Kingswood which had lately rung with the voice of Whitefield now rang with the voice of Wesley; and then the friends met in London, and Wesley preached on Blackheath to twelve or fourteen thousand; " the Lord," says Whitefield, "giving him ten thousand times more success than He has given me."

But Wesley's preaching at Bristol and Kingswood produced effects which Whitefield's apparently more exciting sermons had not done. A single extract from Wesley's Journal will show of what nature these were.

"April 26, 1739, at Newgate [Bristol], I was led to pray that God would bear witness to His word. Imme-

H

diately one, and another, and another sunk to the
earth; they dropped on every side as if thunderstruck.
One of them cried aloud. We besought God in her
behalf, and He turned her heaviness into joy. A second
being in the same agony, we called upon God for her
also; and He spoke peace unto her soul. In the evening one was so wounded by the sword of the Spirit,
that you would have imagined she could not live for a
moment. But immediately His abundant kindness was
shown, and she loudly sang of His righteousness."

This is only one out of numerous similar entries
in the Journal for the spring of 1739. In fact these
physical phenomena, some of them in the form of the
most awful convulsions, were every-day occurrences
during Wesley's sojourn at Bristol.

In the midst of all this wild excitement, Wesley had
an interview with the Bishop of the diocese. This
Bishop was none other than the great Joseph Butler,
who had already published *The Analogy*, and whose
mental powers were at their zenith. Now it surely
will not be contended that the author of *The Analogy*
deliberately set himself against a work which he knew
to be the work of God. And yet he was more hostile
to Wesley than any prelate had yet been. The upshot
of the conversation was this. The Bishop said—"Well,
sir, since you ask my advice, I will give it freely. You
have no business here; you are not commissioned to
preach in this diocese; therefore I advise you to go
hence." To which Wesley replied—"My Lord, my
business on earth is to do what good I can. Wherever,
therefore, I think I can do most good, there must I stay
so long as I think so. At present I think I can do
most good here, therefore here I stay. Being ordained

a priest, by the commission I then received, I am a priest of the Church Universal; and being ordained as Fellow of a College, I was not limited to any particular cure, but have an indeterminate commission to preach the word of God in any part of the Church of England. I conceive not, therefore, that in preaching here by this commission I break any human law. When I am convinced I do, then it will be time to ask, Shall I obey God or man? But if I should be convinced in the meanwhile that I could advance the glory of God and the salvation of souls in any other place more than in Bristol, in that hour, by God's help, I will go hence, which till then I may not do."

It is deeply to be regretted that any misunderstanding should have arisen between two great and good men, both of whom had done, and were doing, in their different ways, more than any two men in England to help the cause of their common Christianity. *The Analogy* was the very best of the many good works which had firmly established Christianity against the bitter attacks which had been made upon it from various quarters. The victory had been complete on the intellectual side; it now remained to give it, in the language of preachers, "a practical application." Bishop Butler had complained in the advertisement to his great work—" It is come, I know not how, to be taken for granted by many persons that Christianity is not so much a subject of inquiry, but that it is now at length discovered to be fictitious. And accordingly they treat it as if, in the present age, this were an agreed point among all people of discernment, and nothing remained but to set it up as a principal subject of mirth and ridicule, as it were, by way of reprisals for its having so long interrupted the pleasures of the world."

This was in 1736; and now in 1739 there stood before him a man who was prepared to devote himself, body and soul, to the work of contending against the godless spirit of the age; no ignorant fanatic, but a highly cultivated gentleman and scholar, a man of intense earnestness and boundless energy, and deeply attached to the Church of which Butler was a bishop. Was he not just the man to do the work which, in the Bishop's own view, was so sorely needed? But Bishop Butler shared the almost universal feeling of his age against everything that savoured in any degree of that dreaded enemy "enthusiasm." The wild extravagances which had been perpetrated during the reign of the Saints, under the pretext of the extraordinary illumination of the Holy Spirit, were too recent to allow even a clear-headed man like Butler to weigh calmly the pretensions of one who would certainly seem to him an enthusiast. "Sir," he said to him, "the pretending to extraordinary revelation and gifts of the Holy Ghost is a horrid thing, a very horrid thing." And Wesley's plea, that when he was ordained priest on the title of his Fellowship, he had a roving commission given to him to preach just where he liked, and set bishops, incumbents, and all parochial order at defiance, could hardly commend itself to an orderly mind like that of Bishop Butler. Wesley, on his side, clearly did not appreciate the sort of man with whom he was dealing. We may be quite sure that in later years, when his own judgment had become more matured, and when he had read and admired "that fine book, Bishop Butler's *Analogy*," he would have addressed its great writer with more respectful consideration.

But he was now in the ardour of his first love, and would allow nothing to interfere with what he regarded as his great work. So the Bishop went on his way, and Wesley went on his.

But surely it is not unreasonable to suppose that many clergy felt as Bishop Butler felt, and that the true ground of their disapproval of Wesley's proceedings was not that they loved darkness rather than light, because their deeds were evil. Take the case of Wesley's own brother. By the confession of all, Samuel Wesley was a good man according to his lights,[1] and yet he could hardly find language strong enough to express his disapproval of the "new departure" of John and Charles. With that blunt outspokenness which was a characteristic of all the Wesley family, he thus ungraciously acknowledges the receipt (whether as a gift or not, we do not know) of one of his brother's publications[2]—"April 16, 1739. I have got your abridgment of Halyburton; and, if it please God to allow me life and strength, I shall demonstrate that the Scot as little deserves preference to all Christians, as the book to all writings but those you mention. There are two flagrant falsehoods in the very first chapter. But your eyes are so fixed upon one point that you overlook everything else. You overshoot, but Whitefield raves." Some months later (September 3) he cross-questions him about the physical phenomena:

---

[1] Mr. Telford, with his usual fairness, owns that "whatever were Samuel Wesley's prejudices against the new movement, he was a devoted Christian."—*Life of Charles Wesley*, p. 77.

[2] *An Abstract of the Life and Death of Mr. Thomas Halyburton.* With recommendatory Epistle by George Whitefield, and Preface by John Wesley. Oswald : London, 1739.

"Did these agitations ever begin during the use of any collects of the Church? or during the preaching of any sermon that had before been preached within consecrated walls without effect? or during the inculcating any other doctrine besides that of your new birth?" And, what must have cost one who had always been the most affectionate of sons the greatest effort, he felt it a duty to unsettle his aged mother by warning her in the strongest terms against countenancing what he thought the delusions of her younger sons. "It was with exceeding concern and grief I heard you had countenanced a spreading delusion, so far as to be one of Jack's congregation. Is it not enough that I am bereft of both my brothers, but must my mother follow too? I earnestly beseech the Almighty to preserve you from joining a schism at the close of your life, as you were unfortunately engaged in one at the beginning of it. It will cost you many a protest, should you retain your integrity, as I hope to God you will. They boast of you already as a disciple. They design separation. They are already forbidden all the pulpits in London; and to preach in that diocese is actual schism. In all likelihood, it will come to the same all over England, if the Bishops have courage." Then he specifies the points, which include most of the distinctive features of John Wesley's system, with the strongest disapproval, and declares, "As I told Jack, I am not afraid the Church should excommunicate him (discipline is at too low an ebb), but that he should excommunicate the Church. It is pretty near it." He evidently thinks it is a pity that more stringent measures could not be taken against his brothers, but "ecclesiastical censures have lost their terrors—thank fanaticism on the one

hand, and atheism on the other. To talk of persecution from thence is mere insult." Within three
weeks of writing these very plain words the writer had
passed away. Now if a good man who loved John
Wesley dearly, and must have known his real goodness,
could be so strongly opposed to his irregular proceedings, is it not more than probable that many other good
men, who knew and cared nothing about him personally,
opposed him simply because they thought he was wrong,
and not because they were hostile to spiritual religion ?

And now to return, from this long but very necessary
digression, to John Wesley's outer life. From 1738 to
1742 the scenes of his work were chiefly Bristol and
London, and the places which lay between them. But
in 1742 he was drawn northwards. John Nelson, a
pious stonemason, persuaded him to come and give him
a helping hand in Yorkshire, and Lady Huntingdon
induced him to try and arouse the colliers on the Tyne,
as he had aroused the colliers on the Avon. Hence Newcastle became a third great centre, and there were few
places which he loved more, and where his labours were
more highly appreciated. His preaching among the
colliers of Newcastle was as successful, if not more so,
than among the colliers of Bristol and Kingswood.
Seventeen hundred and forty-two was an eventful year
in Wesley's itinerant work ; in that year he began to
plant the seed in many different counties; in that
year he visited Epworth after seven years' absence.
As his invariable custom was, he offered his services in
the old church where he had so often ministered and
worshipped. Of course the curate-in-charge, Mr.
Romley, was quite within his rights when he rejected
them, but it was an instance of "summum jus, summa

injuria." He owed his own position in life entirely to
the Wesley family; he might at least have remembered
that John was the son of his late benefactor; and, however much he might have disagreed with John Wesley's
views, it was neither a graceful nor a grateful act to
preach a sermon obviously directed against them. But
he could not possibly have pursued a policy better
calculated to defeat his own ends. John Wesley, not
being allowed to preach in the church, took up his
position on his father's tomb, and every evening for a
week preached to congregations such as had never been
seen before at Epworth. No wonder that there were
" few places where his preaching was attended with
greater or more permanent effect than at Epworth on
this his first visit."[1] No wonder that Wesley himself was more than content with the result. So dramatic
an incident of course took hold of the popular mind;
and among the many pictures of John Wesley, none
is more effective than that which represents him
delivering from this coign of vantage the message
which he was not permitted to deliver within the
venerable walls hard by. Nothing has tended more
to encourage the popular idea that Wesley was " turned
out of the Church." If he might not preach in the
church of which his father had been rector, and himself
curate, where might he preach? The argument is not
logical; for exclusion from a building and exclusion from
a society are different things. But simple people do
not discriminate; and the Church owes a deep grudge
to Mr. Romley, who half a year later completed the
disastrous work which he had begun by repelling

[1] *Southey*, i. 382.

Wesley from the Holy Communion. The story must be told in Wesley's own words. " Jan. 2, 1743.—At Epworth. Many from the neighbouring towns asked if it would not be well, as it was Sacrament Sunday, for them to receive it. I told them, ' By all means; but it would be more respectful first to ask Mr. Romley, the curate's leave.' One did so in the name of the rest, to whom he said, ' Pray tell Mr. Wesley I shall not give him the Sacrament, for he is not fit.' How wise a God is our God! There could not have been so fit a place under heaven where this should befall me first as my father's house, the place of my nativity, and the very place where, ' according to the straitest sect of our religion,' I had so long ' lived a Pharisee.' It was also fit in the highest degree, that he who repelled me from that very table where I had myself so often distributed the Bread of Life, should be one who owed all in this world to the tender love which my father had shown to his, as well as personally to himself." For the credit of Epworth Church I hasten to add some further extracts, which show that at a later period her most distinguished son was better received by his spiritual mother.

"July 3, 1748.—Epworth. Mr. Hay, the rector, reading prayers, I had once more the comfort of receiving the Lord's Supper at Epworth. I was peculiarly pleased with the deep seriousness of the congregation at church, both morning and evening; and all the way as we walked down the Church Lane, after the sermon was ended, I never saw one person look on either side, or speak one word to another."

" March 12, 1758.—Epworth. I was much comforted at church, both morning and afternoon, by the serious behaviour of the whole congregation, so different from what it was formerly."

From the commencement of Wesley's itinerant work, mob violence was one of the forms of opposition which he had to encounter. It broke out both in London and Bristol, when those places were the only great centres; but though the magistrates would not interfere at first, they very soon checked it with a firm hand; and the admirable courage and coolness of Wesley himself helped them to stamp out the nuisance. But as soon as the work began to spread, the violence broke out again with redoubled force. It reached a climax among the wild colliers of Staffordshire in the summer of 1743. Wednesbury was one of the chief scenes of these disgraceful riots. In the January John Wesley had visited the place with considerable success, the vicar, Mr. Egginton, encouraging his work. But in the spring Wesley found, he says, "things surprisingly altered. The inexcusable folly of Mr. W——s [one of his preachers who had railed against the Church] had so provoked Mr. E——n, that his former love had turned into bitter hatred; but he had not yet had time to work up the poor people into the rage and madness which afterwards appeared." In June Wesley received "a full account of the terrible riots in Staffordshire," and with his usual courage set out at once for the scene of danger. But it was not till the close of October that the storm burst out in all its fury. Then the mob besieged the house in which he was staying, and cried, "Bring out the minister; we will have the minister." "I desired one to take their captain by the hand and bring him into the house. After a few sentences interchanged between us, the lion was become a lamb. I desired

him to go out and bring one or two more of the most
angry of his companions.   He brought in two who were
ready to swallow the ground with rage, but in two
minutes they were as calm as he.   I then bade them
make way that I might go out among the people.   As
soon as I was in the midst of them, I called for a chair,
and standing up, asked, ' What do any of you want with
me ? '   Some said, ' We want you to go with us to the
Justice.'   I replied, ' That I will, with all my heart.'
I then spoke a few words which God applied ; so that
they cried out with might and main, ' The gentleman
is an honest gentleman, and we will spill our blood in
his defence.'"   But unfortunately the matter did not
end here.   The Justice was timid, and would not interfere.   So Wesley was hurried on to another magistrate
at Walsal, who was equally timid.   It was now dark,
and as they were returning to Wednesbury they were
met by a Walsal mob ; Wesley's convoy deserted him,
and he was left alone in the midst of an infuriated
rabble.   They seized him by the collar and strove to
pull him down ; one struck him on the breast, another
on the mouth with such force that the blood gushed
out ; another lifted up his arm to strike, but then let it
drop, and stroked his head, saying, " What soft hair he
has !"   He was dragged back to Walsal and paraded
through the main street.   " Are you willing," he cried,
" to hear me speak?"   They replied, "No, no; knock out
his brains ; down with him ; kill him at once !"   "What
evil," asked Wesley, " have I done ?   Which of you all
have I wronged in word or deed ? "   " Bring him away !
bring him away ! " was the reply.   And then he began
to pray ; and one of the ringleaders turned and said,
" Sir, I will spend my life for you ; follow me, and no

one shall hurt a hair of your head." Two or three others joined, one of them, luckily, a prize-fighter, and so he was rescued; and " a little before ten o'clock," he writes, " God brought me safe to Wednesbury, having lost only one flap of my waistcoat, and a little skin from one of my hands. From the beginning to the end I found the same presence of mind as if I had been sitting in my own study. But I took no thought for one moment before another; only once it came into my mind, that if they should throw me into the river, it would spoil the papers that were in my pocket. For myself, I did not doubt but I should swim across, having but a thin coat and a light pair of boots."

Similar scenes had taken, or were about to take place at various other places. At Pensford, he tells us (March 19, 1742), " The rabble brought a bull they had been baiting, and strove to drive it among the people. But the bull was wiser than his drivers; it ran on either side of us, while we quietly sang praise to God, and prayed for about an hour. They drove the bull against the table. I put aside his head with my hand, that the blood might not drop upon my clothes, intending to go as soon as the hurry was over." At Whitechapel (Sept. 12, 1742) 'they drove cows among the congregation, and threw stones, one of which struck me between the eyes; but I felt no pain at all; and when I had wiped away the blood, went on testifying that God hath not given us the spirit of fear." At St. Ives, in Cornwall, (Sept. 16, 1743), " Satan began to fight for his king-dom. . . . I would fain have persuaded our people to stand still, but the zeal of some and fear of others had no ears. So that, finding the uproar increase, I went into the midst, and brought the head of the mob up

with me to the desk. I received but one blow on the
side of the head; after which we reasoned the case till
he grew milder and milder, and at length undertook to
quiet his companions." At Buckland (Sept. 10, 1753)
"the curate had provided a mob with horns, and other
things convenient, to prevent the congregations hearing
me." He always made a point of facing a mob. At
Falmouth in 1745, when the panic about a Stuart
invasion was at its height, and Wesley was absurdly
suspected of being a Papist and a Jacobite, the rabble
broke into the house where he was staying; but Wesley
went boldly out into their midst, and asked one after
another, "To which of you have I done any wrong? To
you? or you? or you?" and speedily silenced them.

And so we might go on citing instances of savage
opposition, met with a courage which was only exceeded
by the calmness and good judgment which always
characterized Wesley in such emergencies. This form
of opposition was chiefly confined to the earlier period
of his itinerant work. There was a recrudescence of it
here and there in later days, but it became more and
more the exception, not the rule, and Wesley's own
Christian conduct was the chief cause of its disappear-
ance. There must be two parties to a quarrel, and he
steadily refused to be one of them. No provocation
could induce him to be disloyal to the "powers that be,"
which he believed from his very soul to be "ordained of
God"; and the opposition which he met with from his
brother clergy filled him with sorrow rather than anger.
He issued a most touching appeal to them in 1745.
"Desire of us," he said, "anything we can do with a safe
conscience, and we will do it immediately. . . . We do
not desire any preferment from Church or State. But

we do desire (1) that if anything be laid to our charge, we may be permitted to answer for ourselves; (2) that you would hinder your dependents from stirring up the rabble against us, who are certainly not proper judges of such matters; (3) that you suppress and thoroughly discountenance all riots;—these things you can certainly do with a safe conscience."

It is impossible to follow Wesley step by step in his wanderings; but it may be said generally that the places in which his influence was most felt, and which he seems to have taken the greatest pleasure in visiting, were the large commercial centres and the country villages. London, Bristol, and Leeds were marked out from all other places in the "Deed of Declaration" of 1784, as the three places in which the annual Conference was to be held in turns; Newcastle, Manchester, Birmingham, Liverpool, Halifax, Huddersfield, Macclesfield, and towns of that stamp were also great strongholds of Wesley. Mining districts, and especially collieries, also furnished rich veins of spiritual ore for John Wesley; hence much of his time was spent in Cornwall, Staffordshire, Derbyshire, and the northern coal-fields. Purely agricultural places, again, were visited by him with great effect and pleasure, and hence, perhaps, the great hold he always had upon his own native county of Lincoln.

On the other hand, places of fashionable resort, such as Bath and Cheltenham, and cathedral cities, were not, as a rule, congenial fields of labour; and neither of the University towns was much affected by him. He used in his earlier itinerant career always to take his preaching turn in the University pulpit at Oxford,[1] and his

---

[1] As there were then far fewer Masters of Arts than there are

preaching produced a flutter in that learned dove-cot; but it cannot be said that either the University or the city was widely influenced. Cambridge he all but ignored.

The reason of this choice of places is obvious. John Wesley, though—or shall we say because ?—he was a refined gentleman and a highly cultivated scholar, always found himself more at home among the poor or among plain men of business than among those whom he calls "the genteel vulgar." Not that he did not appreciate culture. He enjoyed chance interviews with men like Dr. Johnson and Bishop Lowth. But with John Wesley it was not a question as to what he would enjoy, but as to where he would do most good ; and he was thoroughly convinced that that was not among the classes who were induced by Lady Huntingdon to attend Whitefield's ministry. He had a mean opinion both of their moral and intellectual qualities. With a grim sort of humour he expresses his surprise when he finds that they know how to behave themselves. " Cockermouth, April 26, 1761.—Even the genteel hearers were decent; many of the rest seemed deeply affected." "Oct. 28, 1765.— Preached at Bath ; but I had only the poor to hear; there being service at the same time in Lady Huntingdon's Chapel. So I was just in my element. I have scarce found such liberty at Bath before." "April 25, 1771, Wexford.—I preached in the market-place at ten. The congregation was very large and very genteel; and yet as remarkably well-behaved as any I have seen in the kingdom." "Aug. 25, 1771, Pembroke.—Many of them were gay, genteel people; so I spake on the first elements of the Gospel. But I was still out of

now, the turn came much more frequently—perhaps about once every three years.

their depth. Oh, how hard it is to be shallow enough for
a polite audience!" Holding such sentiments, it was no
wonder that he shrank from fashionable congregations.

Two country villages claim special notice, because
the incumbents were not only friends and supporters
of John Wesley, but itinerants themselves. These are
Haworth, a village in the heart of the wild hills and
moors of the West Riding, and Everton, amid the tamer
scenery of the Midlands. The incumbent of the one
was William Grimshaw, of the other, John Berridge.
Both were eccentric almost to the verge of insanity; both
grate upon one terribly by their incessant exhibitions of
bad taste—a fault of which John Wesley never was
guilty; but both were thoroughly good, self-denying,
hard-working men; and both paved the way for Wesley
not only in their own parishes, but in the wide circles
through which they itinerated. Hence his visits to
Haworth and Everton were always triumphant successes.
He mentions, as he always does when he can, with
especial satisfaction, the vast number of communicants
he found at Haworth Church; and at Everton he was
partly pleased, partly embarrassed by the fact, that his
preaching was so effective that it revived, in an aggra-
vated form, those physical convulsions which in the
early period of his itinerant work had appeared at
Bristol, Kingswood, and Newcastle.

"Aug. 28, 1759.—I preached at Mr. Berridge's church.
One sunk down, and another, and another; some cried
aloud in an agony of prayer. One young man and one
young woman were brought into Mr. Berridge's house,
and continued there in violent agonies both of body and
soul." With much more to the same effect.

All this will appear to many minds very shocking,

but easily to be accounted for. The heat of the crowded church, the electric spark of sympathy running through the excited masses, the wild terror and the ecstatic joy arising from the treatment of the most awful subjects with the most vivid realism, will appear quite enough to throw sensitive minds off their balance, and then to react upon their bodily frames. But such explanations would never satisfy one who had so intense a belief in the super-natural as John Wesley had. He had no doubt what-ever that the phenomena were solely attributable to an agency outside the natural world; but he *was* in doubt in particular cases as to whether that agency was from below or from above; and he characteristically concludes that both had a share in it; sometimes it was God's work, sometimes Satan mimicked the work of God. Few things more tended to prejudice his contemporaries against John Wesley than these results of his preaching; and perhaps he *was* sometimes deceived in the matter. His very virtues prevented him from being the best man to detect imposture or to check extravagance. His intense belief in the intervention of Divine Providence in human affairs, and his guileless readiness to believe the best of every one, may have led him to regard with too favourable an eye manifestations which should have been sternly repressed. But when he *was* convinced— as he not unfrequently was—of their unreality, no one could have been more prompt or more effective in putting a stop to them.

Wesley's itinerant labours were not confined to his own country. He frequently crossed over the border into Scotland, and the Channel into Ireland, and did not neglect the isles dotted about our coasts. His first visit to Ireland took place in 1747, and he afterwards

I

crossed the Irish Channel no less than forty-two times.
Considering the strong hold which Roman Catholicism
had upon that class of people who were most likely to
be attracted by Wesley, it is wonderful that he should
have had so great a measure of success in Ireland. At
Dublin there was a larger body of his followers than
at any other place except London; some of his most
efficient helpers came from Ireland; and, as a rule, he
was well received wherever he went. He loved the
Irish, though he was not blind to their faults; he
applied to them the description of Reuben, "unstable
as water," and told them, with his usual plainness, of
the danger of such instability. But their warm-hearted-
ness, their generosity, and perhaps, we may add, their
excitability, were qualities which he greatly admired,
and which rendered them peculiarly susceptible to the
influence of his preaching. But their impulsiveness
and impetuosity also made them a very inflammable
material; and we are not surprised at finding riots
breaking out in Ireland after they had all but died
away in England. Wesley's farewell to Ireland, when he
was long past eighty years of age, was quite an ovation.

It is a curious instance of the predominance of
temperament over training that Wesley was more
successful in Ireland than he was in Scotland. According to the principles of the majority of the Irish, Wesley
was a pestilent heretic; according to those of the
Scotch, a true evangelist. But in Ireland feeling ruled
over intellect; in Scotland intellect ruled over feeling.
Of all things, John Wesley disliked controversy; and
if the Scotch were not controversial, they were nothing.
They wanted to argue with him; and John Wesley
preferred being pelted with mud and rotten eggs to

being pelted with arguments. We hear of no riots in Scotland; in fact he was, as a rule, received most kindly and respectfully there; but he could make little way. It is fair to remember that the Scotch were a decent, orderly people, better educated than either the English or the Irish, and quite familiar with theological questions. Hence, the message which John Wesley had to deliver was not so new to them, nor the threats he had to denounce so formidable, as to their neighbours. Moreover they were Calvinists, almost to a man, and would listen, therefore, with some prejudice to one who was known to be a strong anti-Calvinist. And once more, John Wesley was a Church of England man to the backbone, and so the discipline, doctrine, and mode of worship of the Presbyterians were distasteful to him. It is no wonder, therefore, to find such entries as these in his Journal—"At Glasgow I preached on the Old Green to a people, the greatest part of whom *hear* much, *know* everything, and *feel* nothing." "The dead, unfeeling multitudes in Scotland." "At Dundee I admire the people; so decent, so serious, so perfectly unconcerned." "There is seldom fear of wanting a congregation in Scotland; but the misfortune is, they know everything, so they learn nothing." "Being informed that the Lord's Supper was to be administered in the West Kirk (Edinburgh), I knew not what to do; but at length I judged it best to embrace the opportunity, though I did not admire the manner of administration. How much more simple, as well as more solemn, is the service of the Church of England!" "Oh, what a difference is there between the English and Scotch method of burial! The English does honour to human nature; and even to the poor remains, that

were once the temple of the Holy Ghost! But when I
see in Scotland a coffin put into the earth, and covered
up without a word, it reminds me of what was spoken
of Jehoiakim, 'He shall be buried with the burial of
an ass!'"

What John Wesley *did* like in Scotland was just
what one would have expected him to like—the services
in the Episcopal chapels. If there was any body of
Christians which he would have preferred to the
Church of England, it would have been the Scotch
Episcopalians. With their doctrines and their ritual
he would be thoroughly in sympathy. He contrasts
the Church with the Kirk, much to the disadvantage of
the latter. "May 19, 1776.—Aberdeen. I attended
the morning service at the kirk, full as formal as any
in England; and no way calculated either to awaken
sinners, or to stir up the gift of God in believers. In
the afternoon I heard a useful sermon in the English
chapel; and was again delighted with the exquisite
decency both of the minister and the whole congregation. The Methodist congregations come the
nearest to this; but even these do not come up to it."
"Glasgow, 1779.—I attended the Church of England
service in the morning, and that of the kirk in the
afternoon. Truly, 'no man, having drunk old wine,
straightway desireth new.' How dull and dry did the
latter appear to me, who had been accustomed to the
former!"

On his way to and from Ireland, John Wesley
generally made a round of visits in Wales; and though
the great body of the Welsh Methodists followed the
lead of Whitefield and became Calvinists, yet Wesley
had considerable success in the Principality. The way

had been prepared for him by Howell Harris, who had been an itinerant evangelist some time before the Wesleys and Whitefield. There is one entry in his Journals in Wales which so aptly illustrates what he desired to do that it may be quoted. "March 27, 1748. Holyhead.—Mr. Swindells informed me that Mr. E. (the clergyman of the parish) would take it a favour if I would write some little thing, to advise the Methodists not to leave the church, and not to rail at their ministers. I sat down immediately and wrote, *A Word to a Methodist*, which Mr. E. translated into Welsh and printed."

When quite an old man (1777) he visited the Isle of Man, "and," he writes, "a more loving, simple-hearted people than this I never saw—and no wonder; for they had but six Papists and no Dissenters in the island." Four years later (1781) he was still more delighted when he "visited the island round, east, south, north, and west." "I was thoroughly convinced," he writes, "that we have no such circuit as this, either in England, Scotland, or Ireland. It is shut up from the world; and, having little trade, is visited by scarce any strangers. Here are no Papists, no Dissenters of any kind"—[to the end of his life John Wesley disliked Dissenters],—"no Calvinists, no disputers." And, what would be a great recommendation to him, "the natives are unpolished, that is, unpolluted; few of them are rich and genteel."

Finally, the hardy old man, now aged eighty-four, visited in the stormiest weather the Channel Islands, and found to his delight that "high and low, rich and poor, received the Word gladly." One can hardly place his two journeys to Holland after he was eighty years of age, under the head of itinerant work, for they really were holiday excursions. They may, however, be mentioned as an additional proof of the marvellous activity of the old man.

Travelling is now made so easy that it is difficult to realize the hardships and even dangers which frequently beset a constant traveller like Wesley in the eighteenth century. Sea voyages were made, not in comfortable steam-packets, but in small sailing vessels which were dependent on the winds, buffeted by the tides, and took six times as long to reach their destination as their fleeter successors do. By land, we "should have seen the roads before they were made" to appreciate what Wesley went through. Till his friends persuaded him, as he grew old, to charter a chaise, he always made his journeys on horseback ; he rode through storms of all kinds ; and had scant sympathy with those who were deterred by such obstacles. "The wind was high and sharp, and blew away a few delicate ones," he contemptuously remarks on one occasion. No difficulty of transit prevented him from keeping an engagement, as the following account, to the truthfulness of which an Isle of Axholme man can testify, will show :—"Oct. 22, 1743. Set out from Epworth to Grimsby ; but at Ferry we were at a full stop, the boatmen telling us we could not pass the Trent. It was as much as our lives were worth to put from shore before the storm abated. We waited an hour ; but, being afraid it would do much hurt if I should disappoint the congregation at Grimsby, I asked the men if they did not think it possible to get to the other shore. They said they could not tell ; but if we would venture our lives, they would venture theirs." They did, and crossed with great danger. Old

age made no difference to his hardiness and intrepidity.
When he was more than seventy years old (1774) his
horses ran away with him, and were only stopped by a
gentleman galloping in between them as they were on
the edge of a precipice ; but Wesley felt, he says, " no
more fear or care (blessed be God !) than if I had been
sitting in my study."   " I am persuaded," he adds,
" both evil and good angels had a large share in this
transaction."   When he was nearly eighty (Aug. 14,
1782), as he was going to Bristol, " We were informed,"
he says, " that the highwaymen were on the road before
us, and had robbed all the coaches that had passed, some
within an hour or two.   I felt no uneasiness on this
account, knowing that God would take care of us ; and
He did so, for before we came to the spot, all the highwaymen were taken, so we went on unmolested, and
came safe to Bristol."

CHAPTER VIII.

JOHN WESLEY'S great success as an organizer was due at least as much to his readiness to accept, and his adroitness in adapting, the suggestions of others, as to the fertility of his own resources. It is a remarkable fact that there was scarcely a single detail of his wonderfully complete system of which he can properly be called the originator. The very name and idea of " the Societies" did not in any way originate with him. Both name and thing had been thoroughly familiar to him from his childhood. "The Religious Societies " were conspicuous features in the Church life of that period to which John Wesley's father belonged ; the Rector of Epworth was a personal friend of one of their most ardent supporters, Robert Nelson,[1] and vindicated the Societies in a sermon preached in 1698, the fire and vigour of which reminds us of John Wesley himself; he also appended to his *Pious Communicant rightly prepared* a forcible "Letter concerning Religious Societies."

[1] In a list of subscribers to a Free School founded at Epworth in the time of Mr. Wesley, I find the name of "Mr. Robert Nelson, £5." I have no doubt also that the lines on the portrait of Robert Nelson, signed "S. W.," were written by Samuel Wesley.

John Wesley frequently speaks in his early Journals of going "to the meeting of a Society," assuming apparently that every one would understand what he meant, for he gives no explanation.

The United Societies with which this chapter is concerned were merely a continuation of what he had organized before, for he himself tells us plainly—" The first rise of Methodism was in November 1729, when four of us met together at Oxford; the second was at Savannah in April 1736, when twenty or thirty persons met at my house ; the last was at London, when forty or fifty of us agreed to meet together every Wednesday evening, in order to free conversation, begun and ended with singing and prayer." [1]

There is no excuse for not knowing all about these Societies; for Wesley himself, with his usual frankness, told all the world, not once, but over and over again, the whole story of them. And first we learn from him that there was " no previous design or plan at all; but everything arose just as the occasion offered." " My brother and I "—it is always " my brother and I "— " were desired to preach in many parts of London." The result of the preaching was to stir up in many a concern for their souls. They met with little sympathy, and much opposition, and naturally came those who had aroused them for advice. "Strengthen you one another," was the advice given. . . . " Talk together as often as you can. And pray earnestly with and for one another, that you may ' endure to the end and be saved.' " They said, " But we want you likewise to talk with us often, to direct and quicken us in our way, to give us

---

[1] *Ecclesiastical History*, iv. 175.

the advice which you well know we need, and to pray with us, as well as for us." "I asked, 'Which of you desire this ? Let me know your names and places of abode.' They did so. But I soon found they were too many for me to talk with severally so often as they wanted it. So I told them, 'If you will all of you come together every Thursday, in the evening, I will gladly spend some time with you in prayer, and give you the best advice I can.' Thus arose, without any previous design on either side, what was afterwards called a *Society ;* a very innocent name, and very common in London, for any number of people associating themselves together."

This, as appears from the first sentence in the General Rules of the United Societies, refers to what took place in the latter end of 1739; but Wesley's Journal speaks of a Society before this.

"May 1, 1738.—This evening our little Society began, which afterwards met in Fetter Lane." He was now under the direction of Peter Böhler, the Moravian ; and the Fetter Lane Society afterwards became a Moravian Society; but it was certainly not so while Wesley belonged to it, nor yet after he had left it, until Molther arrived in England. We have John Wesley's own word for this.[1]

As we saw in the last chapter, Wesley was at this period much at Bristol, and there too a Society was founded which, among other things, "passed a resolution that all the members should obey the Church to which they belonged by fasting on Fridays," a rule about which Wesley, as a strong Churchman, was always very particular in all his Societies. Quite at the close of

---

[1] See his "Letter to Mr. Church," *Works*, viii. 424.

1739, Wesley returned to London, and found the Fetter Lane Society " in the utmost confusion." The squabbles which ensued need not here be recorded; Wesley showed, as he always did on such occasions, not only great self-command, but also the courtesy of the gentleman combined with the meekness of the Christian; but the result was a split with the Fetter Lane Society, and the formation of another, whose head-quarters was the Foundry. This Foundry was a dilapidated building or shed in Windmill Street, near Finsbury Square, which had been formerly used for the casting of cannon. Wesley obtained a long lease of it, and had erected there " a preaching house "—that is his own deliberately chosen word—a band-room where the classes met, the north end being also used for a school-room and a book-room for the sale of Wesley's publications; while over the band-room were John Wesley's own modest apartments,—his only home on earth for many years. Bristol, in this as in other respects, was in advance of London, the first " preaching house " having been erected in that city, near the Horse Fair, earlier in 1739. On July 23, 1740, John Wesley records—" Our little company met at the Foundry instead of Fetter Lane," and from that time forward the movement spread rapidly: London, Bristol, Kingswood, Newcastle-upon-Tyne were the earliest homes of the Unitied Societies, and then they were founded in all parts of the kingdom; and in 1743 it was found necessary to draw up a set of " general rules." This was done at Newcastle with characteristic brevity. The rules fill little more than two octavo pages, and were signed " John Wesley, Charles Wesley." In this interesting little document we have the founders' own definition of what they meant by such a Society—

" A company of men having the form and seeking the
power of godliness, united in order to pray together, to
receive the word of exhortation, and to watch over one
another in love, that they may help each other to work
out their salvation."

It is abundantly evident that John Wesley's intention
in founding his Societies was not to weaken and paralyze,
but to strengthen and vivify, the Church of his baptism,
and that the very last thing he desired was any separation from that Church. "Wesley's object," writes one
who will not be suspected of taking too Church-like a
view, "was to revive the spirit of religion in the Church
of England. To this he thought himself called; for
this he commenced and continued his labours."[1] And he
believed that the organization of Societies would be an
effectual means of doing so; and surely he had reason
for thinking this. Fifty years before, the Church of
England had been wonderfully revived by " the Religious Societies." More than a century earlier the
Church of Rome had been greatly strengthened by the
establishment of " The Society of Jesus," the life of the
great founder of which John Wesley had read with
deep interest.[2] But, in point of fact, John Wesley went
back much further than the seventeenth or the sixteenth century, even to the fountain-head, to the constitution of the Early Church before its division into
East and West. This he endeavoured to make his
model in all his arrangements; and almost all his so-called
" innovations " found a precedent in the constitution of
the Early Church. He dearly loved the Church of

[1] *Observations of Southey's Life of Wesley*, by Richard Watson,
p. 125.
[2] See his *Journal*, vol. i. p. 369.

England, and when he varied from her at all in practice—(in doctrine he never knowingly varied from her)—it was because he thought he was justified in so doing by the customs of primitive times.[1]

Turning to details, we find at almost every stage of our inquiry illustrations of both points. We find it in the first constitution of the Societies in their most rudimentary form. They arose, as we have seen, simply from the desire of the new converts to be united more closely together; but " upon reflection," writes John, " I could not but observe, This is the very thing which was from the beginning of Christianity. In the earlier times, those whom God had sent forth 'preached the gospel to every creature.' And the οἱ ἀκροάται, 'the body of hearers,' were mostly either Jews or heathens. But as soon as any of them were so convinced of the truth, as to forsake sin and seek the gospel salvation, they immediately joined them together, took an account of their names, advised them to watch over each other, and met these κατηχούμενοι, 'catechumens' (as they were then called), apart from the great congregation; that they might instruct, rebuke, exhort, and pray with them, and for them, according to their several necessities." [2]

---

[1] This point is well brought out by Mr. Denny Urlin, in his *John Wesley's Place in Church History*, and in his later volume, *The Churchman's Life of Wesley*.

[2] "*A Plain Account of the People called Methodists*, in a Letter to the Reverend Mr. Perronet, Vicar of Shoreham in Kent, written in the year 1784," *Works*, viii. 250. To prevent needless references, it may be said, once for all, that the quotations from Wesley in this chapter are taken from this letter, which only consists of twenty pages, unless otherwise specified. It is the clearest of the many accounts which Wesley gives of his Societies.

Following Wesley's own order, we next come to the
Class Meetings. These also arose from apparently accidental circumstances. Wesley found there was a need
of further discipline, which he knew not how to supply.
"Several grew cold, and gave way to the sin which
had long easily beset them." But how was he to get
rid of such unsatisfactory members, or bring them to a
better mind, scattered as they were in all parts of the
town, "from Wapping to Westminster"?

"At length, while we were thinking of quite another
thing, we struck upon a method for which we have had
cause to bless God ever since. I was talking with
several of the Society in Bristol concerning the means
of paying the debts there, when one [1] stood up and said,
'Let every member of the Society give a penny a week
till all are paid.' Another answered, But many of
these are poor, and cannot afford to do it.' 'Then,'
said he, 'put eleven of the poorest with me; and if
they can give anything, well—I will call on them
weekly; and if they can give nothing, I will give for
them as well as for myself. And each of you call on
eleven of your neighbours weekly; receive what they
give, and make up what is wanting.' It was done. In
a while, some of these informed me, they found such
and such a one did not live as he ought. It struck me
immediately—'This is the thing; the very thing we
have wanted so long.' I called together all the Leaders
of the classes (so we used to term them and their companies), and desired that each would make a particular
inquiry into the behaviour of those whom he saw weekly.
They did so. Many disorderly walkers were detected.

---

[1] This was a certain Captain Fry.

Some turned from the evil of their ways. Some were put away from us. Many saw it with fear, and rejoiced unto God with reverence." The plan, commenced at Bristol, soon spread elsewhere. It was found impracticable, for various reasons, for the class leader to visit each person at his own home; and it was agreed that those of each class should all meet together under the guidance of their leader; and "it can scarce be conceived," writes Wesley, "what advantages have been reaped from this little prudential regulation."

The next institution is the *Watch-night*. This, again, was not Wesley's own idea; he "was informed that several persons in Kingswood frequently met together at the school; and, when they could spare the time, spent the greater part of the night in prayer, praise, and thanksgiving." "Some," he says, "advised me to put an end to this; but, upon weighing the thing thoroughly, and comparing it with the practice of the ancient Christians, I could see no cause to forbid it. Rather, I believed it might be made of more general use. So I sent them word, I designed to watch with them on the Friday nearest the full moon, that we might have light thither and back again." And so the Watch-night, closely corresponding with the "Vigiliæ" of the Early Church, became a settled institution, being held at first monthly, and then annually on New Year's Eve.

Then arose the *Quarterly Meeting* in the most natural manner possible; and its distinctive feature again bore analogy to the custom of the Early Church. "As the Society increased, I found it required still greater care to separate the precious from the vile. In order to this, I determined at least once in three months to talk with every member myself. . . . To each of those of whose

seriousness and good conversation I found no reason to
doubt, I gave a testimony under my own hand, by
writing their name on a ticket prepared for that purpose; every ticket implying as strong a recommendation
of the person to whom it was given, as if I had wrote at
length, ' I believe the bearer hereof to be one that fears
God, and works righteousness.' " And then he compares
these tickets to " the σύμβολα, or *tesseræ*, as the ancients
termed them, being of just the same force as the ἐπιστόλαι
συστατικαὶ, *commendatory letters*, mentioned by the
apostle. These supplied us with a quiet and inoffensive method of removing any disorderly member. He
has no new ticket at the quarterly visitation (for so
often the tickets are changed), and hereby it is immediately known that he is no longer of the community."

The next institution was the *Band Meeting ;* and again
we find the impulse coming to Wesley from without.
Even his best converts found that the " war was not over,
as they had supposed ; but they had still to wrestle both
with flesh and blood, and with principalities and powers ;
so that temptations were on every side ; and often
temptations of such a kind as they knew not how to
speak of in a class ; in which persons of every sort,
young and old, men and women, met together." They
wanted some means of closer union ; and in compliance
with their desire Wesley divided them into smaller
companies or bands, putting the married or single men,
and married or single women, together. " Confess your
faults one to another, and pray one for another, that ye
may be healed," was the text on which these bands
were formed. The Leader of each band was to
describe " his own state first, and then to ask the rest,
in order, as many and as searching questions as may be,

concerning their state, sins, and temptations." *The Select Society* was a sort of inner circle within the Bands, which were themselves an inner circle within the United Society.

In close connection with these Band Meetings arose the *Love-feasts*, which, unlike most of his institutions, originated with Wesley himself, or rather were revived by him, for they were the "Agapæ" of the Primitive Church. "In order," he says, "to increase in them a grateful sense of all God's mercies, I desired that, one evening in a quarter, all the men in band; on a second, all the women, would meet; and, on a third, both men and women together; that we might together 'eat bread,' as the ancient Christians did, 'with gladness and singleness of heart.' At these Love-feasts (so we termed them, retaining the name, as well as the thing, which was in use from the beginning) our food is only a little plain cake and water. But we seldom return from them without being fed, not only with 'the meat which perisheth,' but with 'that which endureth to everlasting life.'" Subsequently the Love-feasts were not confined to the bands, but open to the whole Society.

The last institution was the *Penitents'-meeting*, the title of which tells its own tale. Hymns, exhortations, and prayers, were all adapted to the circumstances of penitent backsliders; and it is curious to observe how Wesley seems to hanker after, though he does not purpose to revive, the ancient discipline. He would bring the penitents back to the great "Shepherd and Bishop of their souls," "not by any of the fopperies of the Roman Church, although in some manner countenanced by antiquity. In prescribing hair-shirts, and bodily austerities, we durst not follow even the ancient

K

Church; although we had unawares, both in dividing οἱ πίστοι, the believers, from the rest of the Society, and in separating the penitents from them, and appointing a peculiar service for them." John Wesley was in advance of his age in his discrimination between that which was primitive and that which was distinctly Roman.

As to the mode of worship prescribed by Wesley for his Societies, he carefully arranged that it should be regarded as a supplement, not a substitute, for the worship at the parish church. "Some may say," he writes in 1776, "our own service is public worship. Yes, in a sense, but not such as to supersede the Church service. We never designed it should. If it were designed to be instead of the Church service, it would be essentially defective, for it seldom has the four grand parts of public prayer—deprecation, petition, intercession, and thanksgiving. Neither is it, even on the Lord's Day, concluded with the Lord's Supper. If the people put ours in the place of the Church service, we *hurt* them that stay with us, and *ruin* them that leave us." In accordance with these sentiments he insisted upon it that the Sunday services in his preaching-houses should not clash with the Church hours, and was very angry when he observed towards the close of his life a tendency to do so. "I met," he writes in 1786, "the classes at Deptford, and was vehemently importuned to order the Sunday service in our room at the same time as that of the Church. It is easy to see that this would be a formal separation from the Church. We fixed both our morning and evening service, all over England, at such hours as not to interfere with the Church; with this very design—that those of the Church, if they

choose it, might attend both one and the other. But to
fix it at the same hour, was obliging them to separate
either from the Church or us; and this I judge to be
not only inexpedient, but totally unlawful for me to do."
He persisted until he carried his point, and at last,
three months later, told them plainly—"If you are resolved, you may have your service in Church hours;
but, remember, from that time you will see my face no
more. This struck deep, and from that hour I have
heard no more of separating from the Church." The
details of the service much resembled those of many
Churches in the present day, though they would be
rarely found in the eighteenth century. Open benches
instead of pews; a separation of the sexes; quick, lively
singing; a weekly celebration of the Holy Communion;[1]
the due observance of all Church festivals and fasts, including the weekly fast of Friday—these were the
things that he loved to the end of his life, and, as far as
he could, with his limited supply of clerical help, carried
out. In 1788 the trustees of the City Road Chapel
tried to alter the rules about the sexes sitting apart,
and about no one being allowed to call any seat his
own; "thus altering," said John Wesley, indignantly,
"the discipline which I have been establishing for fifty
years." But, as usual, John Wesley had his way. "We
had," he says, "another meeting of the committee, who,
after a calm and loving consultation, judged it best (1)
that the men and women should sit separate still; and
(2) that none should claim any pew as his own, either

---

[1] This may seem to contradict Wesley's own words, quoted in
p. 130; but the explanation is, that the Holy Communion was
celebrated only in those chapels (not "preaching houses") which
were served by regular clergymen.

in the New Chapel or in West Street." The Holy Communion was celebrated weekly in the New Chapel.

Among the officers of the Societies, passing over the Leaders of the Classes and the Bands, whose duties are sufficiently expressed by their names, and the clergy, who, when they would join with Wesley, held a position quite distinct from any others, we come to the *Lay-Assistants*. It is very characteristic of John Wesley that he would allow no higher title than the humble one of *Assistants* or *Helpers*, if they were not in Holy Orders, to the men whose office was really a very responsible one, far more so than that of any other except Wesley himself. That office was, "in the absence of the minister [that is, a regular clergyman]: (1) to expound every morning and evening; (2) to meet the united society, the bands, the select society, and the penitents once a week; (3) to visit the classes once a quarter; (4) to hear and decide all differences; (5) to put the disorderly back on trial, and to receive on trial for the bands or society; (6) to see that the stewards, the leaders, and the school-masters faithfully discharge their several offices; (7) to meet the leaders of the bands and classes weekly, and the stewards, and to overlook their accounts." It is perfectly marvellous how Wesley could keep men who had so much power put into their hands, in the strictest subordination; but he determined to do it, and he did it.

In what are called "The Large Minutes," the following questions and answers occur—

Q. 23.—What is the office of a Christian Minister?

A.—To watch over souls, as he that must give account.

Q. 24.—In what view may we and our helpers be considered ?

A.—Perhaps as extraordinary messengers (that is, out of the ordinary way) designed (1) To provoke the regular ministers to jealousy ; (2) To supply their lack of service towards them who are perishing for want of knowledge. But how hard is it to abide here ! Who does not wish to be a little higher ?—suppose, to be ordained.

Q. 25.—What is the office of a helper ?

A.—In the absence of a minister,[1] to feed and guide the flock.

John Wesley had to overcome a violent prejudice before he could reconcile himself to the idea of laymen preaching at all; and had it not been for his mother's advice, he would probably not have overcome it as soon as he did. "To touch this point," he says, "was to touch the apple of my eye." But those who say that his " High Church principles " were the hindrance, only show that they know less of Church history than John Wesley did. He was perfectly right when he contended that lay-preaching was forbidden by no law of the Church. He was quite clear as to what was, and what was not, the exclusive office of the priesthood. " They " (his lay-preachers) " no more take upon them to be priests than to be kings. They take not upon them to administer the sacraments—an honour peculiar to the priests of God. Only, according to their power, they exhort their brethren to continue in the grace of God." [2] When his brother-in-law Hall had the impertinence to urge him to leave the Church in 1745, he replied—" We believe it would not be right for us to administer either

---

[1] That is, a clergyman of the Church of England.
[2] *Farther Appeal*, &c., *Works*, viii. 224.

Baptism or the Lord's Supper, unless we had a commission so to do from those bishops whom we apprehend
to be in a succession from the apostles. We believe
there is, and always was, in every Christian Church
(whether dependent on the Bishop of Rome or not), an
outward priesthood, ordained by Jesus Christ, and an
outward sacrifice offered therein by men, authorized to
act as ambassadors for Christ, and stewards of the
mysteries of God." [1]   His later views on the ministry
will be noticed presently; they do not appear to me in
the slightest degree to affect the distinction he here
draws between what *is* and what is *not* the exclusive
work of the priesthood; he then proceeds to justify, as
a Churchman, field-preaching, and with less confidence—
in fact, far more hesitatingly than he need have done
—lay-preaching. Like so many institutions in Wesley's
system, that of lay-preaching arose from the press of
circumstances rather than from design; and was at first
reluctantly permitted, not originated, by the founder.
And when it became a distinctive feature of Methodism,
it was still hedged in by the strictest precautions.
Every preacher had to be a " local " before he was permitted to be an " itinerant," and Wesley kept a tight
hand upon them all, impressing upon them strongly,
over and over again, that their duty was to obey him
implicitly. As there has sometimes been a little confusion about the names, it may be added that John
Wesley termed his itinerants " preachers " or " helpers,"
and that the preacher who had to superintend the work
of the whole circuit in which he was placed, and who is
now termed " the superintendent," was then called " the
assistant."

[1] *Tyerman,* i. 496.

The next officers were the *Stewards*, who, as their name implies, had to manage the temporal affairs of the Societies, which Wesley found "a burden he was not able to bear." Here again one observes with wonder how Wesley was able to secure without fee or reward the services of busy men who gave up a vast amount of time and trouble to their labour of love. Among other duties of the Stewards was that of visiting and relieving the sick; but as the Societies grew, this became too great a burden, and hence arose the appointment of *Visitors of the Sick*, an office which again seemed to Wesley an exact copy of the Primitive Church; for "what," he asks, "were the ancient Deacons? What was Phœbe the Deaconess but such a visitor of the sick?"

The last office which Wesley notices is that of the *School-masters*, and this introduces us to his experiment in Christian education. From the early days of Methodism (1740), there had been a school at Kingswood for the children of the colliers. But in 1748 another school was opened there (the earlier one still going on) for the children of Methodists generally, and preachers in particular. John Wesley took the deepest interest in this school, making the most stringent rules, and writing and editing school-books for its express use. The scholars, who were all to be boarders, "were to be taken in between the years of six and twelve, in order to be taught reading, writing, arithmetic, English, French, Latin, Greek, Hebrew, history, geography, chronology, rhetoric, logic, ethics, geometry, algebra, physics, and music." There was to be no play, for "he who plays when he is a child will play when he becomes a man." Every child was to rise at four a.m., and spend

an hour in private reading, meditation, singing, and
prayer. Every Friday, as the Fast-day of the Church,
all the children, whose health would bear it, were to
fast till three p.m. Sundays were, of course, devoted to
religious exercises, including attendance at the parish
Church. Well might Wesley say—"The children of
tender parents so called (who are indeed offering up their
sons and their daughters unto devils) have no business
here; for the rules will not be broken, in favour of
any person whatever. Nor is any child received unless
his parents agree that he shall observe all the rules of
the house; and that they will not take him from
school, no, not a day, till they take him for good and
all;"—so there were to be no holidays.

Instead of being surprised that the experiment was not
more successful, one is astonished that it could ever have
been carried on at all. What *was* to become of the
poor little minds and the poor little bodies of children
under such high pressure? John Wesley was alternately
in the height of exultation and in the depth of despair
about his school; but in spite, or rather in consequence
of, the troubles and disappointments in which such an
impossible scheme naturally involved him, he clung to
it with all the tenacity of his strong nature. "Surely,"
he writes in 1753, "the importance of this design is
apparent, even in the difficulties that attend it. I have
spent more money, and time, and care on this than
almost any design I ever had, but it is worth all the
labour." In 1766, "I will kill or cure. I will have one
or the other; a Christian school or none at all." In
1769 he is full of elation; it "comes nearer a Christian
school than any I know in the kingdom." In 1781 this
elation reaches its climax: Kingswood is infinitely

superior to either Oxford or Cambridge! An elaborate comparison is drawn greatly to the disadvantage of the earlier educational establishments. But alas! in 1783 he is down in despair again. "The school does not, in any wise, answer the design of its institution, either with regard to religion or learning. The children are not religious; they have not the power, and hardly the form, of religion. Neither do they improve in learning better than at other schools; no, nor yet so well." Among other misdemeanours, "they run up and down in the wood, and mix, yea, fight, with the colliers' children. They ought never to play, but they do every day, yea, in the school." [1] Adam Clarke more than bears out this sad account. It is fair to add that the officials at this time were very unsatisfactory; but surely it was the tendency of such a system as John Wesley, in the simplicity of his heart, with the best of motives, but with a strange ignorance of child-nature, instituted at Kingswood, to make the children either little hypocrites or little rebels; and of the two the latter alternative was perhaps the best. John Wesley took a deep interest in children; but in his treatment of them, his own mother's mantle does not seem to have fallen upon him. It is curious to observe how his theory and his natural feelings were sometimes at variance. "I met," he writes on one occasion, "a large number of children, just as much acquainted with God and with the things of God as a wild ass colt, and just as much concerned about them. And yet who can believe that those pretty little creatures have the wrath of God abiding on them?" If we did not know the thorough goodness and sincerity of the man, it would make us quite

[1] Minutes of Conference, 1773.

indignant to read how he worked upon their tender
natures and roused the most unwholesome excitement
in them.

The organization of the Societies may be said to have
been completed by the institution of *Conference* in 1744.
The growth of the movement rendered it necessary to
make a systematic arrangement of *circuits*, and appoint
a certain number of preachers for each circuit. This
was perhaps one, but only one, of the reasons which led
Wesley to gather a few clergymen and lay preachers
together at the Foundry. Wesley himself mentions only
the names of the six clergymen who attended this first
Conference, but there were also four assistants present.
It was a small, informal gathering, hardly equal in point
of numbers and dignity to a modern "clerical meeting,"
but the most important questions of doctrine and
discipline were discussed by the little assembly. Wesley
very characteristically terms the discussions merely
"conversations," but the "minutes" in their quaint
form of question and answer are deeply interesting, and
of inestimable value to those who desire to know what
Wesley's system really was. Year by year the Conference was duly held in London, Bristol, or Leeds; and
the proceedings are carefully chronicled. It grew in
importance, until in 1784 it assumed a new phase
which will be noticed in connection with Wesley's old age.

Such were the Societies, growing in numbers and
weight year by year, of which John Wesley was for
more than half a century the absolute and supreme
ruler. Not that he was impervious to the influence of
others, or that he exercised an over-strict discipline in
one sense; on the contrary, he was sometimes too liable
to be influenced when he would have acted more wisely

if he had followed his own judgment, and he was often too lenient in reproving or excluding offenders. But his will, when he chose to assert it, was law. Few ventured to dispute it, and those who did, invariably had to yield. If it be asked how he attained this complete ascendancy over a vast body of men upon whom he could bring no other than a moral influence to bear, many reasons may be given, but certainly not among them that one which has often been cited as the sufficient explanation. He did not wish to form a sect with himself at the head of it. "I should rejoice," he writes, "(so little ambitious am I to be at the head of any sect or party,) if the very name (of Methodist) might never be mentioned more, but be buried in eternal oblivion"—and I believe the assertion was literally true. He only regarded his elaborate system as means to an end, that end being the promotion of scriptural holiness in heart and life; and the general and profound conviction that this was so, was the chief cause of the unbounded deference that was paid to him. If there had been the faintest suspicion of any ulterior motives, besides the simple and avowed one of doing good, this would have so far weakened his influence. His plainness of speech; his promptitude in action; his habit of command; that air of authority which was natural to all the Wesleys, but to John above all; the transparent simplicity of his life and character; his utter disregard of wealth, position, and high connection; his superior education, and the patent fact that he was a gentleman born and bred; his aptitude for organizing, preaching, and writing—all these combined to confirm his authority; but all would have been of no avail had there not been this sheer confidence in his goodness.

The preachers would, one might have thought, have
been the most difficult to manage; hence the following
testimony of a good representative of the body is
valuable. "I am persuaded," writes Mr. Pawson, "that
from the creation of the world there never existed a
body of men who looked up to any single person with a
more profound degree of reverence than the preachers
did to Mr. Wesley; and I am bold to say, that never
did any man, no, not St. Paul himself, possess so high
a degree of power over so large a body of men as was
possessed by him. He used his power, however, for the
edification of the people, and abused it as little perhaps
as any one man ever did. When any difficulty occurred
in governing the preachers, it soon vanished. The
oldest, the very best, and those of them that had the
greatest influence, were ever ready to unite with him,
and to assist him to the utmost of their power. If the
preachers were in any danger at all, it was of calling
Mr. Wesley 'Rabbi,' and implicitly obeying him in
whatsoever he thought proper to command."[1]   And as
he ruled the preachers, so he did all the members of the
Societies. They read what he told them to read, went
where he told them to go, dressed as he told them to
dress, managed their bodily health as he told them to
manage it, nay, married as he told them to marry, and
educated their children as he told them to educate
them. His government of the Societies was a strictly
paternal government; but he showed the love and
tenderness and unselfish consideration as well as the
unbounded authority of a father. He was never a
bishop, but he was in the truest sense of the term a
'Father in God.'

[1] Quoted by Tyerman, iii. 299.

It may be added that he used his vast power over his Societies in trying to make their members good citizens as well as good Christians. It was not *his* fault if they did not set their faces against the prevalent abuses of the day, against which he warned them in his own plain, direct, and forcible way. Take, for instance, his outspoken utterances against smuggling—" Neither sell nor buy anything that has not paid the duty. Defraud not the king any more than your fellow-subject. Never think of being religious unless you are honest. What has a thief to do with religion ? "[1] " A smuggler is a thief of the first order, a highwayman or pickpocket of the worst sort. Let not any of those prate about religion ! Government should drive these vermin away into lands not inhabited ! "[2] And he records with great satisfaction : " That detestable practice of cheating the king is no more found in our Societies. And since that accursed thing has been put away, the work of God has everywhere increased. This Society [Port Isaac] is doubled."[3] It was the same with the very common custom of receiving bribes at elections. " July 1, 1747, St. Ives, Cornwall. I spoke severally to all those who had votes in the ensuing election. I found them such as I desired. Not one would even eat or drink at the expense of him for whom he voted ; " and he issued a sort of Pastoral against treating and other malpractices. He was one of the first to protest against " that execrable sum of all villanies, commonly called the Slave Trade " (*Journal*, Feb. 12, 1772). In his *Serious Advice to the People of England* (1778) he writes— " ' But we have lost our Negro Trade.' I would to God

---

[1] To the Societies at Bristol in 1764.
[2] *A Word to a Smuggler*, 1767· [3] *Journal*, Sept. 17th, 1762.

it may never be found more! That we may never more steal and sell our brethren like beasts; never murder them by thousands and tens of thousands. Oh, may this worse than Mahometan, worse than Pagan abomination be removed from us for ever! Never was anything such a reproach to England since it was a nation, as the having a hand in this execrable traffic." He published a tract entitled *Thoughts on Slavery;* and his very last letter (Feb. 24, 1791) was addressed to William Wilberforce, who had just brought the question before Parliament, bidding him, "Go on, in the name of God, and in the power of His might, till even American slavery, the vilest that ever saw the sun, shall vanish away before it." When the time came, the strongly-expressed opinion of their venerable founder was not lost upon his Societies. He spoke in terms that could not be mistaken on the subject of common honesty, which he evidently regarded as by no means common. "What servants, journeymen, labourers, carpenters, bricklayers, do as they would be done by? Which of them does as much work as he can? Set him down for a knave that does not. Who does as he would be done by, in buying and selling, particularly in selling horses? Write him knave that does not; and the Methodist knave is the worst of all knaves." [1] He saw the danger of covetousness, into which the very virtues of his followers might lead them, and gave them advice which has become proverbial. "Methodists are diligent and frugal; therefore they increase in goods. We ought not to prevent them from being diligent and frugal; we *must* exhort all Christians to gain all they can, and to save all they can; that is, grow rich. What way,

[1] Minutes of Conference at Leeds, 1766.

then, can we take, that our money may not sink us into the nethermost hell ? There is one way, and there is no other under heaven. If those who *gain* all they can, and *save* all they can, will likewise *give* all they can, then the more they gain, the more they will grow in grace, and the more they will lay up in heaven." [1] And finally, both by precept and example, he fostered the spirit of loyalty to the "powers that be." He distinctly regarded loyalty as a part of his religion, and he impressed this feeling upon his followers. There were no better soldiers in the British army than the Methodist soldiers; and their letters to Wesley, which he frequently copies into his *Journal*, show how completely they and their spiritual director agreed on this part of their duty. On the death of George II., he writes, "King George was gathered to his fathers. When will England have a better prince ? " [2] The following Friday was set apart, at Wesley's command, by the Societies at Bristol, "as a day of fasting and prayer, for the blessing of God upon the nation, and in particular on his present Majesty." All his old aristocratic feelings were aroused by the Wilkes' riots. " Cobblers, tinkers, porters, and hackney-coachmen think themselves wise enough to instruct both king and council." He himself " is not so deeply learned. Politics were beyond his province ; but he would use the privilege of an Englishman to speak his naked thoughts." [3] In his *Calm Address to the Inhabitants of England*, he tells the Methodists that "though many who go under that name, hate the king and all

---

[1] *See* Alexander Knox, *Remains*, i. 88, for a criticism on this.
[2] *Journal*, Oct. 25, 1760.
[3] *Free Thoughts on the Present State of Public Affairs*, 1768.

his ministers only less than they hate an Arminian, he would no more continue in fellowship with them than with thieves, drunkards, and common swearers." And in his extreme old age, 1789, he preached a most vigorous thanksgiving sermon at Bristol, on "the grand day of rejoicing for his Majesty's recovery." John Wesley has been termed *par excellence* "The Reformer," [1] but surely there never was a more conservative reformer.

[1] *The Reformer* is the heading of the chapter on John Wesley, in Mrs. Oliphant's *Sketches of the Reign of George II.*

CHAPTER IX.

IN an account of John Wesley's friends, the first thing to notice is that by far the most weighty and prominent among them were all clergymen. The clergy, as a body, were, it is said, opposed to Wesley and his system; and so they were. But in spite of that, the clerical element was so far the backbone of the movement, that if you remove it, the whole thing collapses at once. Abstract the part which the clergy took in it, and you sweep away at one fell swoop John and Charles Wesley, Fletcher, Coke, Perronet, Whitefield, Berridge, Grimshaw, Piers, Meriton, and others of minor importance; and what is the residuum? A number of excellent men, no doubt, who worked admirably as subordinates; but the motive force is gone. In short, early Methodism was, strange as it may sound, essentially a clerical movement. Nor can it be said that the prime movers, John and Charles Wesley, were clergymen by accident; they were rocked in the cradle of clericalism, and were steeped with clerical ideas through and through.

This will appear clearly when we turn to him, who, in spite of some differences, in spite of the fact that he

L

partially withdrew himself from an important branch of the work, must still be regarded as second only to John Wesley himself, and in some respects hardly second even to him.

Charles Wesley was some years his brother's junior, and had early learned to look up to John as his guide. But it was not in the Wesley nature to submit blindly to any man; and Charles Wesley soon showed that he had a will of his own, and was both competent and ready to act on his own independent judgment. On his return from Georgia he fell under the same powerful influence which affected John; and the two brothers went hand in hand in their revival work. Charles was as active an itinerant, as vigorous and successful a preacher, as fearless and calm a confronter of mobs, for several years as John himself. In John Wesley's many accounts of his early work as a revivalist, he always links his brother's name with his own, and evidently regards him, not as a follower, but as a coadjutor quite on a level with himself. It is always "my brother and I." But the differences of temperament between the two brothers soon began to show themselves. Charles was of a warmer, more impetuous, less placable disposition than John; but he was a keener judge of character, and far less easily imposed upon. He regarded with grave suspicion the physical convulsions which resulted from his brother's preaching, and when similar phenomena began to accompany his own, he took remarkably efficacious measures for testing their reality, and for putting a stop to them when he thought them unreal. On the other hand, he was rescued by his brother from the dangerous attraction of Moravian "stillness," though his latest biographer gives good reason for believing

that his peril in this direction has been exaggerated.[1]
Charles Wesley was quite free from a tendency, which
seems to have run in the Wesley family, to fall in love
with the wrong people, and to make ill-assorted matches.
No Sophia Hopkeys, Grace Murrays, or Widow
Vazeilles ever disturbed *his* peace. He married a lady
in his own sphere of life, and found in her a true helpmeet; and he had no scruple about interfering to
prevent John from marrying unsuitably.   In 1753,
when John seemed likely to die, Charles flatly refused
to be his successor, declaring with the true Wesley
frankness and promptitude that he had "neither the
body, nor the mind, nor grace, nor talents for it." His
most serious disagreement with his brother was about
the relations of the Societies to the Church.   Both
brothers were strong Churchmen; but Charles was by far
the most consistent and clear-sighted of the two.   He
saw, what everybody except John Wesley himself seems
to have seen, that the Societies, and especially the
preachers, were drifting away from the Church, and he
exerted himself with characteristic energy to stop what
he deemed the dangerous tendency.   In his *Reasons
against Separation*, John concludes with asserting that
it is *inexpedient* to separate ; but Charles, in affixing his
signature, added that it was also *unlawful*.   He had a
much lower opinion of the lay preachers than John had ;
and when the chapel in the City Road was opened in
1776, would not hear of their officiating in it on the
Lord's day.   The Anti-Church feeling in the Societies
was probably the chief reason why Charles Wesley
ceased to itinerate from 1756 onwards, though the

[1] See Telford's *Life of Charles Wesley.*

fact of his being happily married, with a family growing
up around him, may also have caused him to desire
comparative rest, or rather a settled home. This fear
of a schism, combined with the fact that Charles never
could take kindly to Mrs. John Wesley, produced a
certain estrangement between the two brothers, of
which John complains touchingly in 1771. But there
was no real diminution of love and respect on either
side; no, not even when the relations were strained to
the utmost by John Wesley's "ordinations" in his old
age. Apart from family affection, which was very
strong among the Wesleys, John always felt that his
brother was his nearest, dearest, and best friend. He
thoroughly appreciated the services which Charles
rendered to the cause by his wonderful gift of sacred
poetry. He regarded his hymns, not only as elegant
and elevated expressions of praise, but as "a body of
practical and experimental divinity." And so they
really were; they answered in effect the purposes of a
creed to the Societies. Abstract confessions of faith
might make little impression upon the poor and un-
educated, who constituted the majority of John Wesley's
followers, and whom he certainly loved and valued most;
but the poorest and most unlettered could remember
the verses of a hymn which had been sung by thousands, with all the fervour of impassioned souls, in the
preaching-houses, at the class meetings, or under the
blue canopy of heaven. The teaching of the sermon
became stereotyped in the hymn, which was enshrined
in the hearts of many, and remembered on a death-bed
when all else was forgotten. John Wesley's keen eye
for the practical thus led him to attach an additional
value to his brother's hymns, while his abhorrence of

anything which savoured of bad taste caused him to welcome with peculiar delight compositions which were more calculated to provoke "the critic to turn Christian, than the Christian to turn critic."[1]

Are we to term the last of the trio who certainly stand pre-eminent in the history of early Methodism, a friend or an opponent of John Wesley? Certainly from John Wesley's own standpoint, a friend. "You may read," he says, "Whitefield against Wesley, but you shall never read Wesley against Whitefield." Until the unfortunate question of "the decrees" intervened, George Whitefield and John Wesley were of one heart and soul in their evangelistic work. It was Whitefield, as we have seen, who set the example of field-preaching, which Wesley followed reluctantly. It was Whitefield who committed the continuance of his work in London, when he went to Georgia, to the Wesleys; and, on his return, was more than satisfied with the result. It was Whitefield whose name was far more prominently connected with the commencement of the movement than Wesley's own. What evil genius led George Whitefield to the conviction that it was his peculiar mission to elucidate the mysteries—for there were many—of what was vaguely termed Calvinism, we know not. But the case is not a peculiar one. As a general rule, one finds that the weaker the divine, the profounder the subjects he aspires to deal with; and Whitefield, though a mighty preacher, was a feeble divine. It is easy enough to see why John Wesley thought it necessary to take any part in the matter. He might, indeed,

---

[1] Let credit be given where credit is due. This terse and epigrammatic sentence was not, as it has been sometimes represented, John Wesley's, but John Byrom's.

have remembered his mother's wise counsel when he
was inclined to puzzle his young mind about these
profound mysteries—"Such studies tend more to con-
found than to inform the understanding." But if
Calvinism tended, as John Wesley thought it did, to
Antinomianism, it struck at the root of his most cherished
project—the spread of scriptural holiness throughout
the land. The unhappy dispute produced a temporary
alienation between the two good men, but the breach
was entirely healed, mainly through the instrumentality
of Charles Wesley; and henceforth Whitefield and the
two brothers became "a threefold cord which could not
be broken," until the death of Whitefield in 1770;
when, in accordance with the dying man's own direction,
John Wesley preached his funeral sermon.

Whitefield, however, was never so much a man after
Wesley's own heart as John Fletcher, with whom he
became acquainted just at the time when he seemed to
be most in need of help; that is, when his own health
seemed to be breaking down, and when his brother
Charles was gradually withdrawing from itinerant work.
"When my bodily strength failed," he says, "and none
in England were able and willing to assist me, He
sent me help from the mountains of Switzerland, and
an helpmeet for me in every respect. Where could I
have found such another?" The personal history of
him who was *par excellence* the saint of Methodism must
be sought elsewhere.[1] Suffice it to say, that Wesley
found in Fletcher a supporter whom he could thoroughly
trust in every way, a man whose piety was a shining
example to all, and whose mind, if of a somewhat thin

---

[1] See *inter alia, The English Church in the Eighteenth Century.*

texture, was elegant and refined, and improved by culture to the finest possible point. So far from their friendship splitting on the rock of Calvinism, Wesley derived from Fletcher by far the most valuable aid he ever received in checking the tendency to Antinomianism, which he trembled to see in some who were called Methodists. He appreciated this aid all the more because it relieved him of a work which of all others he abhorred most—the work of writing on controversial divinity. So highly did he value Fletcher, that he wrote to him in 1773, when he expected that, in the course of nature, he must soon let fall the reins of government which he had long held with so firm a hand :—" The wise men of the world will say, ' When Mr. W. drops, then all comes to an end.' And so surely it will, unless, before God calls him hence, one is found to stand in his place. For οὐκ ἀγαθον πολυκοιρανίη. Come out then in the name of God ! Come to the help of the Lord against the mighty ! Come while I am alive, and capable of labour ! Come while I am able, God assisting, to build you up in the faith, and introduce you to the people ! " [1]

The hardy old man, however, was destined to survive his younger and more delicate friend several years. He preached his funeral sermon in 1785, from the suggestive text, "Mark the perfect man," &c., and at once set about writing his life. Wesley always thought it a pity that Fletcher should waste his sweetness on the desert air of Madeley, which he calls "an exceeding pleasant village, encompassed with trees and hills." [2] He believed that even in that narrow sphere, " the

---

[1] Quoted from *Tyerman*, iii. 148.   [2] *Journal*, July 1764.

immense pains which Mr. Fletcher took with his
people " was not so successful as it ought to have been,
owing to the want of discipline in the Church.

Another clerical friend of John Wesley who, in one
sense, should be ranked higher than even Fletcher or
Charles Wesley himself, was Mr. Vincent Perronet,
Vicar of Shoreham. Charles Wesley called him "the
Archbishop of the Methodists," and he was regarded by
both the brothers as a sort of ultimate Court of Appeal.
In 1751, when they were in great anxiety about the
preachers, they conferred with Mr. Perronet as a confidential adviser, and drew up a formal agreement between themselves, of which the following was one of
the articles : " That if we should ever disagree in our
judgment, we will refer the matter to Mr. Perronet."
Earlier in the same year John Wesley had consulted
Mr. Perronet on the delicate question of marriage, and
was unfortunately guided by his advice : " Feb. 2, 1751.
Having received a full answer from Mr. P., I was clearly
convinced that I ought to marry." It was at Mr.
Perronet's vicarage, and after much consultation with
its master, that John wrote to Mr. Fletcher, urging him
to be his successor. In short, Shoreham Vicarage was a
favourite retreat of John Wesley. There he combined
the double advantage of rest and leisure with the
trusted counsel of the Vicar : " Oct. 11, 1746. I had
the pleasure of spending an hour with Mr. P."; " Nov.
20, 1749. I rode to Mr. Perronet's of Shoreham, that I
might be at leisure to write." Such entries are very
frequent in the Journals; they end with a touching
notice of the good old man's death : " May 2, 1785. So
ended the holy and happy life of Mr. Vincent Perronet,
in the 92nd year of his age. I follow hard after him in

years.   O, that I may follow him in holiness, and that
my last end may be like his!"   Mr. Perronet is the
very first-named among the evangelical clergy with
whom John Wesley proposed to enter into a kind of
informal union.   It was, however, as a "guide, philo-
sopher and friend," rather than as an active worker in
any larger sphere than his own parish, that Mr. Perronet
was valued by John Wesley, who never complains, as
he complained about Fletcher, that the Vicar of Shoreham confined his labours to Shoreham, but on the
contrary, frequently notices the immense amount of
good he was doing there.

It was not until late in life (1776), that John Wesley
met the last of the five who may be said to stand
in the first rank of his clerical friends.   "Aug. 14,
1776.   Here [Kingston, Somerset] I found a clergyman,
Dr. Coke, a gentleman-commoner of Jesus College in
Oxford, who came twenty miles on purpose.   I had
much conversation with him ; and a union then began
which I trust shall never end."   And it never did.   It
was at the time when Fletcher's health had begun to
break down, while Charles Wesley had long ceased to
itinerate.   One can well understand, therefore, the
ardour with which John Wesley welcomed an ally who,
by position and education, was qualified to take their
place ; and the way in which he welcomed him was
very characteristic—"The Doctor expressed his doubts
respecting the propriety of confining himself to one
congregation.   Wesley clasped his hands, and in a
manner peculiarly his own, said, 'Brother, go out, go
out, and preach the gospel to all the world.'"[1]   In the

---

[1] Tyerman, iii. 214.

following year Wesley records—"Oct. 19, 1777. I
went forward to Tiverton with Dr. C., who, being
dismissed from his curacy, has bid adieu to his
honourable name, and determined to cast in his lot
with us." It is only fair to add that this dismissal from
his curacy can hardly be regarded as an act of tyranny.
"On Sunday," we are told,[1] "after the second lesson, he
(Coke) would read a paper of his appointments for the
ensuing week, with the place and time of service"—that
is, in connection with the Methodists. Now how many
incumbents in the present day would approve of their
curates reading, entirely on their own responsibility,
when they had no right to read anything at all except
what they were told to do, announcements which were
extremely distasteful to the body of their hearers?
However, Dr. Coke became John Wesley's first lieu-
tenant; and a most vigorous and efficient one he was.
He was full of zeal and energy, but he was not always,
at least from a Churchman's point of view, the best
adviser that Wesley could have found. It must be
repeated that though John Wesley ruled his Societies
with absolute sway, he was himself singularly liable to
be swayed by those in whom he had confidence; it was,
therefore, highly important, considering the immense
power he possessed, that his trusted counsellors should
not only be pious and earnest, but judicious men. Dr.
Coke had many excellent qualities, but "judicious" is
not the epithet that would be most appropriate to him.
In the later years of Wesley's life, he was certainly
second only to Wesley himself. He used to visit the
Societies in Ireland alternately with Wesley, having

---

[1] Tyerman, iii. 214.

equal power. He was one of the three clergymen who were joint incumbents, as it were, of the new chapel in the City Road. He was the father of Wesleyan Foreign Missions, and grudged no labour or hardship in that most important branch of work. He was one of John Wesley's executors, and the joint-author of the earliest biography of him.

There were many other clergymen who did Wesley yeoman's service by paving the way for him, and countenancing his efforts in their respective parishes and neighbourhoods. Two such have been noticed, Grimshaw of Haworth, and Berridge of Everton. Others were the four clergymen who attended the first Conference, Messrs. Piers, Meriton, Taylor, and Hodges ; [1] Mr. Richardson, a "curate" of the Wesleys, in the City Road chapel; Mr. David Simpson, a clergyman of Macclesfield, a place which John Wesley dearly loved ; Mr. Baddiley of Hayfield in Derbyshire ; Messrs. James Creighton, Peard Dickinson, and E. Smyth, of all of whom space forbids any lengthened notice.

But the clergy of the Evangelical school, which almost reached its zenith before the old man's long life closed, were never, as a body, very cordial admirers of John Wesley. And no wonder; for they really belonged to a different school of thought. It is true that *his* cardinal doctrine, justification by faith, was also *their* cardinal doctrine. But even on this point, when it came to be explained, there was a marked difference,

[1] A short account of these will be found in Mr. R. Denny Urlin's *Churchman's Life of Wesley*, p. 121. And here I must venture to express my deep obligations to this and the earlier volume, *John Wesley's Place in Church History*. The admirable Christian tone of these books on the one hand, and of Mr. Telford's *Life* on the other, must be recognized by all impartial readers.

—so marked, that it was one point of the fiercest controversy in which John Wesley, to his sorrow, was ever
engaged.   In fact, Wesley throughout took a different
standpoint from theirs.   *They* took their stand on the
Reformation in the sixteenth century; *he* on the
Primitive Church.   *They*, again, were all, more or less,
inclined to Calvinism; *he* was a vehement anti-Calvinist.
He was at once too much and too little of a Churchman
for them : too much, for he laid great stress upon many
distinctly Church usages, about which they were either
absolutely indifferent, or positively disliked; too little,
for he made light of the parochial system, and had no
scruple about invading any man's parish, whether the
incumbent was an Evangelical or not, and planting his
Societies there.   This brought him into collision with
such men as Mr. Venn of Huddersfield, Mr. Walker of
Truro, and Mr. Adam of Winteringham, and drew forth
a letter of remonstrance from his old college pupil,
Mr. Hervey of Weston Favell, though the latter was
not personally affected by any invasion of the Societies.
In fact there does not seem to me to be the least
reason for wondering that John Wesley's repeated
attempts at establishing an *entente cordiale* between
himself and the Evangelical clergy by the formation of
a sort of union, in which everybody was to be allowed
to think pretty much as he pleased, should have proved
abortive.

Another and far more numerous class of clerical
opponents were those who, for one cause or another,
hated above all things every form of what they vaguely
called "enthusiasm."   It is unjust to set this class down
indiscriminately as men without any sense of religion.
Such sweeping censures are far too common, and have

sometimes been passed by men who ought to have
known better.   The 18th century clergy were not, as a
body, irreligious men;[1] they did not, indeed, take a
very high spiritual standard; but their religion, as far
as it went, was real; and there was a robust manliness
about them, which, though it sometimes degenerated
into coarseness, might yet teach some useful lessons to
the present age.   Bishops Warburton and Lavington
were types of this class.   They strangely misunderstood
John Wesley, and laid themselves open to his unanswerable retorts; the one, when in his *Doctrine of Grace* he
affirmed the direct, personal influence of the Holy Spirit
to be limited to the Apostolic age; the other, when in
his *Enthusiasm of the Papists and Methodists compared* he
described in effect Methodism as Popery in disguise;
but they were not mere heathens.

It should be remembered, too, that both language
and manners were rougher in those days than they are
now.   Bishops do not talk now, as Bishop Warburton
talked then about "crews of scoundrels," and about
"trimming the rogues' jackets for them"; and in times
when bull-fighting and cock-fighting were favourite
amusements, deeds were regarded as mere horse-play
which would now be accounted downright cruelty.
The men who would now be content with writing an
indignant letter to *The Times*, would have thought it
no harm then to show their disapproval by sanctioning
a ducking in a horsepond, or a shower of rotten eggs.

---

[1] Of course there were very many exceptions, far more than I
am happy to believe there are at the present day.   But I make
the statement in the text most deliberately, after long study, not
of second-hand, but of original, sources; and I can fully bear
out what Canon Hockin states about the clergy of one particular
district in an appendix to *John Wesley and Modern Methodism.*

Nor is it at all wonderful that quiet clergymen, who, in a sleepy sort of way, were trying to do some good in their parishes, did not welcome with open arms men who certainly set their people by the ears, and raised a spirit of disturbance which they could not quell. There is a passage in one of Charles Wesley's letters to his brother which speaks volumes. John had reminded him of one of his early poems in which he speaks of "Heathenish priests and mitred infidels," and Charles replied—"That juvenile line of mine I disown, renounce, and with shame recant. . . . I never knew of more than one 'mitred infidel,' and for him I took Mr. Law's word." [1] Now if a cultured clergyman, a warm friend of the Church, and a most amiable and charitable man like Charles Wesley, had yet to admit that he had thus spoken without the book, is it likely that men of a different stamp, whose very *raison d'être* as revivalists depended upon the badness of the clergy, would be more particular about investigating the truth of their accusations? And is it reasonable to expect that the clergy would like to hear themselves thus recklessly accused?

This is not intended as a justification of the treatment which John Wesley too frequently met with in the outset of his career as a reformer. It is admitted that there is another side of the question; but that side has been so frequently and prominently put forward, that it seemed necessary to redress the balance by insisting upon what, after many years' study of the 18th century, I am persuaded ought to be taken into account. It is most deplorable that a reformer, who was so warmly attached

---

[1] Tyerman, iii. 446.

to the Church as John Wesley was, could not have been utilized, instead of repelled.   But it is an easy thing to be wise after the event; and, looking at the matter from an 18th century point of view, I venture to think that the difficulties in the way of cordial co-operation were far more numerous, and far less easy to be sur-mounted than is commonly supposed.[1]

The obstacles, however, which John Wesley met with from without, were less formidable than those he met with from within; but this is so important a subject that it must be treated of in a separate chapter.

[1] Mr. Abbey's remarks on this point, in his *English Church and its Bishops* (1700—1800), are, in my opinion, unanswerable.

CHAPTER X.

" WHAT can hurt the Methodists so-called, but the Methodists? Only let them not fight one another, let not brother lift up sword against brother, and no weapon forged against them shall prosper." So wrote John Wesley on May 29, 1764, when he had already had much painful experience of the damage which internal disputes did to the cause he had at heart. Quite from its commencement, the course of the revival began to be checked by this hindrance. On his return from Herrnhuth in 1738, Wesley found the little Society in London torn with disputes, which, however, the awe of his presence soon checked. But at the close of the next year they had broken out again with redoubled force. "Dec. 29, 1739," he writes, "came to London. Here I found every day the dreadful effects of our brethren's reasoning and disputing with each other. Scarce one in ten retained his first love, and most of the rest were in the utmost confusion, biting and devouring one another." Half a year later (June 19, 1740), he found that old bone of contention, predestination, fiercely disputed at Deptford. The account of a conversation with one of these hot disputants illustrates alike his wonderful forbearance, which was one of the secrets of his success, and the sort of material he had to deal with. "Mr. Acourt said, 'What, do you refuse admitting a person into your Society, only because he differs from you in opinion?' I answered, 'No; but what opinion do you mean?' He said, 'That of election. I hold a certain number is elected from eternity, and those must and shall be saved; and the rest of mankind must and shall be damned; and many of your Society hold the same.' I replied, 'I never asked whether they hold it or no. Only let them not trouble others by disputing about it.' He said, 'Nay, but I will dispute about it.' 'What, wherever you come?' 'Yes, wherever I come.' 'Why, then, should you come among us, who you know are of another mind?' 'Because you are all wrong, and I am resolved to set you right.' 'I fear your coming with this view would neither profit you nor us.' He concluded, 'Then I will go and tell all the world that you and your brother are false prophets. And I tell you, in one fortnight you will be all in confusion.'"

The dispute which led to the transference of Wesley's Society from Fetter Lane to the Foundry in 1740 has already been noticed. Then Kingswood became the scene of disorder. John Cenwick, Wesley's master at the school for colliers there, and one of his first lay-preachers, was the ringleader, and many members of the Band Society had to be expelled, "not for their opinions, but for scoffing at the word and ministers of God; for tale-bearing, back-biting, and evil-speaking; for dissembling, lying and slandering." They had "made it their common practice to scoff at the preaching of Mr. John and Charles Wesley" (Journal, Feb. 28, 1741).

M

Whitefield had now returned from America, and the paper war which had been waged between him and the Wesleys when the Atlantic divided them, was exchanged for another form of hostility, and produced another split in the camp.

At Epworth in 1751 Wesley found "a poor, dead, and senseless people," and was informed that "some of our preachers there had diligently gleaned up and retailed all the evil they had heard of me; some had quite laid aside our hymns as well as the doctrine they had formerly preached; one of them had frequently spoke against our rules, and the others quite neglected them."

Norwich was for many years a troublesome place. "I met," he writes, Sept. 9, 1759, "the Society at seven, and told them in plain terms that they were the most ignorant, self-conceited, self-willed, untractable, disorderly, disjointed Society that I knew in the three kingdoms. And God applied it to their hearts; so that many were profited, but I do not find that one was offended." But alas! the improvement was not lasting; for four years later, Oct. 14, 1763, he had to tell them again—"For many years I have had more trouble with this Society than with half the Societies in England put together. With God's help, I will try you one year longer; and I hope you will bring forth better fruit." Nov. 4, 1770 he writes—"In all England I find no people like those at Norwich. They are eminently as unstable as water;" and as late as Oct. 22, 1785, he had to tell them—"Of all the people I have seen in the kingdom, for between forty and fifty years, you have been the most fickle, and yet the most stubborn." It was the misfortune of Norwich to have in the early

stage of the movement a baneful element of disorder in
an able and very influential but thoroughly bad man,
James Wheatley, who combined a high profession with
a low practice.

About the year 1763 fresh troubles broke out among
the London Societies, Thomas Maxfield and George
Bell being the ringleaders of the malcontents. Maxfield was one of the first of John Wesley's lay-
preachers, and had, through the kind offices of Wesley
himself, obtained Holy Orders from the Bishop of
Londonderry, who said to him, "Sir, I ordain you to assist
that good man, that he may not work himself to death."
Bell had so exalted an idea of his own powers that he
had the monstrous impiety to touch a blind man's eyes
with spittle, and say, "Ephphatha." Both were jealous
of the authority of the two brothers, and raised a
rebellion against them. John Wesley puts the matter
very mildly when he says that he "disliked in Bell and
Maxfield something that had the appearance of
enthusiasm—overvaluing feelings and inward impressions; mistaking the mere work of imagination for the
voice of the Spirit; expecting the end without the
means; and undervaluing reason, knowledge, and
wisdom in general." He behaved with his usual forbearance. "I desired," he says (Journal, Jan. 7, 1763),
"George Bell, with two or three of his friends, to meet
me with one or two others. We took much pains to
convince him of his mistakes, particularly that which
he had lately adopted—that the end of the world was
to be on Feb. 28. But we could make no impression
upon him at all. He was as unmoved as a rock."
Wesley persevered, and on Jan. 23, he says, "In order
to check a growing evil, I preached on 'Judge not, and

ye shall not be judged.' But it had just the contrary
effect on many, who construed it into a satire upon
G. Bell, one of whose friends said, 'If the devil had been
in the pulpit, he would not have preached such a sermon','"—as he certainly would have not. Bell and the
rest seem to have been tools in the hands of Maxfield.
"All this time," proceeds Wesley, "I did not want for
information from all quarters, that Mr. M. was at the
bottom of all this; that he was continually spiriting up
all with whom I was intimate against me; he told
them that I was not capable of teaching them, and
insinuated that none was, but himself." Wesley, however, was very firm; he would not allow Bell to pray at
the Foundry. "The reproach of Christ," he said, "I am
willing to bear, but not the reproach of enthusiasm, if I
can help it." The upshot of it all was that some in
the London Societies threw up their tickets, saying,
"Blind John is not capable of teaching us; we will
keep to Mr. Maxfield."

By far the bitterest opponents John Wesley ever had
were the Calvinists. I place their opposition under
the head of internal disputes, because, though there was
a marked distinction between the Calvinistic and the
Arminian Methodists, they both professed to join in
one great cause, viz. the revival of spiritual religion,
to promote which was John Wesley's grand object. It
really is difficult at the present day to understand why
the minds of these good men should have been lashed
into a fury by the discussion of a profound mystery,
which far more able and learned divines had, long
before *their* time, in vain tried to solve. Not only
Christian charity but common decency was thrown to
the winds in the language used *to*, and *about*, John

Wesley in the miserable squabble which is dignified by the name of the Calvinistic controversy. If it were not for the awful solemnity of the subject, it would be difficult to repress a smile at the ludicrous way in which, with quite unconscious humour—the dreary vituperations are not relieved by one gleam of *conscious* humour—some of his adversaries expressed themselves. Thus, as early as 1740, Whitefield wrote—" With Universal Redemption brother Charles pleases the world; brother John follows him in everything "—which, by the way, was very unlike "brother John." " I believe no atheist can more preach against predestination than they "—as if atheists were in the habit of preaching either for or against predestination. Whitefield's Christian, placable character, however, prevented him from indulging in abuse. But in 1744, a Mr. Cudworth, an Antinomian, gave vent to the remarkable utterance that he "abhorred John Wesley as much as he did the Pope, and ten times more than he did the devil "—a strange estimate of the relative harm which these three enemies of religion were doing. These, however, were but preludes to the Calvinistic controversy proper; the germs of which may perhaps be traced to a little dispute which arose between Wesley and his old Oxford pupil and son in the Gospel, James Hervey. It was natural that the latter should consult his old tutor and spiritual father about a work which he was preparing for publication, *Theron and Aspasio;* but he could scarcely have expected that a book which strongly advocated Calvinistic views, and which was written in a most florid and lymphatic style, should find favour with one who was known to be a decided anti-Calvinist, and who above all things aimed at plainness, terseness, and strength in his writings. After Hervey's death, his letters to Wesley on the subject were published, to Wesley's great annoyance. This was in 1765; three years later the expulsion of six Methodist students from St. Edmund's Hall, Oxford, was made the subject of a dispute between the Calvinists and the Arminians. These premonitory sputterings issued at last in a violent explosion. In 1770, Lady Huntingdon excluded from her college at Trevecca all Arminians, including the saintly Fletcher, whose office was something like that of a Visitor at an Oxford or Cambridge college, and Joseph Benson, its able head-master. Both were intimate friends and allies of John Wesley, and he remonstrated with Lady Huntingdon on the proceeding. He was not sorry for the opportunity of doing so; for "I had been convinced deeply," he says, "for several years that I had not done my duty to that valuable woman; that I had not told her what I was convinced no one else would dare to do, and what I knew she would bear from no other person, but possibly might bear from me." In the famous Minutes of the Conference in 1770, Wesley stated plainly but temperately enough his anti-Calvinistic views. Lady Huntingdon and her relative, Mr. Shirley, were up in arms at once; and, not to enter into the complications of the dispute, it may be said briefly that the storm now burst forth in all its fury, and raged at intervals for nearly eight years. The whole matter was most distasteful to John Wesley, who was only too glad to allow his friends, Mr. Sellon, Mr. Olivers, and above all Mr. Fletcher, to fight the battle instead of him. But the weight of the storm fell upon the devoted head of him who was regarded as the chief offender. Wesley exasperated them all the more because he persisted in holding aloof from the fray. "Let Mr. W.," writes Toplady, "fight his own battles, but let him not fight by proxy; let his cobblers keep to their stalls, his tinkers mend their brazen vessels, his barbers confine themselves to their blocks and basins, his blacksmiths blow more suitable coals than those of controversy; every man in his own order." Wesley is elegantly described as "slinking behind one of his drudges." "An old fox tarred and feathered," "Pope John," "Little John" (a delicate allusion to his short stature), "a designing wolf," "the most perfect and holy and sly, that e'er turn'd a coat, or could pilfer and lie," "a dealer in stolen wares," "as unprincipled as a rook, and as silly as a jackdaw," "a gray-headed enemy of all righteousness," "a venal profligate," "an apostate miscreant," "the most rancorous hater of the Gospel system that ever appeared in this land," "a low and puny tadpole in divinity"—these and similar expressions actually occur *da capo* in the writings of Sir Richard and Rowland Hill, Toplady, and Wesley's old friend and coadjutor, Berridge, respecting a man who, like themselves, had the revival of spiritual religion most deeply at heart. It must be confessed that the writers on Wesley's side (Fletcher always excepted) showed themselves almost as great adepts in the art of calling names as their antagonists, who culled a choice selection of flowers of rhetoric to show that the Arminian Oliver could match the Calvinistic Roland. Happily we have only to do with the quarrel so far as John Wesley was concerned in it, and as it would undoubtedly have been his mind that the whole matter should pass into deserved oblivion, there let it rest.

After the subsidence of the Calvinistic controversy, there was comparative quiet within the camp of John Wesley; but disorder still broke out now and then. In 1779, "for the first time Wesley's supreme and absolute power was professedly and openly resisted," [1] which led to the expulsion of Alexander McNab from the pulpit at Bath in spite of the Conference. John Wesley not only asserted but carried his point, that the Conference had literally no power whatever, but that the whole and sole authority over every Society rested ultimately in himself. It was an amazing claim, and it was well that his aims were as pure and unselfish as they were, for this unlimited sway over a large and increasing body of men would have been a dangerous weapon in the hands of any one who was not uniformly actuated by the love of God and the love of man for God's sake.

If he met with an exceptional amount of opposition, it was counterbalanced by an amount of authority which it has fallen to the lot of few men to wield.

[1] Tyerman, iii. 308.

CHAPTER XI.

THE very last thing of which John Wesley was ambitious was literary fame. In nothing does the intensely practical character of his mind come out more strongly than in his writings. Whether it is long treatise or short tract, whether it is prose or poetry, whether it is original composition or the reprinting or abridging of the works of others, whether it is a simple school-book or one on controversial divinity, whether it is a sermon or a commentary or a journal, it is all the same ; he has always some immediate practical end in view; and in almost every case we can trace the reason of his writing what he did write in the particular circumstances which were at that particular time before him. Hence we may admit, to a certain extent, the truth of the remark of a very thoughtful critic, that " on ' The Works of the Rev. John Wesley,' the funeral formula is already uttered, ' Dust to dust,' " [1] and at the same time maintain with perfect consistency that John Wesley was an

---

[1] *Wesley and Methodism*, by Isaac Taylor, p. 208. A very different estimate, however, of the value of John Wesley's writings is given by Mr. Alexander Knox, who was at least as thoughtful a man as Mr. Isaac Taylor. See Knox, *Remains*, i. 278, &c.

exceedingly .... and ....
it is too much the ....
him off mentally ....
mind do so, if he would ....
writings.

It would of course, ...
thing which John Wesley ....
as the great work of his ....
or Whitefield; but if we ....
writings as classics in ....
is ....., we are standing ....
picture of the truest ....
of one of the most ....
tho ....

nothing of the religious, point of view, it would, as a
great mistake to be satisfied with regarding Wesley as
he appears when filtered through the mind of any
critic or biographer, however able, without contemplating
him as he appears in his own pages.

But in considering John Wesley as a writer, the same
difficulty occurs which we found in considering him as
an itinerant. As in the one capacity he appeared to be
here, there, and everywhere in body, so in the other he
appears to be here, there, and everywhere in mind.
For more than half a century, scarcely a year elapsed
without the press being busy with something, generally
with several things, for which John Wesley was
responsible. How did he find time for it all? Simply
by being in the literal sense of the term "a Methodist";
that is, by methodically parcelling out every hour,
almost every minute, so that there should never be any
waste. "You do not," he writes in 1777, "understand
my manner of life. Though I am always in haste, I am

never in a hurry, because I never undertake more work than I can go through with perfect calmness of spirit. It is true I travel four or five thousand miles a year; but I generally travel alone in my carriage, and, consequently, am as retired ten hours in a day as if I was in a wilderness. On other days I never spend less than three hours, frequently ten or twelve, in a day alone. Yet I find time to visit the sick and poor—a matter of absolute duty." Let us see how he employed his time, so far as literary work was concerned.

He first appeared in print in 1733 with *A Collection of Prayers for every Day in the Week ;* this was followed in 1734 by an abridgment of John Norris' *Treatise on Christian Perfection.* In 1735 three publications appeared—a reprint of his father's *Letter of Advice to a Young Clergyman ;* a sermon on *The Trouble and Rest of Good Men ;* and an edition, with a long Preface, of the *De Imitatione Christi,* the volume which is referred to in his correspondence with Law. In 1737 he published his first Hymn-book at Charlestown in America. Then in 1739 came *Hymns and Sacred Poems, by John and Charles Wesley,* twenty of them being translations from the German by John. In 1740 another Hymn-book came out with many Hymns on Christian Perfection. In 1741 appeared *An Extract from the Life of M. de Renty,* whom John Wesley regarded as a great saint, Roman though he was [1]; and an *Abridgment of Norris' Reflections on the Conduct of Human Life.* The first publication of 1742 was again a work of Norris, his

---

[1] In the Preface of his *Life of Mr. Fletcher,* written many years later, he says he had long despaired of finding so holy a person as the Marquis de Renty. Mr. Fletcher alone had in his view appeared to equal him.

Treatise of Christian Prudence. John Norris, it may be observed, was a personal friend of Wesley's father, and was the only Oxford man who was prominent among the English Platonists; he was the worthy successor (several intervening) of the saintly George Herbert at Bemerton, and belonged to the same type of Churchmen. It is interesting to notice that among the very first books with which Wesley supplied his followers were two written by such a man. In the same year he most reluctantly became a controversial writer. "I now," he writes, "tread an untried path with fear and trembling —fear not of my adversary, but of myself." The work was, *The Principles of a Methodist, in Answer to the Rev. Josiah Tucker.* The year 1743 produced his first Tract, in the modern sense of the term, and the First Part of one of the most telling of all his writings, *An Earnest Appeal to Men of Reason and Religion.* In 1744 came out, *A Collection of Moral and Sacred Poems,* dedicated to Lady Huntingdon; an Abridgment of Law's *Serious Call;* and a reprint of Scougal's *Life of God in the Soul of Man,* the very book which his mother had recommended to him twenty years before. The year 1745 commenced with two works of a very different type; an Abridgment of Jonathan Edwards' *Thoughts on the Revival in New England,* and *Extracts from Baxter's Aphorisms on Justification;* and in the same year came out that very remarkable volume, *Hymns on the Lord's Supper,* by John and Charles Wesley, with Dr. Brevint's *Preface concerning the Christian Sacrament and Sacrifice.* Several Tracts were written in this year: *An Earnest Persuasion to keep the Sabbath-day holy; A Word for a Swearer; A Word in Season, or Address to an Englishman,* which was called forth by the alarm about the

Pretender, and was of course an exhortation to loyalty
to King George; *A Word to a Drunkard;* and *Advice
to the People called Methodists;* and this busy year
saw also the First Part of *The Farther Appeal,* &c.,
which was even more telling than its predecessor, *The
Earnest Appeal.* In 1746 we have another Tract, *A
Word of Advice to Saints and Sinners; Lessons for
Children;* a controversial piece entitled *The Principles
of the Methodists further explained,* in answer to the
Rev. T. Church, an able writer; and Parts II. and III.
of the *Farther Appeal.* In 1747 appeared two Tracts
on political subjects: *A Word to a Protestant,* on the
duty of keeping out Romanism in the shape of the
Pretender; and *A Word to a Freeholder,* written on
the eve of the Exeter election; *A Letter to the Bishop
of London* (Dr. Gibson) defending himself very temperately against the strictures upon the Methodists in his
lordship's "Charge"; and a curious book, *Primitive
Physic,* in which Wesley put into print the medical
advice which he had given gratuitously to his people.
The year 1748 produced several Class-books in Latin
for Kingswood School; *A Word to a Methodist on his
Duty of adhering to the Church; A Letter to a Friend
concerning Tea* (Wesley at this time waged a fierce
war against tea-drinking); and *A Letter to a Person
lately joined to the People called Quakers*—a step of
which Wesley strongly disappproved. In 1749 we have
some more school-books; *A Letter to Dr. Conyers
Middleton on his Free Enquiry,* one of the few instances
in which John Wesley took the initiative in theological
controversy; and the *Plain Account of the People called
Methodists,* in a letter to Mr. Perronet, which has been
largely quoted above; a reprint of Law's powerful

Answer to Dr. Trapp's Sermon on being Righteous overmuch; a *Roman Catechism,* in which he showed the unscriptural character of Romanism; and the first volume of *The Christian Library,* containing the principal works of the Apostolical Fathers, whom Wesley regarded as all but inspired, or at any rate as standing on a higher level than any other writers outside the Sacred Canon. The year 1750 produced only a few school-books, including the Colloquies of Erasmus, Phædrus, and a Compendium of Logic, taken from Aldrich and Sanderson; and the *First Letter to the Author of The Enthusiasm of the Methodists and Papists compared* (Bishop Lavington). In 1751 we have only a pamphlet, *Thoughts on Infant Baptism;* and a Hebrew, a Greek, and a French Grammar, all quite short. In 1752 appeared his first anti-Calvinistic production, *Predestination calmly considered,* and his *Second Letter to Bishop Lavington.* The year 1753 is the date of his *Complete English Dictionary;* and 1754 is a blank. John Wesley was now, for the first time in his wonderfully healthy life, seriously ill; but he was very busy during his convalescence; and in 1755 appeared the most important work he ever produced—his *Explanatory Notes on the New Testament.* They are chiefly founded on Matthew Henry and Bengel, whose *Gnomon* had lately appeared and had interested him deeply. The notes are short, but his own remarks are very pungent and pithy, and his selections good. This work, besides its intrinsic value, has an interest as being one of the doctrinal standards of Methodism. In this year the fifty volumes of *The Christian Library* were completed. This was the year of the great earthquake at Lisbon, and "being much importuned thereto," writes John Wesley, "I wrote

Serious Thoughts on the Earthquake at Lisbon, directed, not as I designed at first, to the small vulgar, but the great; to the learned, rich, and honourable Heathens, commonly called Christians." In 1756 he republished his father's treatise on Baptism, and wrote his *Letter to Mr. Law* on Jacob Behmen, and an *Address to the Clergy*, in which, among other things, he urged them not to despise "human learning." The year 1757 produced only one work, but that a very able one, *The Doctrine of Original Sin*, in answer to a well-known Socinian, Taylor of Norwich. The year 1758 was a time of great unsettlement about the relations of the United Societies to the Church; so we have a Tract, *Reasons against a Separation from the Church of England against all Dissenters*, and *A Preservative against unsettled notions in Religion*, which consists of selections, partly from his own works, and partly from those of others, including Charles Leslie's *Short Method with the Deists*. The *Preservative* was specially intended for his preachers who were drifting away from the Church. Then we have a blank for two years; but it should be mentioned that in 1760 was completed his first series of fifty-three *Sermons* in four volumes (1746-1760), which have a value above the rest, because they are, with the *Notes on the New Testament*, the doctrinal standard of the Methodists. In 1762 appeared a *Letter to Mr. Horne*, afterwards Bishop of Norwich, occasioned by his sermon at Oxford in which he reflected upon the Methodists. This letter is couched in very respectful terms, for John Wesley always respected an able and sincere man, as Horne undoubtedly was. Some Tracts on Imputed Righteousness, against the Calvinists, belong to this year. In 1763 he published a *Letter to the Bishop*

of Gloucester (Dr. Warburton) against his "Doctrine of
Grace." The unusual bitterness of this *Letter* may find
some apology in the far greater bitterness of his opponent. He also in this year struck out quite a new line
in *A Summary of the Wisdom of God in Creation—a
Compendium of Natural Philosophy.* In 1764 appeared
A Short History of Methodism, in which, after having
shown how others connected with the revival had drifted
from the Church, he says, "Those who remain with Mr.
Wesley are mostly Church of England men ; they love
her articles, her homilies, her liturgy, her discipline, and
unwillingly vary from it in any instance." In 1765 we
have a very curious production, *Thoughts on a Single Life,*
in which Wesley the married man strongly asserts the
same opinions which Wesley the bachelor had asserted
in favour of celibacy. The year 1767 produced *A
Word to a Smuggler,* a tract which Wesley desired, like
several others of his tracts, to be distributed gratuitously ;
and two reprints, *Christian Letters of Joseph Alleine,* and
Extracts from the Letters of Mr. Samuel Rutherford. In
1768 the country was agitated by the "Wilkes and
Liberty" contest, so we have a tract, *Free Thoughts on
Public Affairs,* of course on the Conservative side. The
year 1770 produced an *Extract from Young's Night
Thoughts,* and two or three pamphlets on the Calvinistic
controversy ; 1772, *Some Remarks on Mr. Hill's Review
of all the Doctrines taught by Mr. John Wesley,* an effu-
sion which he was almost forced in self-defence to notice;
and *Thoughts on Liberty,* on the Wilkes question, in
which he plainly intimated his opinion that his country-
men had quite as much liberty as was good for them,
especially religious liberty. "In the name of wonder,
what religious liberty can you desire or even conceive,

which you have not already ? Where is there a nation
in Europe, in the habitable world, which enjoys such
liberty of conscience as the English ? Let us be thankful for it to God and the King." In 1773 we have *Some
Remarks on Mr. Hill's Farrago double distilled*, a publication again forced on him by necessity; and *A short
Roman History* drawn from popular sources. In 1774
came *Thoughts upon Necessity*, a product of the Calvinistic controversy. On Jan. 1st, 1776, appeared the first
number of *The Arminian Magazine*, and henceforth the
indefatigable old man had a fresh burden laid upon him
in writing for, and editing, with the very inadequate
aid of Thomas Olivers as sub-editor, this new literary
organ. In this year also he printed an *Extract from
the Life of Madam Guion*, a life singularly unlike his
own, the only point in common being the intense piety
of both ; and *A Seasonable Address occasioned by our
unhappy Contest with our American brethren*, in which,
as a staunch "Church and King" man, he was all
against the Americans. In 1780 he edited *The History
of Henry Morland, or, The Fool of Quality, by Henry
Brooke*, to the dismay of some of his followers, who shared
the prejudice of the religious world of that day against
all works of fiction. In 1781 he published *A Concise
Ecclesiastical History*, which is, in fact, an abridgment
of Mosheim. In 1786 appeared *The Life of Fletcher*,
who only died in 1785; and in 1788 the second series of
Sermons, which consisted of those which he had prepared for his Magazine in four volumes. In the same
year he edited five volumes of *Poems* by Charles Wesley,
who had just died, and alas ! in the same year appeared
also the *Revised Psalter and Prayer-book for America*,
the publication of which all good Churchmen must

N

deeply deplore. All this time he was writing, and continually publishing, extracts from his Journal from Oct. 14th, 1735, when he embarked on board the *Simmonds* for Georgia, to Oct 24th, 1790, though the last four years were not revised by himself.

At the risk of wearying the reader's patience, it has been thought necessary to give this long, and, it is to be feared, tedious, list; otherwise it would be difficult to realize the wonderful energy, mental as well as bodily, of John Wesley. Even as it is, this does not pretend to be a complete list of his publications; but it is sufficient for the point aimed at.

As to John Wesley's style of writing it cannot be better described than in his own words—"What is it that constitutes a good style? Perspicuity, purity, propriety, strength, and easiness joined together. . . . As for me, I never think of my style at all, but just set down the words that come first. . . . Clearness, in particular, is necessary for you and me, because we are to instruct people of the lowest understanding. We should constantly use the most common, little, easy words (so they are pure and proper) which our language affords. When I had been a member of the University about ten years, I wrote and talked much as you do now. But when I talked to plain people in the castle or the town I observed they gaped and stared. This quickly obliged me to alter my style, and adopt the language of those I spoke to. And yet there is a dignity in this simplicity, which is not disagreeable to those of the highest rank."[1]

[1] Quoted in Tyerman, ii. 183.

CHAPTER XII.

PERSONAL TRAITS.

UNLIKE most reformers, John Wesley's private was not so entirely swallowed up in his public life that the former is of comparatively little interest and importance. On the contrary, his marked personality so tinged the whole of his public work that it furnishes a clue which enables us to unravel many of the complications and apparent inconsistencies which would otherwise puzzle us in estimating that work.

The first feature which strikes us in Wesley's personality, is his strong family affection. He carried Epworth about with him to the end of his life. "My father," "my brother," and above all "my mother," are constantly referred to, not only in his Journals, but also in his sermons and other public utterances. In the midst of one of his addresses he suddenly remembers that the day was the anniversary of his father's death, and proceeds at once to give a full account of the death-bed scene. He frequently refers to the way in which his mother trained her children. He publishes in his Magazine the account of the fire at Epworth Rectory, and the unexplained mystery of the Epworth ghost. He reprints more than one of his father's works. He

revisits Epworth, ever with an increased delight. He
takes his widowed mother with him to his humble
home, is influenced by her in one at least of the most
important crises of his work, witnesses her happy
departure in 1742, and preaches over her grave in
Bunhill Fields. No differences of opinion can in the
least degree affect his love of his brothers, both Samuel
and Charles, nor yet of his sisters, alienated though
most of them were from him by their unhappy
marriages. In short, it is impossible to understand
John Wesley's character aright without taking into full
account his family ties. These, for example, clearly
laid the foundation of one of his most marked characteristics throughout life ; his intense realization of a
particular Providence in the minutest affairs of daily
life. It is idle to deny that this frequently led him
into a readiness to accept as marvellous and super-
natural what might easily have been explained by
natural causes, and into practices which can only be
described as superstitious. The whole Wesley family,
with the exception of Samuel, seems to have believed
in the Epworth ghost. When the father alone was
undisturbed by it, the rest were afraid that it portended
some evil to him, according to a superstitious notion of
the time. When, to their great relief, the Rector was
also haunted by the visitor, his first idea was that his
eldest son was the victim of fate—" If thou be the
spirit of my son Sammy, knock three times and no
more." In 1769, John Wesley writes to Lady Maxwell
—" I have heard my mother say, ' I have frequently
been as fully assured that my father's spirit was with
me, as if I had seen him with my eyes;' but she did
not explain herself farther." Assuredly, John Wesley's

credulity, as well as his piety, was hereditary; and the two are so blended together that it is difficult to disentangle them. His piety made him resolve to be *homo unius libri;* but his credulity led him to use that one book in a way in which it was never intended to be used. He was more than once led astray by having recourse to the objectionable practice of the *Sortes Biblicæ.* His piety led him to believe in the direct interposition of Divine Providence in human affairs; but his credulity prevented him from remembering that second causes frequently intervene. This is his remark upon the case of a poor woman who was attacked with fits—"The plain case is, she is tormented by an evil spirit; yea, try all your drugs over and over, but at length it will plainly appear, 'This kind goeth not out, but by prayer and fasting.'" He deeply regretted the dying out of the belief in witchcraft. "The English in general," he says, "and indeed most of the men of learning in Europe, have given up all accounts of witches and apparitions. I am sorry for it; and I willingly take this opportunity of entering my solemn protest against the violent compliment which so many that believe the Bible pay to those that do not believe it." [1] When he had a narrow escape for his life in a carriage accident, he remarks—"I am persuaded both evil and good angels had a large share in this transaction." [2] He quite believed that the elements were controlled for the convenience of his work—"Just as I began to preach, the sun broke out, and shone exceedingly hot on the side of my head. I found, if I continued, I should not be able to speak long, and lifted

---

[1] *Journal*, May 25th, 1768.   [2] *Journal*, June 1774.

up my heart to God. In a minute or two it was covered with clouds, which continued till the service was over. Let any who please call this chance; I call it an answer to prayer." [1] "The wind kept off the rain while I was preaching. As soon as I ended, it began." [2] "Just as I began preaching the rain began; but it stopped in two or three minutes, I am persuaded, in answer to the prayer of faith; incidents of the same kind I have seen abundance of times; and they are nothing strange to those who sincerely believe : ' the very hairs of your head are all numbered.' " [3] Old-world superstitions found a ready believer in John Wesley— " About two in the morning a dog began howling under our window in a most uncommon manner. We could not stop him by any means. Just then, William B—r died." [4]

Another personal characteristic near akin to that above-mentioned, was his extreme guilelessness, his readiness to believe the best of everybody, his utterly unsuspicious nature. This weakness—for it amounted to a weakness—showed itself most glaringly in his relations to the other sex. We have seen one instance in Georgia; but unfortunately Wesley did not profit by his dearly-bought experience there. Caution was not a conspicuous feature in any phase of his life; but least of all was it so in regard to the delicate questions of love and marriage. It would have been well for him if his first love passage had been his last. Ten years before the Hopkey episode, he had been smitten with the charms of a sister of Robert Kirkham, one of the Oxford Methodists, who was himself most anxious

[1] *Journal*, April 24, 1755.   [2] *Ibid.* June 2, 1758.
[3] *Ibid.* June 8, 1763.   [4] *Ibid.* Oct. 26, 1786.

that his spiritual adviser should become his brother-in-law. And so far as one can judge, Betty Kirkham would have suited him; she was in the same social position, and was evidently struck with him; but the matter proceeded no further than a little philandering, carried on after the curiously stilted manner of the day, the prosaic Betty being transformed into the romantic "Varenese." Grace Murray succeeded Sophia Hopkey; and, without saying a word against her in any way, we may still admit that she was in no way fitted to be the wife of John Wesley. She accompanied him in his travels, both in Ireland and in the northern counties of England; and when he was taken ill at Newcastle in 1749, she tended him as a nurse. Times of convalescence are *mollia tempora fandi*, and the natural result followed. Wesley made her an offer of marriage, which was accepted with as much surprise as pleasure. "This is too great a blessing for me; I can't tell how to believe it. This is all I could have wished under heaven." But, like Miss Hopkey, Mrs. Murray had a second string to her bow, and by the prompt interference of Charles Wesley, who had no idea of having a ci-devant servant-maid for his sister-in-law, the marriage was prevented in the most effectual way, by her union with her other suitor, John Bennett.

Unfortunately in his next venture John Wesley was only too successful. What were the attractions of the widow Vazeille it is quite impossible to say; but, whatever they were, they were sufficient to lead him to make her an offer, which was accepted. Charles was too late to prevent it. "My brother," he says, "told me he was *resolved to marry*. I was thunderstruck. Trusty Ned Perronet followed, and told me the person was Mrs.

Vazeille, one of whom I had never had the least suspicion. I refused his company to the chapel, and
retired to mourn with my faithful Sally."

Perhaps under no circumstances could the marriage
have turned out happily. Wesley's wandering life was
in itself an obstacle; he was wedded to his work; and
no one who could not throw herself heart and soul into
that work could expect to lead a comfortable life with
him. Neither could any one who was of a jealous and
suspicious nature; for Wesley had a host of female
friends with whom he conversed and corresponded in
the frankest possible manner. Mrs. Wesley had both
these disqualifications; and when she was provoked, she
was a perfect virago, and it must be owned that Wesley
gave her provocation. To place such a woman as Sarah
Ryan, who had three husbands living, and lived with
none of them, in the confidential position of housekeeper
at Kingswood School; to correspond with her, and make
her the confidante of his marital troubles; to write
religious letters to other members of his Society, of
whom his wife was jealous, was, to use the mildest term,
injudicious to the last degree. Wesley meant no harm;
he loved his wife in spite of their disagreements, as
many letters written to her after his marriage prove.
Charles, who was by no means inclined to regard too
favourably John's conduct in the matter, yet owns that
"nothing could exceed his brother's patience in bearing
with his perverse and peevish wife." That patience was
at last exhausted, and he exploded thus,—" Know me,
and know yourself; suspect me no more, asperse me no
more, provoke me no more; do not any longer contend
for mastery, for power, money, or praise; be content to
be a private, insignificant person, known and loved by

God and me. Attempt no more to abridge me of my liberty, which I claim by the laws of God and man; leave me to be governed by God and my own conscience; then shall I govern you with gentle sway, even as Christ the Church. . . . Of what importance is your character to mankind? If you was buried just now, or if you had never lived, what loss would it be to the cause of God?" This is not exactly pouring oil upon the troubled waters; and we are not surprised to learn that matters did not go on more smoothly. It is, however, a mistake to suppose that the ill-assorted pair parted finally, a mistake arising, no doubt, from Wesley's own words— "Jan. 23, 1771. For what cause I know not, my wife set out for Newcastle, purposing 'never to return.' *Non eam reliqui; non dimisi; non revocabo.*" She returned, however, without being recalled.

It is a relief to turn from this painful episode, which a faithful biographer was bound to notice, to more pleasing phases of John Wesley's personal history. The reader has already learned from Wesley's own words how he managed to secure a considerable amount of time at his own disposal. This time he employed, not only in writing, but in an extensive and somewhat desultory course of reading. Unlike his quondam mentor, William Law, he by no means despised "human learning"; and he felt it a pleasure as well as a duty to keep himself in touch with the current literature of the day. In his early wanderings he used to read as he rode on horseback; and when, by his friends' advice, he exchanged that mode of travelling for a carriage, he had a book-shelf fitted up in the conveyance.

His Journals are full of shrewd, though sometimes rather eccentric, comments on the books which he read.

The eccentricity seems to me to have arisen from the fact that he did not judge books by a purely intellectual standard, but very much according to whether they tended to edification or not. For instance, a very inferior mind would surely have been able to perceive the intellectual superiority of Swift to Byrom, and of Hume to Beattie. But Wesley deliberately asserts, after having read John Byrom's poems, that " he has all the wit and humour of Dr. Swift, together with much more learning, a deep and strong understanding, and, above all, a serious vein of piety." Byrom is delightful; but to compare him intellectually with the great Dean is absurd; there was, however, undoubtedly, "a serious vein of piety" in the one which is not conspicuous in the other; hence, perhaps, the amazing dictum. Wesley, again, agreed with his royal master, whom he venerated in the highest degree, that Beattie had entirely demolished Hume; in which judgment he must again surely have allowed his piety to overrule his intellect. He read "Mr. Jones' (of Nayland) ingenious essay on the Principles of Natural Philosophy," and remarks that, " he seems to have entirely overthrown the Newtonian principles," a remark with which the world at large will scarcely agree with him, though, by the way, the writings of Jones of Nayland deserve to be far better known than they are. He saw no merit whatever in Sterne, whose writings were at the time (1772) creating a great sensation. " I casually took up a volume of what is called *A Sentimental Journey through France and Italy. Sentimental!* What is that? It is not English; he might as well have said *continental.* It is not sense." We can well understand that Sterne would be far from being a clergyman after John Wesley's heart, whose religious sense would revolt from the loose, not to say, prurient, tone of the popular writer. But the orthodox divines of his own Church, Wesley greatly and most justly admired. He praises highly the writings of Dean Prideaux (*Journal*, Nov. 1767); he reads with delight "that fine book, *Bishop Butler's Analogy;*" he thinks Dr. Horne's *Commentary on the Psalms* "the best that ever was wrote," though on some points he does not agree with him (*Journal*, March 27, 1783). "Dr. Blair" (the Presbyterian), he says, "is quite too elegant for me; give me plain, strong Dr. Horne." He reads Bishop Lowth's Lectures *De Poesi Hebraicâ*, and thinks them "far more satisfactory than anything on that subject which he had ever seen before." "Lighting on a volume of Mr. Seed's sermons," he says, "I was utterly surprised. Where did this man lie hid, that I never heard of him all the time I was at Oxford?" (*Journal*, May 23, 1765.) Jeremiah Seed, however, ranked high among the noted preachers of the day. Alexander Knox, who must have known, tells us that Wesley was an admirer of the English Platonists, and that "the attachment he conceived to Taylor, Smith, Cudworth, Worthington, and Lucas," all of whom except the last belonged to the Platonic School, "retained all its cordiality to the last hour of his life;" but I can find few traces of the influence of those divines in Wesley's own writings. With a curious eclecticism, however, he certainly read and admired some of the great Puritan divines.

John Wesley was very particular about the minor details of life; he was scrupulously neat and correct in his dress; generally appearing in full canonicals, a habit which in his time was fast dying out. "His cassock, black silk stockings, and large silver buckles,"

which are familiar to us all through the portraits, were
specially noticed by an eye-witness.[1]   The custom of
wearing his hair long, which he had formed in his early
Oxford days, that he might save the money for the
poor—it should be noted that the dressing of the
natural hair or the arrangement of wigs was a much
more elaborate and expensive operation than it is now
—he retained to his old age; and when the raven locks
were changed to silvery white, his venerable appearance must have been very striking.   His habits were as
regular as clockwork.   For more than fifty years he
rose at four a.m., and he seems to have regarded this
early rising as quite a religious duty.   He speaks of
the laxity in some of the Societies about the daily
morning preaching (at five a.m.!) in terms which would
be appropriate to moral laxity; and when it was
pleaded "the people will not come—at least, not in the
winter"—he remarks, "If so, the Methodists are a fallen
people. . . .   If they will not attend now, they have
lost their zeal; and then it cannot be denied they are a
fallen people. . . .   Let all the preachers that are still
alive to God join together as one man; fast, and pray,
lift up their voice as a trumpet; be instant, in season,
out of season, to convince them they are fallen; and
exhort them instantly to repent and do their first
works; this in particular—rising in the morning, without which neither their souls nor bodies can long
remain in health."[2]

As one might infer from the raciness of his writings,
he was a pleasant companion.   "Mr. Wesley had," writes
Dr. Whitehead, who knew him intimately, "most

---

[1] See Tyerman, ii. 409.   [2] *Journal*, April 4, 1784.

exquisite talents to make himself agreeable in company, and having been much accustomed to society the rules of good-breeding were habitual to him."[1] And here it may be observed that though John Wesley had, as we have seen, an almost ludicrous abhorrence of a "genteel congregation," and is never tired of girding at their shallowness, their inattention and evil behaviour generally, yet he was by no means insensible to the compliment of proper attention when paid by the upper classes, but always repaid it with the courtesy of a well-bred gentleman. It was hardly to be expected that a scion of the Wellesleys and the Annesleys could regard himself as an inferior being even to "a member of the noble house of Shirley"; and John Wesley felt it to be part of his mission to counterbalance some of the painful adulation by which Lady Huntingdon was being rather spoilt by some of her humble followers. But when the good countess recommended him to Lady Buchan as chaplain, he wrote her a courteous letter of thanks, and showed his gratitude to Lady Buchan by preaching before her a faithful sermon on her duty as a rich lady.[2] He records with evident satisfaction the attention and hospitality shown to him by more than one Bishop. Dr. Johnson delighted in his conversation, and only complained that Wesley had not leisure to give him as much of it as he desired. Wesley, by the way, never joined in the contemptuous pity which some had the impertinence to express for the Doctor's religion, but always spoke of

---

[1] *Life of John Wesley, some time Fellow of Lincoln College,* by John Whitehead, M.D., author of the *Discourse delivered at Mr. Wesley's Funeral,* p. 468.
[2] See *The Faithful Steward.*

him and his writings with the respect that was their
due. His last entry is touching—"Feb. 18th, 1784. I
spent two hours with that great man, Dr. Johnson, who
is sinking into the grave by a gentle decay." There
were in fact several points of resemblance between the
two men. Both combined a most loyal allegiance to
the reigning family with a sort of sentimental regard
for the ancient race. (This of course is obvious in Dr.
Johnson; it is not so obvious in John Wesley; but the
attentive observer will find traces of the feeling. He
regarded his father's troubles as a judgment upon him
for his treatment of Mrs. Wesley in her refusal to say
Amen to the prayers for the new Royal Family; he
was a strong upholder of Mary Stuart, Queen of Scots;
he was a great admirer of John Byrom, who, to say the
least, was a hankerer after the Stuarts, and certainly
agreed with several of the Nonjurors on many points.)
Both were bluff, downright Englishmen who spoke out
just what they thought, and came to the point at once;
both had a way of addressing their friends in a most
unceremonious way, and telling them home-truths with
an abruptness which, but for their real kindness of
heart and genuine sincerity, would have been rather
offensive. The "Bozzys" and "Goldys" and "Lankys"
of Johnson found their counterparts in the "Tommys"
and "Jemmys" and "Sammys" of Wesley. Here
is a specimen of the way in which Wesley used to
address his friends, which reminds us, *mutatis mutandis,*
of the way in which Johnson used to address Boswell.
"Dear Jemmy,—Unto you it was given to suffer a little
of what you extremely wanted—obloquy and evil
report. But you did not acknowledge either the gift
or the Giver. You saw only Thomas Olivers, not God.

'O Jemmy, you do not know yourself. You cannot bear to be continually steeped in the esteem and praise of men. Therefore I tremble at your stay at Dublin; it is the most dangerous place for *you* under heaven." [1]

The extreme openness of John Wesley's character showed itself in his habits. It would have been dangerous for any one to have written to him a private and confidential letter. "He never," writes Dr. Whitehead, "travelled alone; and the person who attended him had the charge of his letters and papers, which, of course, lay open to his inspection. The preachers, likewise, who were occasionally with him, had access to his letters and papers, especially if he had confidence in their sincerity and zeal in religion, which it was not very difficult to obtain. It was easy for these persons to see the motive that influenced him, and the end he had in view in every action of his life, however remote from public observation; and he took no pains to conceal them, but seemed rather to court the discovery." [2] In fact, he could conceal nothing; whatever he felt at the moment came straight out—sometimes in a rather embarrassing way. One of his travelling preachers went over to the Friends in 1777, a course of which John Wesley would vehemently disapprove. In his indignation he let out circumstances which should not have been disclosed. The preacher seems to have told his grievance to Charles Wesley, who replied, "You expect he will keep his own secrets. Let me whisper it in your ears; he never could do it since he was born. It is a gift which God has not given him.

---

[1] Quoted by Tyerman, iii. 24.   [2] Whitehead, ii. 370.

But I shall speak to him, and put a stop to what you justly complain of. I wish you may never have an uneasy thought on our account. Speak not, therefore, of my brother; think no evil of him; forget him if you can entirely, till you meet above." Being perfectly open himself, he believed everybody to be the same, and was thus, no doubt, often imposed on. "My brother," said Charles, "was, I believe, born for the benefit of knaves."

About money, or the luxuries which money brings, John Wesley cared literally nothing. His writings became a very valuable property; for with an amusing *naïveté*, he recommended or rather insisted upon his people buying and reading the books he wrote or edited; and of course they obeyed him in this as in everything else. The sale, therefore, was naturally very large; but Wesley himself received no pecuniary profit whatever from it. In several notices of bishops' palaces and grounds that he visited, which occur in his *Journal*, there is not a hint that he envied them, or contrasted his own poor lot with theirs. His orderly habits prevented him from running into debt; but when his modest, personal wants were supplied, he was all but penniless, and was quite content to be so.

Other circumstances in his personal history will appear in the account of his last years, which is the subject of the next chapter.

CHAPTER XIII.

THE last six years of John Wesley's life form an epoch of their own, and require separate treatment. In ordinary cases it would be rather late to date the commencement of a man's old age from his eighty-second year; but in this case, we rather owe him an apology for venturing to call him an old man so soon. He was still a youth, both in mind and body. In making his usual entry on his birthday, he writes—"June 28, 1784. To-day I entered on my eighty-second year, as fit for any exercise of body or mind as I was forty years ago. I am as strong at eighty-one as I was at twenty-one; but abundantly more healthy, being a stranger to the headache and other bodily disorders which attended me in my youth." Even two years later he declares—"June 28, 1786. I am a wonder to myself. It is now twelve years since I have felt such a sensation as weariness. I am never tired either with writing, preaching, or travelling." It is not till he is turned eighty-five that he begins to feel that he is getting on in years; and then the only symptoms are that he is "not quite so agile as he was in times past, and that his sight is a little decayed." He will only allow one cause to explain this marvellous vitality—"The good pleasure of God, who doeth whatsoever pleaseth Him." But he specifies three "chief means.

O

1. My constantly rising at four for about fifty years. 2. My generally preaching at five in the morning; one of the most healthy exercises in the world. 3. My never travelling less, by sea or land, than 4500 miles in a year." It is not then because of his age, but because his work entered upon a new phase, that the last stage of his life may be dated from 1784. Dr. Whitehead calls this year "the grand climacterical year of Methodism," on account of two changes which now took place in the form of its original constitution, and "laid the foundation of a *new* order of things among the Methodists, hitherto unknown." [1] These changes were—1. The Deed of Declaration. 2. The Ordinations.

The first need not detain us long. Even John Wesley could not live for ever; and what was to become of the Societies after he was gone? "During the time Wesley governed the Societies, his power was *absolute.* There were no rights or privileges; no offices of power or influence, but what were created and sanctioned by him; nor could any persons hold them but during his pleasure." [2] It was obviously necessary to provide for a contingency, which in the course of nature could not be very remote. So John Wesley executed and enrolled in Chancery a Deed Poll, which "substituted for the Founder a permanent body of a hundred, who, meeting annually as 'the Conference,' fill the place which Wesley filled during his life-time." [3] This "Legal Hundred," "being preachers and expounders of God's Holy Word, under the care of, and in connection with, John Wesley," were to be the supreme governing body, vacancies being filled up by co-optation.

---

[1] *Life of Wesley*, ii. 404.   [2] *Ibid.* ii. 474.
[3] Mr. Denny Urlin's *John Wesley's Place in Church History*, p. 125.

The deed was simply "to explain the words 'Yearly Conference of the people called Methodists,' and to declare what persons are members of the said Conference, and how the succession and identity thereof is to be continued."[1] It need only be added that the choice of the first "Legal Hundred" rested entirely with John Wesley, and that out of the 191 preachers in full connection, he made a selection which was thought by some rather arbitrary, and which hurt the feelings of some who were excluded; but in this, as in everything else, there was no appeal against John Wesley's decision.[2]

The other events which make 1784 an epoch in John Wesley's life, will require much longer notice. Hitherto, there really had been nothing in his proceedings which can fairly be called a violation of Church principles. The utmost that can be said is, that he had not paid the obedience which was due to his ecclesiastical superiors, in matters in which no real principle was involved; and, considering the urgent need there was of a revival of the dormant energies of the Church; considering that the great majority of the multitudes who were aroused by him to a consciousness of their spiritual wants were practically, as he said, no more members of the Church of England than they were of the Church of Muscovy; considering that the rulers of the Church themselves complained, with a mournful unanimity, of the little influence for good that religion then exercised; considering that Wesley's strict obedience to the requirements of the Church authorities would simply have cut him off altogether from doing the work which he felt himself called to do, we may well be slow to condemn him for irregularities which were concerned

[1] See Tyerman, iii. 418.
[2] See Southey's *Life of Wesley*, ii. 342-344.

with matters of detail, not with matters of principle.
The parochial system may be an excellent arrangement
for ordinary times; but it is, at best, only of the *bene
esse*, not of the *esse* of the Church; and it had completely broken down as an adequate religious agency
in the early part of the Georgian era.

John Wesley was perfectly right in contending that
not one part of his complicated machinery for a religious revival was in any way inconsistent with his
position as a good Churchman. On the contrary, without any overstraining, he found a precedent for almost
every one of the methods he adopted in the earliest
and purest ages of the Church. The formation of
Societies, with all their arrangements of class-meetings,
and so forth, the employment of lay-preachers, the
adoption of field-preaching—all this was perfectly consistent with the soundest Churchmanship. Wesley had
steadily refused, though much pressure had been put
upon him, to sanction anything which would have really
compromised him as a clergyman; he never called his
Society *a* Church or *the* Church; he absolutely forbade
his preachers to usurp any priestly functions; he would
have no meetings to interfere with the Church hours.

But now, in 1784, he took a step, or rather commenced a series of steps, which, if they really were
what they have generally been represented as being
(which is doubtful), come under a very different category.
But we must begin at the beginning, and for that
purpose have to go back nearly forty years. "Jan. 20th,
1746," he writes—"On the road to Bristol I read over
Lord King's account of the Primitive Church. In spite
of the vehement prejudice of my education, I was ready
to believe that this was a fair and impartial draught;
but if so, it would follow that bishops and presbyters

are (essentially) of one order ; and that originally every
Christian congregation was a Church independent of
all others." Accordingly, in his *Notes on the New
Testament*, a few years later, he says doubtfully—" Perhaps elders and bishops were the same, or no otherwise
different than are the rector of a parish and his curates."
" The names of bishop and presbyter or elder were pro-
miscuously used in the first ages." In 1756 he writes—
" I still believe the episcopal form of Church government to be scriptural and apostolical—I mean, well
agreeing with the practice and writings of the Apostles.
But that it is *prescribed* in Scripture I do not believe.
This opinion, which I once zealously espoused, I have
been heartily ashamed of ever since I read Bishop
Stillingfleet's *Irenicon*." One turns with some curiosity
to the two books which exercised so powerful an influence over John Wesley's mind; and one finds that
both of them were written by mere boys. Peter
King (afterwards Lord Chancellor) was only twenty-one
when he wrote his treatise on *The Primitive Church ;* [1]

[1] The full title is, *An Enquiry into the Constitution, Discipline,
Unity and Worship of the Primitive Church that flourished within
the first* 300 *years after Christ. Faithfully collected out of the
Extant Writings of these Ages. By an Impartial Hand,* 1691.
The writer justifies his title. From his own point of view he
certainly *does* write with "an impartial hand"; and, as a matter
of fact, his "enquiry" led him to become a Churchman instead
of a Dissenter. Curiously enough, he condemns by anticipation
John Wesley's own conduct in the strongest possible terms :
" When," he writes, " Churches had been regularly formed under
the jurisdiction of their proper Bishops, it had been unaccountable
impudence and a most detestable act of schism, for any one,
though never so legally ordained, to have entered those parishes,
and then to have performed ecclesiastical administrations, without
the permission, or, which is all one, in defiance to the Bishops or
Ministers thereof." (" Enquiry," p. 57.) When Wesley read
these words, did he remember his interview with Bishop Butler,
and his arguments with the many clergy whose parishes he
invaded ?

Stillingfleet only twenty-four when he wrote his *Irenicon*. It seems a strange thing that a well-read, thoughtful man of mature age like John Wesley should have attached so much weight to the opinions of two youths, who, when they grew older and wiser, virtually recanted what they had written. However, we must take John Wesley as we find him ; and the fact is undeniable that the dicta of these two young gentlemen made a deep impression upon his mind ; they acted upon it like leaven, and the results at last appeared in the events which have now to be recorded.

It has been seen that properly ordained clergymen had been the very backbone of the Wesley movement; and John Wesley sincerely desired to strengthen the clerical element in it. But the body of the clergy held aloof, or were openly hostile; and the Bishops, though many of them were personally kind to the Wesleys, did not encourage his work ; among the numerous Bishops' charges, from 1740 to the end of the century, which are still extant, there are few in which some blow is not aimed at the Methodists. In default of English Bishops, John Wesley had, in 1764, enlisted the services of a rather shadowy Greek Prelate, Erasmus Bishop of Arcadia, to ordain some of his lay-preachers. There seems to be no reason to doubt that Erasmus was a genuine Bishop; but Charles Wesley disapproved of the proceeding, and would never allow preachers ordained by the Bishop of Arcadia to assist him at the Holy Communion. We have seen also how John Wesley made futile overtures to the evangelical clergy. Matters did not improve with years, and John Wesley was, to use a homely phrase, at his wits' end to know how to gain clerical assistance. We can well understand, therefore, how he would welcome Dr. Coke as an invaluable accession, not only as a most energetic, earnest worker, but as a genuine clergyman, about whose Orders there could be no mistake; and how he would be ready to stretch a point to meet his views. But surely Mr. Southey has made a mistake when he says that John Wesley "*summoned* Dr. Coke to Bristol, and Mr. Creighton, a clergyman, who had become Methodist; and with their assistance ordained Richard Whatcoat and Thomas Vasey presbyters, for America; and afterwards Dr. Coke[1] as superintendent." The initiative was clearly taken by Dr. Coke himself, as his own letter proves. In 1784 he wrote to Wesley—"The more maturely I consider the matter, the more expedient it appears to me that the power of ordaining others should be received by me from you, by imposition of your hands; and that you should lay hands on brother Whatcoat and brother Vasey. You can do all this in Mr. C——n's house, in your chamber; and afterwards (according to Mr. Fletcher's advice) give us letters testimonial of the different offices with which you have been pleased to invest us. For the purpose of laying hands on brothers Whatcoat and Vasey, I can bring down Mr. Creighton with me, by which you will have two presbyters with you. In respect to brother Rankin's argument that you will escape a great deal of odium by omitting this, it is nothing. Either it will be known, or not known. If not known, then no odium will arise; but if known, you will be obliged to acknowledge that I acted under your direction, or suffer me to sink under the weight of my enemies, with perhaps your brother at the head of them. I shall entreat you to ponder these things."

---

[1] *Life of Wesley*, ii. 299.

John Wesley's action upon this, and his reasons for it, had better be told in his own words. " The case," he said, " is widely different between England and North America. Here there are Bishops who have a legal jurisdiction. In America there are none, neither any parish minister; so that for some hundreds of miles together there is none either to baptize, or to administer the Lord's Supper. Here therefore my scruples are at an end; and I consider myself at full liberty, as I violate no order, and invade no man's right by appointing and sending labourers into the harvest." And more at length—" I have appointed Dr. Coke and Mr. F. Asbury to be joint superintendents over our brethren in North America; as also Rich. Whatcoat and T. Vasey, to act as elders among them, by baptizing and administering the Lord's Supper. And I have prepared a liturgy, little differing from that of the Church of England (I think the best constituted National Church in the world), which I advise all travelling preachers to use on the Lord's Day, in all congregations, reading the Litany only on Wednesdays and Fridays, and praying extempore on all other days. I also advise elders to administer the Supper of the Lord on every Lord's Day. If any one will point out a more rational and scriptural way of feeding and guiding these poor sheep in the wilderness, I will gladly embrace it. At present I cannot see any better method than I have taken. It has been indeed proposed to desire English Bishops to ordain part of our preachers for America. But to this I object:—(1) I desired the Bishop of London to ordain one, but could not prevail. (2) If they consented, we know the slowness of their proceedings; but the matter admits of no delay. (3) If they would ordain them now, they would expect to govern them, and how grievously this would entangle us! (4) As our American brethren are now totally disentangled, both from the State and the English hierarchy, we dare not entangle them again, either with the one or the other. They are now at full liberty, simply to follow the Scriptures and the Primitive Church. And we judge it best that they should stand fast in that liberty wherewith God has so strangely set them free." In his Journal he records—"Sept. 1, 1784. Being now clear in my own mind, I took a step which I had long weighed in my mind, and appointed Mr. Whatcoat and Mr. Vasey to go and serve the desolate sheep in America." "Sept. 2.—I added to them three more ; which I verily believe will be much to the glory of God."

Now let us give full weight to the undoubted fact that the Christians in America were in a desolate state —remembering, however, that the fault really lay with the English State, not the English Church, which had been incessantly pleading for many years for bishops and for more clergy for America. Let us also note that John Wesley carefully avoids using the word "ordain," or "bishop," or "priest"; let us moreover observe how he still clings to Church usages—the weekly celebration, the use of the Litany on Wednesdays and Fridays, the following of the Primitive Church, &c. Yet, after all, into what a sea of difficulties and inconsistencies he launches himself as a duly ordained clergyman ! If bishops and priests were of the same order, what was the object of one priest laying his hands upon a brother priest? What could Wesley confer upon Coke, which Coke might not equally well have conferred upon Wesley? Does not the whole force of the argument derived from the independence of America, turn upon the question whether the church is a mere creature of the civil government, or a spiritual society which is not in the least affected in its essence by its connection or disconnection with the civil power ? Wesley had always maintained the latter ground. He had spoken rather slightingly of "the establishment." "If, as my lady says, all outward establishments are Babel, so is this establishment. Let it stand for me. I neither set it up, nor pull it down. But let you and I build up the City of God."[1] But surely the independence of America could only affect the *establishment* of the Church, not the Church itself. Then again, Wesley, as a well-read divine, must have known that ordinations were always public. But this service was conducted in the strictest privacy. In the small hours of the morning, in his own private chamber, without the knowledge of even his brother, who was close at hand, he made Dr. Coke and Mr. Asbury——what? Certainly not bishops. He repudiated the title himself, and was extremely annoyed when those whom he had "set apart as superintendents" assumed it in America. In his own plain way he wrote to Asbury—"Sept. 20, 1788. In one point, my dear brother, I am a little afraid both the Doctor (Coke) and you differ from me. I study to be little; you study to be great. I creep; you strut along. I found a school, you a college; nay, and call it after your own names [Cokesbury = Coke, Asbury]. . . . One instance of your greatness has given me great concern. How can you, how dare you, suffer yourself to be called bishop? I shudder, I start at the very thought! Men may call me a knave or a fool, a rascal, a scoundrel, and I am content; but they shall never by my consent call me bishop! For my sake, for God's

[1] To his brother Charles, Jan. 28th, 1755.

sake, put a full end to all this ! Let the Presbyterians do what they please, but let the Methodists know their calling better. Thus, my dear Franky, I have told you all that is in my heart."

Charles Wesley had of course something to say on the matter :—" Alas !" he wrote to his brother, " what trouble are you preparing for yourself as well as for me, and for your oldest, truest, and best friends ! Before you have quite broken down the bridge, stop and consider. Go to your grave in peace, or at least suffer me to go before this ruin. So much I think you owe to my father, my brother, and to me; as to stay till I am taken from the evil. This letter is a debt to our parents and to our brother, as well as to you." John replied—" For these forty years I have been in doubt what obedience is due to ' heathenish priests and mitred infidels.' In obedience to the laws of the land I have never exercised in England the power which I believe God has given me. I firmly believe I am a scriptural *episcopos* as much as any man in England, for the uninterrupted succession I know to be a fable that no man can prove. But this does nowise interfere with my remaining in the Church of England, from which I have no desire to separate now more than fifty years ago. I still attend all the ordinances of the Church at all opportunities, and I earnestly advise all that are connected with me to do so," with much more to the same effect; and he adds the remarkable words— " Perhaps if you had kept close to me, I might have done better." Charles answered him point by point. After having recanted his own line "Heathenish priests,"[1] " I do not," he says, " understand what obedience to the Bishops you dread. They have let us alone, and left us

[1] See *supra*, p. 158.

to act just as we pleased, for these fifty years. At
present, some of them are quite friendly to us, particularly towards you. The churches are all open to you,
and never could there be less pretence for a separation.
That you are a scriptural ἐπίσκοπος or overseer, I do not
dispute; and so is every minister who has the cure of
souls. Neither need we dispute whether the uninterrupted succession is fabulous, as you believe; or real,
as I believe; or whether Lord King be right or wrong.
If I could prove your separation, I would not. But do
you not allow that the doctor has separated? You ask,
'What are you frighted at?' At the approaching
schism, as causeless and unprovoked as the American
rebellion; at your own eternal disgrace, and all those
frightful evils which your own reasons describe. 'Kept
closer to you!' When you took that fatal step at
Bristol, I kept as close to you as close could be; for I
was all the time at your elbow. You might certainly
'have done better,' if you had taken me into your
counsel. I thank you for your intention of remaining
my friend. Herein my heart is as your heart. Whom
God hath joined, let not man put asunder. We have
taken each other for better or worse, till death us do
part—part? no, but unite eternally!"

Charles Wesley made no secret of his opinion about
his brother's conduct. To a clergyman returning from
America, he wrote—"I can scarcely yet believe it, that
in his eighty-second year, my brother, my old, intimate
friend and companion, should have assumed the episcopal character, ordained elders, consecrated a bishop, and
sent him to ordain our lay-preachers in America. I
was then in Bristol, at his elbow; yet he never gave
me the least hint of his intention. How was he surprised into so rash an action? He certainly persuaded

himself that it was right. Lord Mansfield[1] told me last year that ordination was separation. This my brother does not, nor will not see, or that he has renounced the principles and practice of his whole life. I have taken him for better or worse, till death us do part ; or rather reunite us in love unspeakable. But I have lived too long that have lived to see this evil day !" He takes a very different view of the future of the Americans from what John took. " What," he says, " will these poor sheep in the wilderness do ? Had they had patience a little longer, they would have seen a real bishop in America, consecrated by three Scotch bishops, who have their consecration from English bishops, and are acknowledged by them as the same with themselves. There is, therefore, not the least difference betwixt the members of Bishop Seabury's Church and the Church of England. He told me he looked upon Methodists in America as sound members of the Church, and was ready to ordain any of their preachers whom he should find duly qualified. His ordinations would be indeed genuine, but what are your poor Methodists now ? "

The ordinations for America were followed by some ordinations for Scotland, in regard to which John Wesley acted on the judgment of others, not on his own ; for he records in his Journal—" Aug. 1, 1785. Having, with a few select friends, weighed the matter thoroughly, I yielded to their judgment, and set apart three of our well-tried preachers—John Pawson, Thomas Hanley, and Joseph Taylor—to minister in Scotland ; and I trust God will bless their ministrations, and show that He has sent them." In Scotland, at any rate,

---

[1] Lord Mansfield had been a schoolfellow with Charles Wesley at Westminster.

there was an ancient Episcopal Church, the services of which John Wesley had always enjoyed. It was just being relieved from the disabilities which had long hampered its work. Had Wesley quite forgotten this Church which he once loved, when he argued that his action was not separation from the Church? "Not from the Church of Scotland, for we were never connected therewith; not from the Church of England, for this is not concerned in the steps which are taken in Scotland. Whatever then is done, either in America or Scotland, is not separation from the Church of England. I have no thought of this; I have many objections against it."

But finally John Wesley "set apart" three of his preachers—Mather, Rankin, and More—for the ministry without sending them out of England. Mr. Denny Urlin, who has studied the question thoroughly, is of opinion that it has never been proved that he intended them for England; and certainly his after conduct in reference to the Scotch ordinees, seems to bear out this theory. In Scotland they had assumed full canonicals, and were addressed by Wesley with the title of "Reverend." But as soon as ever they crossed the border, they sunk back again into plain "Mr.," and had to doff their canonicals. They murmured a little, but there was no appeal against Mr. Wesley's fiat.

It has been said that John Wesley's mental powers were failing when he began to "set apart" his preachers; and Charles Wesley himself has countenanced the idea by exclaiming—

"'Twas age that made the breach, not he."

But there really appear to be no traces of mental decay in any other respects. There *are*, however, several

traces of his mind being not quite at ease about what
he had done. His correspondence with his brother,
already quoted, hints as much; and the testimony of
Mr. Alexander Knox is unimpeachable. Knox remonstrated with him on the subject, and "from the
manner," he says, "in which he heard me, and from
what he said in reply, I saw clearly that he felt himself
in a vortex of difficulties; and that, in the steps he
had taken, the yielding to what he thought pressing
exigencies, he nevertheless had done violence to un-
dissembled and rooted feeling."

It is a curious fact that the time when his own Church
had the strongest reason to complain of John Wesley's
proceedings was the very time when almost all opposition to him on the part of Churchmen had died away.
During the last six years of his life he was universally
treated with the utmost reverence. He was no more
suspected of being a Jacobite, a Papist, or—worst of all—
an enthusiast. He himself was utterly amazed at the
change. "I am become," he writes in 1785, "I know
not how, an honourable man. The scandal of the cross
is ceased; and all the kingdom, rich and poor, Papists
and Protestants, behave with courtesy; nay, with
seeming good will." This was written respecting
Ireland, but it was just the same in England. He had
more invitations to preach in churches than he could
possibly accept; and the last pages of his Journal are
full of notices of churches in which he officiated. The
very last entry of all is this—" Oct. 24, 1790. I explained, to a numerous congregation in Spitalfields
church, 'the whole armour of God.' St. Paul's, Shadwell,
was still more crowded in the afternoon, while I enforced
that important truth—'one thing is needful'; and I
hope many, even then, resolved to choose that better

part." The pure motives of the good old man were
now recognized on all sides; he was treated with
affectionate regard wherever he went; and among his
own people his authority was, if possible, greater than
ever. "What an astonishing degree of power," writes
Mr. Pawson, "does our aged father and friend exercise!
However, I am satisfied, and have nothing but love in
my heart towards the good old man."

This change of treatment may have been in part due
to a change in Wesley himself. Some of his angu-
larities were rubbed off by age and experience. With
his usual frankness, he owns, in so many words, that he
had modified his opinions on several points. He had
always been in advance of his age in recognizing real
good wherever it might be found; and this large-
heartedness certainly increased with his increasing
years. His interests were widened, and his sympathies
both widened and deepened in his old age. "As Wesley
grew older," writes Mr. Tyerman, "he took far more interest in visiting scenes of beauty and historic buildings
than in earlier life" (iii. 475). Pious Romans Catholics
and even virtuous heathen became objects of his admira-
tion; and, in spite of his late inconsistent conduct, there
can be no doubt that his attachment to the Church of
his Baptism was stronger than ever in his last years.

He outlived all the friends of his youth and middle
age, but he kept himself wonderfully in touch with the
life of the day, and never sank into a mere obsolete
relic of the past. George Whitefield, Thomas Walsh,
John Fletcher, and Charles Wesley were all younger
men than himself, and all passed away before him; but
he had the enviable faculty, so rare in old men, of
attaching himself to new friends. He was more than
sixty when he made the acquaintance of two of the

warmest friends of his later life, Dr. Whitehead and
Mr. Alexander Knox; and more than seventy when he
took Dr. Coke and Dr. Adam Clarke to his heart. One
of the most interesting links between the generation
that was passing away and the generation that was
coming on, is found in the notices in his Journal of
Mr. Simeon—"Dec. 20, 1784. I went to Hinxworth,
where I had the satisfaction of meeting Mr. Simeon, of
King's College. He has spent some time with Mr.
Fletcher at Madeley; two kindred souls, much re-
sembling each other both in fervour and spirit and in
the earnestness of their address." "Oct. 29, 1787,
Hinxworth. Mr. Simeon from Cambridge met me;
who breathes the very spirit of Mr. Fletcher." Mr.
Fletcher, more than any man he ever met, realized
John Wesley's ideal of Christian Perfection. It is not
often that an old man can see in the coming race a
reproduction of the hero of his prime. But John
Wesley always seems to have acted on the principle,

> Uno avulso, non deficit alter
> Aureus.

Even when his brother Charles was taken to his rest
in 1788, John Wesley did not break down—except on
one occasion, when he speedily recovered himself—but
showed his regard for the beloved memory in a more
practical way by treating the widow and children with
the greatest liberality and kindness. He threw himself
also with all the ardour of youth into the new schemes
for good which were being formed when his own day
was nearly over. He records more than once with
great delight how the new institution of Sunday Schools
seemed to be spreading throughout the land; and his
very last letter was, as we have seen, a letter of en-
couragement to William Wilberforce on his crusade

P

against the slave-trade. He was also quick-sighted enough to perceive the danger which arose from the increasing worldliness of his more opulent followers, and some of his latest utterances were vigorous denunciations of this tendency. "Why," he asks in 1789, "is self-denial in general so little practised among the Methodists? Why is so exceedingly little of it to be found even in the oldest and largest Societies? The more I observe and consider things, the more clearly it appears what is the cause of this in London, in Bristol, in Birmingham, in Manchester, in Leeds, in Dublin, in Cork. The Methodists grow more and more self-indulgent because they grow rich. Although many of them are still deplorably poor ('tell it not in Gath; publish it not in the streets of Askelon!'), yet many others in the space of twenty, thirty, or forty years, are twenty, thirty, yea, a hundred times richer than they first entered the Society. And it is an observation which admits of few exceptions, that nine in ten of these decreased in grace in the same proportion as they increased in wealth."[1] His mind was especially exercised in his old age on the subject of female dress— "O, ye pretty triflers!" he writes in 1787; "I entreat you not to do the devil's work any longer. . . . Let me see, before I die, a Methodist congregation full as plainly dressed as a Quaker congregation. Let your dress be *cheap* as well as plain; otherwise you do but trifle with God and man, and your own souls. No *Quaker linen*, no Brussels lace, no elephantine hats or bonnets, those scandals of female modesty."

[1] This is from the sermon on "*The Causes of the Inefficacy of Christianity*," dated Dublin, July 2, 1789. The same subject is treated in the sermon on "*The Rich Fool*," written at Balham, Feb. 19, 1790, and in the one on "*If riches increase*," &c., written at Bristol, Sept. 21, 1790.

To the last he clung to that two-fold idea of what his system was intended to be; it was to be simply an agency for good which required for admission into it no particular opinions, but at the same time it was to be kept closely in union with that Church of which John Wesley never ceased to be a most attached member. How this two-fold idea could be realized in fact is another question; but John Wesley clung with equal tenacity to both sides of it, if one may use the expression, and never more so than in his last days. Two of his latest utterances bring out respectively the one and the other side of the conception. May 18, 1788, he writes—" There is no other religious society under heaven which requires nothing of men in order to their admission into it but a desire to save their souls. Look all around you; you cannot be admitted into the Church, or Society of the Presbyterians, Anabaptists, Quakers, or any others, unless you hold the same opinion, and adhere to the same mode of worship. The Methodists alone do not insist on your holding this or that opinion; but they think, and let think. Neither do they impose any particular mode of worship; but you may continue to worship in your former manner, be it what it may. Now I do not know any other religious society, either ancient or modern, wherein such liberty of conscience is now allowed, or has been allowed since the days of the Apostles. Here is our glorying, and a glorying peculiar to us. What Society shares it with us?" And he repeated the same in effect fifteen months later.

This is one side of the shield. Let us now turn to the other side. In 1790 he wrote what has been termed his valedictory address [1] to his followers, in the *Arminian*

[1] *John Wesley's Place in Church History*, by R. Denny Urlin, p. 172.

Magazine, and in it are these words—" I never had any
design of separating from the Church; I have no such
design now; I do not believe the Methodists in general
design it. I do, and will do, all in my power to prevent
such an event; nevertheless, in spite of all I can do,
many will separate from it, although. I am inclined to
think not one half nor perhaps a third of them. These
will be so bold and injudicious as to form a separate
party, which consequently will dwindle into a dry, dull,
separate sect. In flat opposition to them, I declare,
once more, that I live and die a member of the Church
of England, and that none who regard my judgment
will ever separate from it."

A few months after these words were written the end
came, on March 2nd, 1791. There was no disease, but
simply a breaking up of nature. He had made all his
preparations both in temporal and spiritual concerns.
His little bequests—they were *very* little ones, for he had
saved absolutely nothing—were carefully considered, and
he gave " £6 to be divided among the six poor men
named by the assistant, who shall carry my body to the
grave ; for I particularly desire there may be no hearse,
no coach, no escutcheon, no pomp, except the tears of
those that loved me, and are following me to Abraham's
bosom." His wishes were, of course, attended to, and
the tears were not wanting ; when the officiating clergyman said, "our dear *father* here departed," instead of
"*brother,*" the vast multitude broke out into loud sobs.

INDEX.

Richard Clay & Sons, Limited, London & Bungay.

18, *Bury Street, W.C., January,* 1891.

MESSRS. METHUEN'S
𝔑ew 𝔅ooks and 𝔄nnouncements.
1891.

CONTENTS.

FICTION.

S. BARING GOULD.

URITH: A Story of Dartmoor. By S. Baring Gould, Author of "Mehalah," "Arminell," &c. 3 vols. [*February.*

HANNAH LYNCH.

PRINCE OF THE GLADES. By Hannah Lynch. 2 vols. [*February.*

W. CLARK RUSSELL.

A MARRIAGE AT SEA. By W. Clark Russell, Author of "The Wreck of the Grosvenor," &c. 2 vols. [*February.*

W. H. POLLOCK.

FERDINAND'S CLAIM. By Walter Herries Pollock. Post 8vo. 1s. [*February.*

R. PRYCE.

THE QUIET MRS. FLEMING. By Richard Pryce. Crown 8vo. 3s. 6d. [*February.*

M. BETHAM EDWARDS.

DISARMED. By M. Betham Edwards, Author of "Kitty." Crown 8vo. 3s. 6d. [*February.*

W. E. NORRIS.

JACK'S FATHER. By W. E. Norris, Author of "Mademoiselle de Mersac." Crown 8vo. 3s. 6d. [*March.*

S. BARING GOULD.

TOM A' TUDLAMS. By S. Baring Gould, Author of "Mehalah" Crown 8vo. 3s. 6d. [*May.*

LESLIE KEITH.

A LOST ILLUSION. By Leslie Keith, Author of "The Chilcotes," "A Hurricane in Petticoats," &c. 3 vols. Crown 8vo.

"Were it only a shade more cheerful it would be a perfect story."—*Manchester Examiner.*
"A really pathetic story full of human nature."—*Graphic.*

G. MANVILLE FENN.

A DOUBLE KNOT. By G. Manville Fenn, Author of "The Vicar's People," "Eli's Children," &c. 3 vols. Crown 8vo.

"A clever novel. The plot is intricate and well managed. The story abounds in strong and exciting situations."—*Speaker.*

L. T. MEADE.

THE HONOURABLE MISS: A Tale of a Country Town. By L. T. Meade, Author of "Scamp and I," "A Girl of the People," &c. 2 vols. Crown 8vo.

"Delightfully fresh and winning."—*Scotsman.*

GENERAL LITERATURE.

S. BARING GOULD.

HISTORIC ODDITIES AND STRANGE EVENTS. Second Series. By S. BARING GOULD, Author of "Mehalah," "Old Country Life," &c. Demy 8vo. 10s. 6d. [*Ready*.

"Mr. Baring Gould has a keen eye for colour and effect, and the subjects he has chosen give ample scope to his descriptive and analytic faculties. The new series of 'Historic Oddities and Strange Events' is a perfectly fascinating book. Whether considered as merely popular reading or as a succession of studies in the freaks of human history, it is equally worthy of perusal, while it is marked by the artistic literary colouring and happy lightness of style."— *Scottish Leader.*

J. B. BURNE, M.A.

PARSON AND PEASANT: Chapters of their Natural History. By J. B. BURNE, M.A., Rector of Wasing. Crown 8vo. 5s. [*Ready*.

"'Parson and Peasant' is a book not only to be interested in, but to learn something from —a book which may prove a help to many a clergyman, and broaden the hearts and ripen the charity of laymen."—*Derby Mercury.*

W. CLARK RUSSELL.

THE LIFE OF ADMIRAL LORD COLLINGWOOD. By W. CLARK RUSSELL, Author of "The Wreck of the Grosvenor." With Illustrations by F. BRANGWYN. 8vo. [*In February*.

P. H. DITCHFIELD, M.A.

OLD ENGLISH SPORTS AND PASTIMES. By P. H. DITCHFIELD, M.A., Author of "Our English Villages." Illustrated. Post 8vo. [*In April*.

Edited by A. CLARK, M.A.

THE COLLEGES OF OXFORD: Their History and their Traditions. By Members of the University. Edited by A. CLARK, M.A., Fellow and Tutor of Lincoln College. 8vo. [*In the Press*.

Edited by J. WELLS, M.A.

OXFORD AND OXFORD LIFE: With Chapters on the Examinations by Members of the University. Edited by J. WELLS, M.A., Fellow and Tutor of Wadham College. Crown 8vo. [*In the Press*.

S. BARING GOULD.

THE TRAGEDY OF THE CÆSARS: The Emperors of the Julian and Claudian Lines. With numerous Illustrations from Busts, Gems, Cameos, &c. By S. BARING GOULD, Author of "Mehalah," &c. [*In the Press*.

W. G. COLLINGWOOD, M.A.

JOHN RUSKIN: His Life and Work. By W. G. COLLINGWOOD, M.A., late Scholar of University College, Oxford. Crown 8vo. [*In Preparation*.

H. H. HENSON, M.A.

DISSENT IN ENGLAND: A Sketch of the History and Constitution of the Principal Nonconformist Sects. By REV. H. H. HENSON, M.A., Fellow of All Souls' College, and Rector of Barking. 8vo. [*In Preparation*.

3

NEW BOOKS for BOYS and GIRLS.

W. CLARK RUSSELL.

MASTER ROCKAFELLAR'S VOYAGE. By W. Clark Russell, Author of "The Wreck of the Grosvenor," &c. Illustrated by Gordon Browne. Crown 8vo. 5s.

"Mr. Clark Russell's story of 'Master Rockafellar's Voyage' will be among the favourites of the Christmas books. There is a rattle and 'go' all through it, and its illustrations are charming in themselves, and very much above the average in the way in which they are produced. Mr. Clark Russell is thoroughly at home on sea and with boys, and he manages to relate and combine the marvellous in so plausible a manner that we are quite prepared to allow that Master Rockafellar's is no unfair example of every midshipman's first voyage. We can heartily recommend this pretty book to the notice of the parents and friends of sea-loving boys."—*Guardian.*

"In the frank and convincing narrative of Master Rockafellar there happens to be set a short story which should make the fortune of the book. 'La Mulette' is as fine a piece of story-telling as ever Mr. Russell has given us, and we heartily commend it to any boy who has the sense to distinguish between the author who has a story to tell, and the author who has to tell a story."—*Speaker.*

G. MANVILLE FENN.

SYD BELTON : or, The Boy who would not go to Sea. By G. Manville Fenn, Author of "In the King's Name," &c. Illustrated by Gordon Browne. Crown 8vo. 5s.

"Who among the young story-reading public will not rejoice at the sight of the old combination, so often proved admirable—a story by Manville Fenn, illustrated by Gordon Browne The story, too, is one of the good old sort, full of life and vigour, breeziness and fun. It begins well and goes on better, and from the time Syd joins his ship exciting incidents follow each other in such rapid and brilliant succession that nothing short of absolute compulsion would induce the reader to lay it down."—*Journal of Education.*

"The pick of the adventure books for this season. There is not a dull page in it. 'Syd Belton' is a capital book."—*Speaker.*

"From beginning to end the book is a vivid and even striking picture of sea-life."—*Spectator.*

Mrs. PARR.

DUMPS. By Mrs. Parr, Author of "Adam and Eve," "Dorothy Fox," &c. Illustrated by W. Parkinson. Crown 8vo. 3s. 6d.

"One of the prettiest stories which even this clever writer has given the world for a long time."—*World.* "A very sweet and touching story."—*Pall Mall Gazette.*

L. T. MEADE.

A GIRL OF THE PEOPLE. By L. T. Meade, Author of "Scamp and I," &c. Illustrated by R. Barnes. Crown 8vo. 3s. 6d.

"An excellent story. Vivid portraiture of character, and broad and wholesome lessons about life."—*Spectator.* "One of Mrs. Meade's most fascinating books."—*Daily News.*

4

METHUEN'S NOVEL SERIES.

THREE SHILLINGS AND SIXPENCE.

MESSRS. METHUEN will issue from time to time a Series of copyright Novels, by well-known Authors, handsomely bound, at the above popular price. The first volumes (ready) are :

F. MABEL ROBINSON.
1. THE PLAN OF CAMPAIGN.

S. BARING GOULD, Author of " Mehalah," &c.
2. JACQUETTA.

Mrs. LEITH ADAMS (Mrs. De Courcy Laffan).
3. MY LAND OF BEULAH.

G. MANVILLE FENN.
4. ELI'S CHILDREN.

S. BARING GOULD, Author of " Mehalah," &c.
5. ARMINELL : A Social Romance.

EDNA LYALL, Author of " Donovan," &c.
6. DERRICK VAUGHAN, NOVELIST. With Portrait of Author.

F. MABEL ROBINSON.
7. DISENCHANTMENT.

M. BETHAM EDWARDS.
8. DISARMED.   [*Shortly.*

W. E. NORRIS.
9. JACK'S FATHER.   [*Shortly.*

S. BARING GOULD.
10. TOM A' TUDLAMS.   [*Shortly.*

Other Volumes will be announced in due course.

English Leaders of Religion.

Edited by A. M. M. STEDMAN, M.A.

Under the above title MESSRS. METHUEN have commenced like publication of a series of short biographies, free from party bias, of the most prominent leaders of religious life and thought in this and the last century.

Each volume will contain a succinct account and estimate of the career, the influence, and the literary position of the subject of the memoir.

The following are already arranged—

CARDINAL NEWMAN. *R. H. Hutton.* [*Ready.*

" Few who read this book will fail to be struck by the wonderful insight it displays into the nature of the Cardinal's genius and the spirit of his life."—WILFRID WARD, in the *Tabl.t.*

" Full of knowledge, excellent in method, and intelligent in criticism. We regard it as wholly admirable."—*Academy.*

" An estimate, careful, deliberate, full of profound reasoning and of acute insight."—*Pall Mall Gazette.*

JOHN WESLEY. *J. H. Overton, M.A.*
 [*In February.*

JOHN KEBLE. *W. Lock, M.A.*

CHARLES SIMEON. *H. C. G. Moule, M.A.*

BISHOP WILBERFORCE. *G. W. Daniell, M.A.*

F. D. MAURICE. *Colonel F. Maurice, R.E.*

THOMAS CHALMERS. *Mrs. Oliphant.*

CARDINAL MANNING. *A. W. Hutton, M.A.*

Other Volumes will be announced in due course.

SOCIAL QUESTIONS OF TO-DAY.

Edited by H. de B. GIBBINS, M.A.

Crown 8vo. 2s. 6d.

MESSRS. METHUEN beg to announce the publication of a series of volumes upon those topics of social, economic and industrial interest that are at the present moment foremost in the public mind. Each volume of the series will be written by an author who is an acknowledged authority upon the subject with which he deals, and who will treat his question in a thoroughly sympathetic but impartial manner, with special reference to the historic aspect of the subject and from the point of view of the Historical School of economics and social science. The Labour Question will be treated of in the volumes on Trades Unions and Co-operation : the Land Question will form the subject of another two volumes ; others will treat of Socialism in England, in its various phases, and of the labour problems of the Continent also. The monograph on Commerce will be of special interest at present in view of the recent development of American commercial policy. Those on Education and on Poverty will be of similar importance in view of current discussion, and the volume on Mutual Thrift will prove a valuable survey of the various agencies for that purpose already in existence among the working classes.

The following form the earlier Volumes of the Series :—

ABOUT
Feb.   **1. TRADES UNIONISM—NEW AND OLD.**
1891.   G. HOWELL, M.P., Author of " The Conflicts of Capital and
               Labour."

March. **2. POVERTY AND PAUPERISM.**
               Rev. L. R. PHELPS, M.A., Fellow of Oriel College, Oxford.

          3. THE CO-OPERATIVE MOVEMENT OF TO-DAY.
               G. J. HOLYOAKE, Author of " The History of Co-operation."

          4. MUTUAL THRIFT.
               Rev. J. FROME WILKINSON, M.A., Author of " The Friendly
               Society Movement."

7

SOCIAL QUESTIONS OF TO-DAY (*continued*).

UNIVERSITY EXTENSION SERIES.

Under the above title MESSRS. METHUEN have commenced the publication of a series of books on historical, literary, and economic subjects, suitable for extension students and home-reading circles. The volumes are intended to assist the lecturer and not to usurp his place. Each volume will be complete in itself, and the subjects will be treated by competent writers in a broad and philosophic spirit.

Edited by J. E. SYMES, M.A.,

Principal of University College, Nottingham.

Crown 8vo.   2*s.* 6*d.*

The following volumes are already arranged, and others will be announced shortly.

THE INDUSTRIAL HISTORY OF ENGLAND.   By H. DE B. GIBBINS, M.A., late Scholar of Wadham Coll., Oxon., Cobden Prizeman.   With Maps and Plans.   [*Ready.*

"A compact and clear story of our industrial development. A study of his concise but luminous book cannot fail to give the reader a clear insight into the principal phenomena of our industrial history. The editor and publishers are to be congratulated on this first volume of their venture, and we shall look with expectant interest for the succeeding volumes of the series. If they maintain the same standard of excellence the series will make a permanent place for itself among the many series which appear from time to time."—*University Extension Journal.*

"A careful and lucid sketch."—*Times.*

"The writer is well-informed, and from first to last his work is profoundly interesting."—*Scots Observer.*

A HISTORY OF ENGLISH POLITICAL ECONOMY.   By L. L. PRICE, M.A., Fellow of Oriel Coll., Oxon., Extension Lecturer in Political Economy.   [*February.*

ENGLISH SOCIAL REFORMERS.   By H. DE B. GIBBINS, M.A., late Scholar of Wadham Coll., Oxon., Cobden Prizeman.

PROBLEMS OF POVERTY : An Inquiry into the Industrial Conditions of the Poor.   By J. A. HOBSON, M.A., late Scholar of Lincoln Coll., Oxon., U. E. Lecturer in Economics.   [*March.*

THE FRENCH REVOLUTION.   By J. E. SYMES, M.A., Principal of University Coll., Nottingham.   [*In the Press.*

9

NAPOLEON. By E. L. S. HORSBURGH, M.A., Camb., U. E. Lecturer in History.

ENGLISH POLITICAL HISTORY. By T. J. LAWRENCE, M.A., late Fellow and Tutor of Downing Coll., Cambridge, U. E. Lecturer in History.

SHAKESPEARE. By F. H. TRENCH, M.A., Fellow of All Souls' Coll., Oxon., U. E. Lecturer in Literature.

VICTORIAN POETS. By A. SHARP. [*April.*

THE ENGLISH LANGUAGE. By G. C. MOORE-SMITH, M.A., Camb., U. E. Lecturer in Language.

AN INTRODUCTION TO PHILOSOPHY. By J. SOLOMON, M.A., Oxon., late Lecturer in Philosophy at University Coll., Nottingham.

PSYCHOLOGY. By F. S. GRANGER, M.A., Lond., Lecturer in Philosophy at University Coll., Nottingham. [*In the Press.*

ENGLISH PAINTERS. By D. S. MACCOLL, M.A., Oxon., Fellow of Univ. Coll., London, U. E. Lecturer in Art and Literature.

ENGLISH ARCHITECTURE. By ERNEST RADFORD, M.A., Camb., U. E. Lecturer in Art. With Illustrations.

THE EVOLUTION OF PLANT LIFE: Lower Forms. By G. MASSEE, Kew Gardens, U. E. Lecturer in Botany. With Illustrations. [*In the Press.*

THE CHEMISTRY OF LIFE AND HEALTH. By C. W. KIMMINS, M.A., Camb., U. E. Lecturer in Chemistry.

MESSRS. METHUEN'S NEW & RECENT BOOKS.

FICTION.

E. LYNN LINTON.

THE TRUE HISTORY OF JOSHUA DAVIDSON, Christian and Communist. By E. LYNN LINTON. Eleventh and Cheaper Edition. Post 8vo, 1*s.*

HISTORY AND POLITICS.

E. LYNN LINTON.

ABOUT IRELAND. By E. LYNN LINTON. *2nd Edition.* Cr. 8vo, bds., 1*s.*

" A brilliant and justly proportioned view of the Irish Question."—*Standard.*

T. RALEIGH, M.A.

IRISH POLITICS: An Elementary Sketch. By T. RALEIGH, M.A., Fellow of All Souls', Oxford, Author of "Elementary Politics." Fcap. 8vo, paper boards, 1*s.*; cloth, 1*s.* 6*d.*

" A very clever work."—MR. GLADSTONE.

" Unionist as he is, his little book has been publicly praised for its cleverness both by Mr. Gladstone and Mr. Morley. It does, in fact, raise most of the principal points of the Irish controversy, and puts them tersely, lucidly, and in such a way as to strike into the mind of the reader."—*The Speaker.*

"Salient facts and clear expositions in a few sentences packed with meaning. Every one who wishes to have the vital points of Irish politics at his finger's end should get this book by heart."—*Scotsman.*

F. MABEL ROBINSON.

IRISH HISTORY FOR ENGLISH READERS. By F. MABEL ROBINSON. *Fourth Edition.* Crown 8vo, boards, 1*s.*

GENERAL LITERATURE.

Edited by F. LANGBRIDGE, M.A.

BALLADS OF THE BRAVE: Poems of Chivalry, Enterprise, Courage, and Constancy, from the Earliest Times to the Present Day. Edited, with Notes, by Rev. F. LANGBRIDGE. Crown 8vo.

" A very happy conception happily carried out. These 'Ballads of the Brave' are intended to suit the real tastes of boys, and will suit the taste of the great majority. It is not an ordinary selector who could have so happily put together these characteristic samples. Other readers besides boys may learn much from them."—*Spectator.*

" The book is full of splendid things."—*World.*

Presentation Edition. Handsomely Bound, 3*s.* 6*d.* (School Edition, 2*s.* 6*d.*) Or, in Three Parts, 1*s.* each, for School Readers.

I. TROY TO FLODDEN. II. BOSWORTH TO WATERLOO. III. CRIMÆA TO KHARTOUM.

P. H. DITCHFIELD, M.A.

OUR ENGLISH VILLAGES: Their Story and their Antiquities. By P. H. DITCHFIELD, M.A., F.R.H.S., Rector of Barkham, Berks. Post 8vo, 2*s.* 6*d.* Illustrated.

" A pleasantly written little volume, giving much interesting information concerning villages and village life."—*Pall Mall Gazette.*

" The object of the author is not so much to describe any particular village as to give a clear idea of what village life has been in England from the earliest historical times. An extremely amusing and interesting little book, which should find a place in every parochial library."—*Guardian.*

A. M. M. STEDMAN, M.A.

OXFORD: ITS LIFE AND SCHOOLS. Ed. by A. M. M. STEDMAN, M.A., assisted by members of the University. *New Edition.* Cr. 8vo. 5*s.*

" Offers a full and in most respects a satisfactory description of the country through which students must travel, and affords to parents who are desirous of calculating the expenses and rewards of University education, a mass of useful information conveniently arranged and brought down to the most recent date."—*Athenæum.*

" We can honestly say of Mr. Stedman's volume that it deserves to be read by the people for whom it is intended, the parents and guardians of Oxford students, present and to come, and by such students themselves."—*Spectator.*

GENERAL LITERATURE *(continued)*.

OLD COUNTRY LIFE. By S. BARING GOULD. With Sixty-seven
Illustrations by W. PARKINSON, F. D. BEDFORD, and F. MASEY. Large
Crown 8vo, cloth super extra, top edge gilt, 10s. 6d. *Second Edition.*

"'Old Country Life,' as healthy wholesome reading, full of breezy life and movement,
full of quaint stories vigorously told, will not be excelled by any book to be published
throughout the year. Sound, hearty, and English to the core."—*World.*

"Mr. Baring Gould is well known as a clever and versatile author ; but he never wrote
a more delightful book than the volume before us. He has described English country life
with the fidelity that only comes with close acquaintance, and with an appreciation of its
more attractive features not surpassed even in the pages of Washington Irving. The illustrations add very much to the charm of the book, and the artists in their drawings of old
churches and manor-houses, streets, cottages, and gardens, have greatly assisted the author."
Manchester Guardian.

HISTORIC ODDITIES AND STRANGE EVENTS. By S. BARING
GOULD. FIRST SERIES. Demy 8vo, 10s. 6d. *Second Edition.*

"A collection of exciting and entertaining chapters. The whole volume is delightful
reading."—*Times.*

"The work, besides being agreeable to read, is valuable for purposes of reference. The
entire contents are stimulating and delightful."—*Notes and Queries.*

HISTORIC ODDITIES AND STRANGE EVENTS. SECOND SERIES.
By S. BARING GOULD, Author of "Mehalah," "Old Country Life," &c.
Demy 8vo, 10s. 6d. [*Ready.*

"Mr. Baring Gould has a keen eye for colour and effect, and the subjects he has chosen
give ample scope to his descriptive and analytic faculties. The new series of 'Historic
Oddities and Strange Events,' is a perfectly fascinating book. Whether considered as merely
popular reading or as a succession of studies in the freaks of human history, it is equally
worthy of perusal, while it is marked by artistic literary colouring and happy lightness of
style."—*Scottish Leader.*

SONGS OF THE WEST: Traditional Ballads and Songs of the West of
England, with their Traditional Melodies. Collected by S. BARING
GOULD, M.A., and H. FLEETWOOD SHEPPARD, M.A. Arranged for
Voice and Piano. In 4 Parts (containing 25 Songs each), 3s. each.
*Part I., Fourth Edition. Part II., Second Edition. Part III., ready.
Part IV., in the Press.*

"A rich and varied collection of humour, pathos, grace, and poetic fancy."—*Saturday
Review.*

YORKSHIRE ODDITIES AND STRANGE EVENTS. By S.
BARING GOULD. New and Cheaper Edition. Crown 8vo, 6s.
[*Now ready.*

JACQUETTA, and other Stories. By S. BARING GOULD. Crown
8vo, 3s. 6d.

ARMINELL: A Social Romance. By S. BARING GOULD. New
Edition. Crown 8vo, 3s. 6d.

"To say that a book is by the author of 'Mehalah' is to imply that it contains a story cast
on strong lines, containing dramatic possibilities, vivid and sympathetic descriptions of Nature,
and a wealth of ingenious imagery. All these expectations are justified by 'Arminell.'"
Speaker.

EDUCATIONAL WORKS.

METHUEN'S SCIENCE SERIES.

MESSRS. METHUEN propose to issue a Series of Science Manuals suitable for use in schools. They will be edited by Mr. R. Elliot Steel, M.A., F.C.S., Senior Natural Science Master in Bradford Grammar School, and will be published at a moderate price. The following are ready or in preparation—

THE WORLD OF SCIENCE. Including Chemistry, Heat, Light, Sound, Magnetism, Electricity, Botany, Zoology, Physiology, Astronomy, and Geology. By R. ELLIOT STEEL, M.A., F.C.S., Senior Natural Science Master in Bradford Grammar School. 147 Illustrations, Crown 8vo, 2s. 6d.

"Mr. Steel's Manual is admirable in many ways. The Book is well calculated to attract and retain the attention of the young."—*Saturday Review.*

"If Mr. Steel is to be placed second to any for this quality of lucidity, it is only to Huxley himself; and to be named in the same breath with this master of the craft of teaching is to be accredited with the clearness of style and simplicity of arrangement that belong to thorough mastery of a subject."—*Parents' Review.*

ELEMENTARY LIGHT with numerous Illustrations. Crown 8vo. [*February.*
  ,,   ELECTRICITY AND MAGNETISM.
  ,,   HEAT.

Other Volumes will be announced in due course.

R. E. STEEL, M.A.
REVISED FOR NEW SESSION.

PRACTICAL INORGANIC CHEMISTRY. For the Elementary Stage of the South Kensington Examinations in Science and Art. By R. E. STEEL, M.A., Senior Natural Science Master at Bradford Grammar School. Crown 8vo, cloth, 1s. [*Now Ready.*

R. J. MORICH.

A GERMAN PRIMER. With Exercises. By R. J. MORICH, Chief Modern Language Master at Manchester Grammar School. [*In the Press.*

H. de B. GIBBINS, M.A.

COMPANION GERMAN GRAMMAR. By H. DE B. GIBBINS, M.A., Assistant Master at Nottingham High School. Crown 8vo, 1s. 6d. [*Ready.*

E. McQUEEN GRAY.

GERMAN PASSAGES for UNSEEN TRANSLATION. By E. McQUEEN GRAY. Crown 8vo, 2s. 6d. [*Ready.*

A. W. VERRALL, M.A.

SELECTIONS FROM HORACE. With Introduction, Notes, and Vocabulary. By A. W. VERRALL, M.A., Fellow and Tutor of Trinity Coll., Cambridge. Fcap. 8vo. [*In the Press.*

SELECTIONS FROM HERODOTUS. With Introduction, Notes, and Vocabulary. By A. C. LIDDELL, M.A., Assistant Master at Nottingham High School. Fcap. 8vo. [*In the Press.*

WORKS BY A. M. M. STEDMAN, M.A.

WADHAM COLLEGE, OXON.

FIRST LATIN LESSONS. *Second Edition, Enlarged.* Crown 8vo, 2s.
[*Ready.*

FIRST LATIN READER. With Notes adapted to the Shorter Latin Primer and Vocabulary. Crown 8vo, 1s. 6d. [*Ready.*

EASY LATIN PASSAGES FOR UNSEEN TRANSLATION. *Second Edition, Enlarged.* Fcap. 8vo, 1s. 6d.

EASY LATIN EXERCISES ON THE SYNTAX OF THE SHORTER AND REVISED LATIN PRIMERS. With Vocabulary. *Second Edition.* Crown 8vo, 2s. 6d. Issued with the consent of Dr. Kennedy.

NOTANDA QUAEDAM: MISCELLANEOUS LATIN EXERCISES ON COMMON RULES AND IDIOMS. With Vocabulary. Fcap. 8vo, 1s. 6d.

LATIN VOCABULARIES FOR REPETITION: arranged according to Subjects. *Third Edition.* Fcap. 8vo, 1s. 6d.

FIRST GREEK LESSONS. [*In preparation.*

EASY GREEK PASSAGES FOR UNSEEN TRANSLATION.
[*In preparation.*

EASY GREEK EXERCISES ON ELEMENTARY SYNTAX.
[*In preparation.*

GREEK VOCABULARIES FOR REPETITION: arranged according to Subjects. Fcap. 8vo, 1s. 6d.

GREEK TESTAMENT SELECTIONS. For the use of Schools. *New Edition.* With Introduction, Notes, and Vocabulary. Fcap. 8vo, 2s. 6d.

FIRST FRENCH LESSONS. [*In the Press*

EASY FRENCH PASSAGES FOR UNSEEN TRANSLATION.
Fcap. 8vo, 1s. 6d.

EASY FRENCH EXERCISES ON ELEMENTARY SYNTAX. With Vocabulary. Crown 8vo, 2s. 6d. [*Ready.*

FRENCH VOCABULARIES FOR REPETITION: arranged according to Subjects. Fcap. 8vo, 1s.

See also School Examination Series, p. 15.

SCHOOL EXAMINATION SERIES.

Edited by A. M. M. STEDMAN, M.A.

Crown 8vo. 2s. 6d. each.

In use at Eton, Harrow, Winchester, Repton, Cheltenham, Sherborne, Haileybury, Merchant Taylors, Manchester, &c.

FRENCH EXAMINATION PAPERS IN MISCELLANEOUS GRAMMAR AND IDIOMS. By A. M. M. STEDMAN, M.A. *Fifth Edition.*

A KEY, issued to Tutors and Private Students only, to be had on application to the Publishers. *Second Edition.* Cr. 8vo, 5s.

LATIN EXAMINATION PAPERS IN MISCELLANEOUS GRAMMAR AND IDIOMS. By A. M. M. STEDMAN, M.A. *Third Edition.* KEY (issued as above), 6s.

GREEK EXAMINATION PAPERS IN MISCELLANEOUS GRAMMAR AND IDIOMS. By A. M. M. STEDMAN, M.A. *Second Edition, Enlarged.* KEY (issued as above), 6s.

GERMAN EXAMINATION PAPERS IN MISCELLANEOUS GRAMMAR AND IDIOMS. By R. J. MORICH, Manchester Grammar School. *Second Edition.* KEY (issued as above), 5s.

HISTORY AND GEOGRAPHY EXAMINATION PAPERS. By C. H. SPENCE, M.A., Clifton College.

SCIENCE EXAMINATION PAPERS. By R. E. STEEL, M.A., F.C.S., Chief Natural Science Master, Bradford Grammar School. In three volumes.

    Part I.   Chemistry.
    Part II.   Physics (Sound, Light, Heat, Magnetism, Electricity).
    Part III. Biology and Geology.   *[In preparation.*

GENERAL KNOWLEDGE EXAMINATION PAPERS. By A. M. M. STEDMAN, M.A.   [KEY. *In the Press.*

EXAMINATION PAPERS IN BOOK-KEEPING, with Preliminary Exercises. Compiled and arranged by J. T. MEDHURST, F. S. Accts. and Auditors, and Lecturer at City of London College. 3s.

ENGLISH LITERATURE, Questions for Examination in. Chiefly collected from College Papers set at Cambridge. With an Introduction on the Study of English. By the Rev. W. W. SKEAT, Litt.D., LL.D., Professor of Anglo-Saxon at Cambridge University. *Third Edition, Revised.*

ARITHMETIC EXAMINATION PAPERS. By C. PENDLEBURY, M.A., Senior Mathematical Master, St. Paul's School. KEY, 5s.

TRIGONOMETRY EXAMINATION PAPERS. By E. H. WARD, M.A., Assistant Master at St. Paul's School. KEY, 5s.

15

www.ingramcontent.com/pod-product-compliance
Lightning Source LLC
Chambersburg PA
CBHW020112030726
47498CB00006B/2072